"Julia, we need to talk."

"What is there to discuss? Did I not make it clear that I wish to sever our engagement?"

"You made that perfectly clear last night."

Last night. Pain gripped her heart. Just thinking of her brother's departure to join the Confederate Army brought tears to her eyes.

"Then you understand," she said.

"Julia, I have nothing to do with the soldiers occupying the city or with Edward's enlistment."

"That's right. You don't. You haven't done a thing to stop it. You abandoned Edward and the rest of the volunteers when they needed your help."

"What is it that you wish me to do?" he asked. "Shall I ride to Virginia tonight? Would a saber and an officer's commission truly make you happy?"

Emotions tore through her. "It is far too late for that, Samuel," she said. She was doing her best to keep her voice steady, in control. It would do no good to argue with him. She had already said everything that needed to be said.

He had made his decision. She had made hers.

SHANNON FARRINGTON

is a former teacher with family ties to both sides of the Civil War. She and her husband of over eighteen years are active members in their local church and enjoy pointing out God's hand in American history to the next generation. (Especially their own children!)

When Shannon isn't researching or writing, you can find her knitting, gardening or participating in living history reenactments. She and her family live in Maryland.

SHANNON FARRINGTON

Her Rebel Heart

Love Inspired

Recycling programs
for this product may
not exist in your area.

 LOVE INSPIRED BOOKS

ISBN-13: 978-0-373-82898-2

HER REBEL HEART

www.LoveInspiredBooks.com

Printed in U.S.A.

And now abideth faith, hope and charity,
these three; but the greatest of these is charity.
—1 *Corinthians* 13:13

For Will and Sarah
May you always remember that God is Sovereign
And history is His Story

Chapter One

~❦~

Baltimore, Maryland
1861

Samuel Ward watched the rising sun and wondered why he had even bothered to go to bed the night before. He hadn't slept, nor had he expected to. How could he when the woman to whom he'd pledged his love and devotion had broken his heart?

Julia's words sliced through his mind.

You are a coward. I will not marry you.

He raked his fingers through his reddish-brown hair, trying to comprehend such a declaration. Just a few weeks ago, they'd been happy and in love. Their future had seemed secure. But the bloody conflict that had divided the nation into North and South had divided Sam and Julia, as well. The final straw had come last night when word had spread that Federal troops were in the process of occupying Baltimore. Angry and frightened, Julia had wanted him to say that he'd support the Confederacy and drive the Northern troops out of their home. But he could not say it. He could not support

States' Rights. And that was something *she* could not accept.

The hole in his heart was vast but as a history and rhetoric teacher at the Rolland Park Men's Seminary, he had a duty to perform. He picked up his watch and gathered his books. He knew the campus would be in an uproar because of what was happening in the city. He prayed for wisdom.

Help me, Lord. Help me follow Your path.

When Sam arrived at the seminary the halls were filled with talk.

"That army is going to arrest anyone with Southern sympathy."

"Those that had it left town last night."

"They won't be the last to leave. You can be certain of that."

Sam walked into his classroom. He stopped briefly to glance at the painting of Francis Scott Key, which hung prominently above the blackboard. The father of the "Star Spangled Banner" had once been caught between two opposing armies. Samuel couldn't help but wonder if Fort McHenry would once again be the center of rockets' red glare.

One month ago, Confederate forces had fired upon Fort Sumter. President Lincoln called for volunteers to put down the rebellion. When Northern troops tried to pass through Baltimore en route to Washington they clashed with pro-secession citizens. Rioting commenced. The soldiers opened fire. People were killed.

His country was at war. So was his family.

He took out his books. When his students filed in he called the roll. Five were missing. He stared at the empty chairs, rumors of their departure circulating around him.

"They rode to Carroll County last night," one student volunteered.

"They packed their haversacks with foodstuffs and took their pistols."

"They will be in Virginia before the week is through."

Julia's brother Edward was a member of the Maryland Guard. He and many other men from the state militia had gone south last night. Sam wondered if his students would fall under Edward's leadership. He prayed that wherever they were this morning that God would protect them.

The remaining men in the classroom wore faces of uncertainty. All they wished to discuss was the army that had invaded Baltimore. They were just as divided as the city. Some were for the occupation.

"Life will get back to normal now because of this show of force."

Others were not so sure. "What do you think General Butler's true intentions are?" one of the men asked.

Sam drew in a deep breath, wanting to remain calm and unaffected by it all, or at least show as much to his students. The last thing they needed was a teacher stirring up their concerns by airing his own fears. But his anxiety over Edward's safety and his despair over the loss of Julia's love made it hard to sound optimistic.

"I should hope that his intentions are as he stated in his proclamation, to '…enforce respect and obedience to the laws.'"

The notice from the Union General had been printed in the local papers that morning. Anyone who could get their hands on one had read it.

For months now the newspapers had been reporting on Maryland's possible political future. The state legislature swung one month toward Federal sovereignty and then unfettered States' Rights the next. Now Maryland's position had been determined for her. She would be kept in the Union by force.

"We have much to attend to today," he said, trying to keep the political discussion limited. "Please open your books to chapter four."

Sam tried to continue with his lesson plans but his heart was heavy and his students were distracted. The combination of which did not make for a very engaging time of study. He ended up dismissing the young men early.

"Look after your families," he told them.

The students seemed grateful to go. They rose quickly from their seats and hurried for the door. Their teacher, wishing to join them, moved to pack his books in his satchel. But where could he go? The Stantons, Julia's family, were the closest thing he still had to family. But her words the previous night had made it quite clear that she would not welcome his company any longer. Her words were still ringing in his ears.

You are a coward. I will not marry you.

A knock on the door frame caused him to look up. There in the opening stood Dr. Charles Carter, the dean of students.

"And how are you today, Mr. Ward?" he said evenly as though it were any other spring day.

Sam had only known the man for a short period of time but he had come to respect him. Dr. Carter was a by-the-book disciplinarian but impartial and evenhanded, as well.

"Well, sir. And you?"

Dr. Carter smiled a tempered smile. "Oh, well enough." He stepped toward Sam's desk. "How was your class? The attendance in particular, if I may ask."

Sam sighed and gave the man his report.

Dr. Carter nodded silently, as though he had suspected such. "I am afraid to say that this is the case in many classrooms this morning," he said. His eyes swept the empty room then turned back. "Do not be discouraged, young man. The hand of Providence still guides."

Sam appreciated the remark but did not have time to express so.

The dean then asked, "Have you a moment?"

"I do, sir."

"Then would you walk with me?"

"It would be a pleasure, sir. I was headed outside myself." Sam quickly packed his satchel and closed his classroom.

"These old rooms get so musty in the springtime," Dr. Carter remarked. "I much prefer the fresh air."

Sam followed the man to the end of the hall. They descended the large, walnut staircase, crossed the main foyer and stepped out onto the tree-lined campus before Dr. Carter spoke again.

"I couldn't help but notice the small volume on your desk just now. Tell me, Mr. Ward, if you will be so kind, do you find Frederick Douglass's words captivating?"

Heat crept up Sam's neck. His tie and collar seemed a little too tight. He hadn't even been aware that an autobiography of the former Maryland slave was lying on his desk. He must have placed it in his satchel with his other school books that morning.

He had bought the book in Philadelphia during his time at the State Street Teacher's College. It was there he had first been exposed to the true realities of slavery. The more he learned, the more his conviction had grown that he could not support an institution that allowed one man to own another. It was a "state right" he could not condone for anyone's sake. Not even Julia's. Sam wondered where Dr. Carter's inquiry was leading but he answered truthfully.

"I do not find them so much captivating, sir, as I do haunting."

Dr. Carter nodded, though his face gave little indication to what he thought of the admission. "Why is that?" he simply asked.

Sam wished now that he hadn't agreed to this walk. Slavery was a dividing issue. The last thing he wanted was to cause controversy between him and one of his colleagues. But he could not deny the certainty that he felt in his heart. He had no wish to offend, but he wouldn't deny his beliefs. He answered the question carefully.

"We are all created in the image of God," he said. "We should treat each other as God treats us."

Dr. Carter stopped beneath one of the maple trees. He turned to Sam and smiled.

"I, too, share your thoughts," he said.

"You do?"

"Yes. Have you ever met Mr. Douglass?"

"I have. A few months ago."

"You were educated in Philadelphia, yes?"

"That is correct, sir."

They started walking once more, choosing the stone path that led to the library.

"Fine work they are doing in Philadelphia," Dr. Carter said. "Fine work, indeed."

Sam wasn't certain if he was referring to education or something else. He sensed it was the latter.

"I met Mr. Douglass once, myself," Dr. Carter said. "In Boston." He glanced at Sam. "There is fine work going on in Boston, as well."

Sam did not reveal that he had once been there, as well; but by now he was beginning to suspect that Frederick Douglass and the *fine work* up north were related. Coupled with Dr. Carter's first question, he reckoned that the Dean of Students had sided with the abolitionist cause. He seemed most curious to know what Sam's position was.

"It is fine work," Sam said. "Something I think that there should be more of."

Dr. Carter's eyes practically sparkled with excitement. From his vest pocket he produced a small scrap of paper. He handed it to Sam. "Then perhaps you would be interested in meeting some of my friends."

Sam studied the note. It was an address in the Fell's Point area. "Are your friends engaged in fine work?" he asked, borrowing the phrase.

"They are and they are always looking for God-fearing young men such as you to be part of such."

He was cautiously intrigued. He had met a few abolitionists in Philadelphia. Most of them were kindhearted, wonderful people. A few, however, had such wild, vengeful looks in their eyes that frankly, they scared him. Sam wanted no part of a group like that. He believed judgment should be reserved for God alone.

A group of students exited the library. They walked toward Dr. Carter and Sam.

Dr. Carter's countenance changed, a firm disciplinary look replacing the smiling excitement his face had just shown.

"Four o'clock, next Friday," he said matter-of-factly. Then he opened the door to the library. Sam watched the white-haired gentleman walk into the building. Then he slipped the scrap of paper the man had given him into his own vest pocket.

Dr. Carter had left him with many questions. Abolitionists were a varying lot, and Sam wasn't exactly certain what he might be getting into. He would appreciate his future father-in-law's counsel. But given what had taken place with Julia, he wondered if Dr. Stanton would receive him. *Does he know about our broken engagement? Will he side with Julia?* He decided to take the chance. After all, he was concerned for their safety.

Heeding his own advice to look after one's family, he hurried to visit the Stantons.

The streets of Mount Vernon were nearly deserted that afternoon. Barricades had filled the streets; but, as of today, the citywide state of "armed neutrality" had given way to at least the appearance of submission. Maryland state flags and the Palmetto flag, the symbol of South Carolina and secession, had been removed. The armed men that had been patrolling the streets for the last month were nowhere to be seen. The Federal guns pointing at Monument Square had discouraged outside activity.

Sam was eager to be indoors as well. To his relief, Dr. Stanton greeted him warmly when he arrived. He invited Sam to join him in the study. The man had surrounded himself with his medical journals.

"I came to see how everyone was," Sam told him, "and to see if you were in need of any assistance." *And, if I may, get your opinion about something,* he thought.

Dr. Stanton nodded. "I thank you. My wife has spent the entire day in bed."

Sam's concern rose. He decided to forgo his planned request for advice. Dr. Stanton had more pressing concerns.

"I am sorry to hear that. Is she ill?"

"Not really. Edward's departure has broken Esther's heart. She doesn't know what to do." He rubbed his mustache. "I suppose we all are that way. All I can seem to concentrate on are my medical books. Julia has busied herself in the kitchen. She has baked four loaves of bread today."

Sam caught himself smiling, though it was a sorrow filled one. Julia had always baked when she was upset or angry.

"Is there any word from Edward?" he asked.

"No, and I fear that there won't be for a very long time."

Neither man knew what to say next. Dr. Stanton went back to his journal. Sam sat quietly and stared at the ceiling. He could hear the rattle of pots and pans coming from the kitchen. He wondered if Julia knew he was here.

"How were your classes?" Dr. Stanton asked.

"I had five missing from my history class alone."

"They left to fight?"

"So the rumors say."

Dr. Stanton sighed long and slow. He tugged at his spectacles. "And those that remained?"

"Their minds were far from the Roman Empire."

"I imagine so."

Sam heard the rustle of her petticoats even before he saw her. Julia's approaching footsteps drew their attention to the door.

"Father, we are in need of wood for the stove…"

The moment she saw Sam an unnerved expression filled her blue eyes. The rest of her words escaped her. He purposefully maintained his gaze. His heart was pounding.

Julia brushed the trace of flour from the front of her green cotton day dress and slowly regained her composure. She looked at her father.

"Will you ask Lewis to fetch some?"

Sam seized the opportunity. "I will see to it."

"Oh, thank you, son."

Son. Dr. Stanton had always called him that. Nothing had changed from his perspective it seemed. Julia, however, did not even acknowledge his presence. She turned her head and looked away as he passed by her.

Sam did not let her actions discourage him. Instead of hunting down Lewis, the family stable hand, he walked to the lean-to.

There was no wood available. He was not surprised. It was Edward's job to see that the kindling box remained full. With all of her baking Julia had depleted the supply that her brother had last chopped. Sam picked out several logs in need of splitting. He could not ease the tensions in his city or his nation. He couldn't protect Edward, his students or Julia. But this was something that needed to be done that he *could* do. He took off his frock coat and set to work.

Julia watched him from the kitchen window. Sleeves rolled up, hair falling over his forehead, arms taut with the ax; in a matter of minutes Samuel had already split enough wood to last for the rest of the day.

He has always been such a hard worker.

She had known Samuel Ward since she was a child. Their families had attended the same church. When his parents had died of typhoid fever when he was but sixteen, he'd practically become a member of their family. Mother doted on him. Father took pride in his accomplishments. Edward treated him like a brother. And she…she fell in love with him. The time he'd spent away from Baltimore, continuing his studies at the teachers' college in Philadelphia, had been almost unbearable.

She'd felt that she couldn't wait for him to come back to her, so they could begin their life together.

He was the quiet, steady type, far different from her outspoken, impulsive nature. As different as he was though, he completed her. And, up until last night, she could not imagine life without him.

The knot in the pit of her stomach tightened. She turned from the window and moved to the stove. She had responsibilities, none of which included watching him.

I am right to break the engagement. I thought I knew him but clearly I did not.

A pot of chicken soup was waiting to be heated. Julia planned to take a bowl up to her mother. She knew it would make her feel better.

She stirred the cold mixture then moved to the counter. She punched down a mound of rising dough then kneaded it carefully. She could hear the chop, chop, chop of Samuel's ax. She tried to ignore it. She slipped the dough into a waiting pan.

A few minutes later, the back door opened with a creak. Julia resisted the urge to turn around. She busied herself by wiping the flour from the table. She then washed her hands. From the corner of her eye she watched him.

Samuel carried in the wood for the kindling box. He quietly loaded the crate then moved to the stove. Julia started to object, ready to say she could light the fire herself. She turned to face him fully. Just one glimpse of his brown eyes brought a lump to her throat.

I promised to love him, she thought. *I promised him forever.*

She backed away and Samuel's attention returned to the stove. He stuffed it with kindling and day-old copies of the local newspaper, *The Baltimore Sun*. He struck a match. The fire ignited and he then turned back to face her.

The lump in her throat grew bigger. *Thank you,* she knew she should say, instead out came, "Why are you here?"

Her words were sharp and accusatory but Samuel did not flinch. He simply looked at her, his eyes melting her hard stance.

"I think you know why," was all he said.

She swallowed hard and watched as he closed the burner lid then went to the pump to wash his hands. Julia held her breath, her emotions drifting through anger and remorse, respect and disdain.

Samuel dried his hands and rolled down his shirt-sleeves. When he turned toward her she quickly busied herself at the table with another pile of dough.

"Julia, we need to talk."

She punched down the soft, sticky mound. "What is there to discuss? Did I not make it clear that I wish to sever our engagement?"

"You made that perfectly clear last night."

Last night. Pain gripped her heart. Just thinking of Edward's departure, of the arguing that had taken place, brought tears to her eyes.

"Then you understand," she said.

"I understand that you are upset," he said, "and rightfully so. You are worried about your brother." He paused. "For some reason you are taking it out on me."

Her spine stiffened. She turned and glared at him. "Some reason?"

"Julia, I have nothing to do with the soldiers occupying the city or with Edward's enlistment."

"That's right. You don't. You haven't done a thing to

stop it. You abandoned Edward and the rest of the volunteers when they needed your help."

"What is it that you wish me to do?" he asked. "Shall I ride to Virginia tonight and join Edward? Would a saber and an officer's commission truly make you happy?"

Emotions tore through her. If he joined Edward, then yes, she believed she would have a measure of peace. Samuel could look after him. But experience told her otherwise.

He cannot be trusted. He is not a man of his word.

"It is far too late for that, Samuel," she said. She was doing her best to keep her voice steady, in control. It would do no good to argue with him. She had already said everything that needed to be said. He had made his decision. She had made hers.

Sam watched her in silence for a few moments. Her face showed fatigue. More than likely she had slept just as little as he. He imagined that after his departure she had spent the long night pleading with Edward not to go south.

Even still, she was beautiful. Her dark curls had escaped her bun. Much of her hair now hung long and loose about her shoulders. Sam had rarely seen it that way. He liked it.

His eyes drifted to her unadorned left hand. He wondered what she had done with his engagement ring. Last night she had ripped it from her hand and held it out to him.

He had refused to take it back.

Look at me, Julia.

Seconds passed. He knew she could feel the weight of his gaze. Finally, she spoke.

"If you will excuse me, Samuel. I have work to tend to."

He drew in a shallow breath, knowing he had a decision to make. He could argue. He could refuse to leave. He could force her to turn around.

But when a lady makes a request, a gentleman will oblige her.

Walking out of the kitchen was one of the hardest things he had ever done. He wanted to take her in his arms, to set things right. He wanted to convince her that her anger toward him was pointless. He loved her. She loved him. He could see it in her eyes.

But Julia Marie Stanton was a stubborn woman. No amount of convincing could change her mind. She would have to do that for herself.

He was determined to wait until she did.

And in that time spent waiting, he'd pray that she would one day see things from his perspective.

He walked back to the lean-to. He placed the ax on the shelf then gathered up his outer clothing. Rather than return to the house by way of the kitchen, he entered through the garden door.

Dr. Stanton was still in the study. His spectacles were perched upon his nose, medical book still in his hands. He looked up.

"Thank you, son. Will you stay for supper?"

The offer was tempting. Goodness knows he wanted to. Even apart from his longing to stay with Julia, there was also the comfort to be found in time spent with Dr. and Mrs. Stanton. The prospect of returning to his lonely, cheerless home held little appeal in comparison.

But he had caused enough tension in the house already.

"Thank you, sir," he said. "But I have some errands to run this evening."

"Ah, I see. Be careful. I was out this morning and I noticed several boys in blue."

Sam nodded. "What do you think the next few weeks will bring?"

Julia's father shrugged. "Hard to say but I hope it is little more than an intimidating presence."

It reminded Sam of the answer he had given his students.

"After all," Dr. Stanton added, "the state legislature voted on their own accord to remain loyal to the Union. Let us hope and pray that that is the end of it."

Sam shook his hand and headed out to the street, praying silently but most fervently that Dr. Stanton's words would prove true. But the sinking feeling in his heart warned him that there was far more trouble awaiting them still.

From a crack in the kitchen door Julia had seen Samuel's broad back as he talked to her father. She had not been able to hear what they said. She wondered if he had told her father of their broken engagement. She wondered if Samuel had taken that moment to seek his advice on how to win her back.

Well, he won't win me back. He has proven his intentions. I will stand on my convictions whether he comes to chop wood or not.

From her vantage point she watched him shake hands with her father. Then as Samuel turned, Julia let the door close. She returned quickly to the stove. As she stood stirring the chicken soup, she heard the front door shut.

She peeked out the window. Samuel was walking down the street in the direction of the harbor. His hands were thrust deep in his pockets. His topper was set low on his forehead but she could tell he was deep in thought. Was he thinking of Edward? Was he thinking of her?

Her father came into the kitchen. Julia immediately left the window.

"He has gone to have a look about the city," he said, knowing exactly whom she was staring after. "Now, do you want to tell me what is going on?"

Julia turned from the stove to look at her father. She could tell that he had also endured a long, sleepless night. Tired lines were prevalent on his face. His left leg, which had been injured in a carriage accident years before, must have been bothering him. He was favoring it.

"I am making soup for Mother," she explained.

"I'm not talking about soup, Julia."

Her father's tone was firm, almost scolding.

Samuel has talked to him, she thought. *I knew he would.* "He told you, didn't he?"

"He?" Her father repeated, eyebrows arched. "I assume you mean Sam. And no, he didn't tell me anything. It was your indifference toward him when you came asking about the wood that caught my attention. Now what is going on?"

Julia could feel her cheeks reddening. She knew her father liked Samuel. He always had. Would he understand her position? Would he support her decision?

She stirred the soup once more, stalling, searching for words.

Her father was drumming his fingers on the kitchen table. She knew he would not leave until she had given him an answer.

I will have to make it known sooner or later. It might as well be now, she thought. "I have decided not to marry him."

The drumming stopped. "Does he know this?" her father asked.

Julia kept her eyes on the soup. Little bits of carrots and chicken were floating in the broth. "Yes. He knows."

He grunted. Then there were several seconds of silence. "When did you decide this?" he asked.

Julia put down her spoon. It was obvious that her business in the kitchen was not going to deter her father's questioning. "Last night."

"Last night?"

"I told him so when Edward—" Fresh grief over her brother's enlistment choked her voice. She looked at her father, hoping her eyes could convey the rest. *Surely you must feel the same.*

Her father drew in a deep breath. "I see. Is this about you and Sam or is it about Edward?"

"It is both," she admitted. "You have seen what has happened here. That day at the train station… Father, the soldiers fired upon us! Our fellow citizens were killed!"

"I know, Julia. I treated the wounded."

"Yes, and Edward has decided to do something! He's gone to Virginia to fight. But Samuel, he won't go! He won't defend what he says he cares about!"

"Because he won't go to Virginia?" Her father sighed. "Perhaps I set a poor example. Perhaps I remained neutral on this issue for too long. The issue of States' Rights, slavery included, never affected us."

"They affect you now," she said, "or they soon will. Northern soldiers have guns turned on this very neighborhood. If we don't stand against them, how can we ever be safe again?"

"And you think Samuel joining the Confederacy will change all of that?"

She blinked, not knowing how to answer.

Her father continued. "Sam has traveled. He has experienced life and drawn from others' life experiences. As a result, he carries a wider perspective of the world. He has spoken to me a few times about a man named Frederick Douglass."

"Yes, I know. The man from Boston. He mentioned him once."

The subject of slavery may have been a contentious topic in the nation for years but not so in the Stanton household. Julia's family did not own any slaves and none of their closest friends did either. Julia had never truly formed an opinion on the subject—and saw no need to now. The plight of a man living in Boston mattered very little to her compared to the safety of her family and friends right here in Maryland.

"Did he tell you he is a former slave?" her father asked. "A former Maryland slave?"

"No."

"Well, perhaps he wished to spare you the indelicate details. The things he spoke of have given me cause to think." He paused. "Rights are all fine and good until they infringe on the rights of others."

Julia shook her head. She still didn't see what that had to do with anything here in Mount Vernon. "But what about the soldiers?"

"I don't like their presence any more than you. Sam doesn't either, for that matter. But, given the scope, the turmoil that this nation is now facing, I understand why they thought it necessary to occupy Baltimore."

Julia let out a disgusted sigh. Her father had always encouraged her and Edward to express their own opinions. She did so now. "How can you even say that? What if their occupation leads to more trouble on the streets? It won't be safe for Mother or me to venture outside."

"Soldiers follow the orders of their commanding officers, of the president. The Bible tells us to pray for those in authority over us. If the military leaders remain honorable then we have nothing to fear." Then he added, "As for your honor, should the worst come, I have no doubt that Samuel Ward would give his life to protect you."

She felt her chin begin to quiver. Samuel had promised her such but she didn't believe him. He had professed loyalty to her family as well; yet he had abandoned her brother when he needed him most.

"Edward and Sam are two very different men," Dr. Stanton said. "They always have been. You know that better than anyone. Their friendship worked because they complemented each other's strengths, each other's weaknesses. They accepted one another's differences."

Scenes of years past flashed through her mind. Edward and Samuel had been schoolmates and best friends for as long as she could remember. Tears filled her eyes when she thought about what their relationship had become.

"And now?" she asked.

"Disagreements come to **every** relationship, some large, some small. It is how **those** disagreements are navigated that determines the future course of the relationship."

Silence hung heavily. Like the steam from the stove pot, it permeated the kitchen. Finally, her father asked, "Is that soup ready?"

Julia had nearly forgotten it. She removed it from the heat. "It's ready."

"Then I will take a bowl up to your mother."

She filled a dish and placed it on a tray. Then she

sliced up a loaf of bread, buttered it and laid it with the soup. She handed it to her father.

"Thank you, child." Then he turned for the door.

Julia was left alone to think about what he had said.

Chapter Two

Sam kept walking until he ended up at the wharf. Sunset was approaching and the local fishermen were making their way back to port. Their vessels were loaded with rockfish and blue crabs, a bountiful harvest from the Chesapeake Bay. He had often come to watch the ships roll in. It was a satisfying sight, a long hard day of work ended, the harbor tranquil and deep.

Tonight the local vessels had to steer and maneuver more than usual for the Baltimore harbor was also full of military ships. Their masts stood stall and black against the orange and purple sky. Sam tried to focus on the crabbing vessels. If he stared at them alone, life appeared to be peaceful.

But life isn't peaceful nor will it be for quite some time.

Sighing, he turned toward Federal Hill. An American flag flapped in the evening breeze while men in blue stood as sentinels over the city. Sam sadly thought how appropriate the hill's identity now was. Named nearly one hundred years before, it was on that very spot that Marylanders had celebrated the ratification of the Federal Constitution. No one then ever dreamed the site would be prime high ground for an occupying army with guns turned on its own citizens.

When I stepped off that train I walked onto a battlefield, he thought.

His fists clenched and his blood raced just thinking of that April day. Sam had returned home having completed his studies and graduation exercises in Philadelphia. As they had planned through their letters, Julia and Edward had met his train.

The President Street station was filled with citizens and Massachusetts soldiers. Sam had assumed the regiment was on their way to Washington, but had paid little attention to them. Though the business in South Carolina and Virginia was tantamount to insurrection, it had not concerned him. His only thoughts were of Julia, their long-awaited reunion and the July wedding they had planned.

She had been waiting for him beneath the clock, a red and black bonnet on her head and the smile on her face that he found so irresistible. Samuel had barely spared a glance in Edward's direction as he'd drawn her in, at least as close as her hoop and ruffled skirts would allow.

"I have missed you," he'd said.

Her eyes had been full of love. "I have missed you as well."

As they'd exchanged words of devotion and promise, neither one noticed that the Massachusetts soldiers had formed a column, that they had begun to march toward the southbound train lines on Bolton Street. None of them had realized how angry the citizens around them had become until someone bumped Julia from behind. She'd crashed into Sam's chest. The crowd was fast becoming a mob.

"We should leave," he'd said to Edward.

"Indeed. This way! Double quick!"

They'd turned for the street. Edward ducked as a stone whizzed past his head. Rocks and bottles were flying. Sam did his best to shelter Julia from the debris while her brother led them through the crowd. The citizens were shouting insults at the soldiers. Some of the soldiers were beginning to answer back. Sam feared they would soon use more than ugly words.

"Where is the carriage?" he'd asked Edward.

"Over here!"

They'd done their best to cross the street. Pressing hard against the angry flow, they had been like salmon swimming upstream. By the time they'd reached Pratt Street, paving stones were being ripped from the road-bed. Carts and wagons were overturned. Julia tripped twice on her skirts.

Tears had silvered her lashes. "What is happening? Why is everyone acting this way?"

"Hurry. We must hurry."

Screams erupted as a volley of gunfire sent the masses scurrying. "They are shooting at us!" Julia cried. "The soldiers are shooting at us!"

Instinctively, Sam shoved Julia into a narrow alley, knocking loose her bonnet. He and Edward then fell in behind.

He'd thought that would be the end of it, that cooler heads would prevail and peace would return. He was wrong. War had come. His best friend had left to fight and the woman he loved now wanted no part of the life they had planned together.

Sam's shoulders fell with another long, labored sigh. He knew the conflict between him and Julia stemmed from that day on Pratt Street. She had recently confessed to having nightmares about the incident and was wary of walking anywhere in public. She loathed and feared the Federal soldiers who had brought such chaos and destruction to her city.

Nearly a dozen Baltimoreans had died and countless others were wounded. Edward sought his solace in taking a stand against troops who would open fire in the presence of innocent civilians. Sam understood such a response but he could not bring himself to join Edward's cause.

And yet to do nothing...

He snatched his topper from his head and raked his fingers through his hair. Standing on the dock, he gazed at the might of the Federal forces. Would scenes like the one at the train station be repeated? Were worse things to come?

Where are You God? Have You turned Your back on us, on this city? What are we supposed to do now?

Though Sam waited, God did not answer. A cool breeze blew over the harbor. The smell of fish drifted past his nose. By now it was almost dark. Replacing his hat and thrusting his hands deep in his pockets, he turned back toward Mount Vernon. The shops along Pratt Street were closing up for the evening. The lamplighter was making his rounds. Sam walked past him. The man nodded pleasantly, then moved on to his next lamppost. Sam couldn't help but wonder which side the man and his family had chosen.

Are they pro-Union or pro-secession? Are they united or divided?

By the time Sam reached Monument Square he met up with a small contingent of Federal soldiers. Even in the semidarkness he could see that their uniforms were new and blue. They had brass buckles on their belts, polished muskets on their shoulders. He wondered if they had ever seen conflict before.

A corporal in the group eyed him suspiciously. Assuming he was just another renegade in a neighborhood full of Southern sympathizers, the man fell out of step long enough to glare at Sam. He nodded politely to the soldier, then kept walking. He had no quarrel with the corporal and he wanted to keep it that way.

The neighborhood doors were shut tight and the curtains drawn. The Stanton home was no exception. As Sam passed by he wondered what Julia was doing at that very moment. Had she baked another loaf of bread? Was the kindling box empty? Resisting the urge to knock on the door and find out, he kept walking.

He lived a few blocks north of Mount Vernon. His was a quieter street and his brick home more modest than those in Julia's neighborhood. Sam's home was furnished sparsely, little more than the necessities. He had never minded the bare solitude before. It was conducive to study. Tonight, however, the house just seemed empty and cold.

I will start the stove, he thought, *warm up something to eat.*

He checked the kindling box. It was running low. He immediately thought of Julia and the look on her face when she saw him in her father's study. Pain squeezed his heart.

She did not wish to see me.

Sam lit a lantern. Once more he took off his frock coat and went outside. He picked up his own ax and set to the task of splitting wood. That which had earlier been done as a labor of love was now an act of drudgery.

* * *

Sunday morning dawned warm and humid, a fore-taste of the oppressive summer to come. Julia dressed for church but found that her mind was far from worship. She was concerned about what the atmosphere of the morning service would be like. Many of her fellow parishioners already knew of Edward's enlistment and those that didn't would soon find out. She wondered what some would say. There had been tension in the congregation before the occupation of the city. Many families supported States' Rights. Just as many others professed loyalty to the Union.

Oh, Lord, please don't let there be a scene.

She climbed into the back of her father's carriage. The seat seemed so empty without Edward beside her. She wondered where her brother was that morning. Had he and the rest of the Guard crossed safely into Virginia? What, if anything, had he had to eat?

After whispering a prayer for his safety her thoughts returned to church. She wondered if Samuel would be waiting on the front steps when they arrived. He always walked to the building early, saying he enjoyed the serenity of the Lord's Day morning. He would wait for her carriage to come to a stop then help her out. He'd give her hand a squeeze. She would smile.

I won't smile this morning, she thought, *even if he is there.*

Her father rolled the carriage to a stop in front of the church. Fellow worshippers clustered about the yard but Samuel wasn't there. Julia felt an odd mixture of disappointment and relief. She climbed slowly from her father's carriage then followed her parents into the building.

The windows were open, yet the room was stuffy.

Creatures of habit, most parishioners sat in their usual pews each Sunday. Today, the people were scattered about. Longtime friends were now on separate sides of the aisle. Even some families were divided. A tension filled the air. No one seemed to be breathing.

Julia knew exactly what had happened. A chill ran through her. *They have chosen sides,* she thought. *And now they will watch to see what we do.*

She glanced at her father. He did not hesitate. Dr. Stanton led his wife to their usual pew, five from the front on the left-hand side. They sat down. Julia adjusted her hoop. She opened her fan. The chill had passed and now she was sweating.

Within seconds after taking their seat, Charlie Johnson, a local businessman and friend of the family, slipped in behind her father. He whispered, though his words were loud enough that Julia could hear them.

"Thomas, for goodness' sake, what are you doing? Edward has enlisted. Why are you sitting on this side of the church?"

Julia blanched. She realized to what Mr. Johnson was referring. They were sitting with those members who had expressed their support for the Federal occupation. Families with sons fighting for the Confederacy were seated on the right side of the congregation. Julia wanted to shrink from view.

Her father did not flinch. "We are sitting where we always have, Charlie," he said calmly. "This is our family pew. It always has been. It always will be."

Mr. Johnson let out a huff but moved back to his seat without further argument. A murmur swept over the congregation. Julia sat frozen, eyes staring straight ahead. She was glad that her bonnet limited her view to what was directly in front of her. She did not want to see what was happening around her. She knew the whispers were about her family.

The pew creaked and Julia realized someone else was approaching. She held her breath, fearing another confrontation about their seating arrangements. She cocked her head ever so slightly, just enough to see who was coming.

It was Samuel.

He was dressed in his finest brown frock coat, Bible in his hand. His face was calm, undisturbed. He looked like he was the only person in the building who had come to worship.

He nodded to Julia's parents. Then he sat down beside her, just as he had every Sunday for years. He gave her a long measured look. The weight of his gaze caused her to tremble. She wanted to ask him what he was doing joining them as if nothing had changed. But given what had just taken place with Charlie Johnson, the last thing she wanted was to cause more contention over the seating arrangements.

He smiled at her. Though she tried to ignore it, her heart was fluttering.

Reverend Perry then took to the pulpit and the service began. Julia could not say what songs they sang or what Scriptures they read. She was distracted by Samuel's presence. Part of her welcomed it, the other couldn't fathom it.

How can he sit beside me as though nothing has happened? I have told him that I do not wish to marry him. Why can't he take no for an answer?

She stole glances at him. There he sat with his Bible on his lap, lost in reading. It was as though, in his mind, there were no guns, no war, as though all the world was right. Julia was even more puzzled. *How can he act this way? Doesn't he care? Doesn't he worry for Edward's sake? For the sake of this city?*

It was only when Samuel bowed his head did she realize that Reverend Perry was closing the service in prayer. Julia also closed her eyes. She tried to focus, to be respectful.

"Lord, we humbly ask Thee to grant President Lincoln wisdom."

A murmur rippled through the right side of the room. Julia was as surprised by his words as the rest of the group was. All thoughts of conversing with the Almighty dissipated and her focus shifted to Reverend Perry's words alone. She held her breath. The Reverend did not stop with his petition for Lincoln. He also prayed for the officers and soldiers occupying the city.

He is making his position known, she thought. *He is obviously siding with the Union.*

"And we ask Thee to guard our young men who have chosen to fight…"

In shock, her head went up. Just when she thought she had him pegged as a supporter of the Federal Army, the Reverend prayed for the safety of eight men who had enlisted for the Confederacy. All eight were sons of the congregation. When Edward's name was mentioned, tears squeezed past her eyelids and a cry escaped her lips. Julia had to fight hard to keep from breaking down completely.

Just when she felt her composure crumbling, she felt the warmth of a hand slide over and around her trembling fingers. Samuel had taken her hand in his. His touch conveyed the love, the strength, the same comfort as it always had. In spite of herself, Julia clasped it tightly while whispering her own prayer on Edward's behalf.

* * *

God comfort her, Sam thought. He stole a glance at Julia's face. Her head was bowed and she was clutching a lace handkerchief to her mouth. He could understand the pain she was feeling. Edward's departure was bad enough but coupled with the way he had parted, the tension in the family that night, it only made things worse. Sam regretted every minute of their conversation.

Edward had been called to the armory during a dreadful thunderstorm. Little did Sam know Federal troops were in the process of occupying the city. When Edward returned home that night he announced the terrible news.

"The armory has been stripped," he'd said, his face a mixture of wild emotions. "Any man who would take a gun and hide it was given one."

I was angry that he had brought the muskets to the house. I know he only hoped to protect his family with them but I didn't see it that way then. All I could think of was Federal soldiers tearing the house apart to find them. All I could think of was what they might do to her.

"Edward," Sam had said, "the Northern troops will realize what has happened. They will search the houses. They will find the guns. If you hide them here you are putting your mother and sister at risk."

"Then I'll take the muskets with me. I'll take them south, tonight."

Everyone in the room realized what he had just said, though shock stole the words of objection from their lips. Only Julia had been able to find her voice.

"No, Edward! No! You can't do such a thing!"

Her mother then also began to plead. "Son, please. Think about this. You don't want to do this."

"Yes, I do. I am going to personally see that the Federal Army is thrown out of Baltimore!"

He'd looked to Dr. Stanton. "It is our duty to protect our city, our state. Father, I know you can't fight. Your leg would never allow it, so the duty is left to those who can."

He then looked at Samuel. He'd held out a musket. "Come with me."

Tossing the invading army out of the city for the sake of Julia's safety so strongly appealed to Sam that he nearly reached for the gun, until he realized, defending States' Rights meant defending them *all*.

"No," Sam had said.

Edward lowered the musket with a look of shock on his face. "What did you say?"

The thoughts fired through his head. *Protect her and freedom! Fight!* It took everything Sam had within him to stand firm.

"I said no."

A scowl crossed Edward's face. "Not even now? You won't fight, even now? You won't defend the rights of your state?"

"By defending rights are you including slavery?"

"I'm not fighting for slaves one way or the other! Look man, a Federal battery has taken aim at our front door! If we don't stand against such tyranny, who will?"

"I won't go with you."

"Then you are a coward." Edward then turned to Julia. "You should give serious consideration to the kind of man you are marrying."

Sam stared now at Julia's ringless hand in his. Hers was so delicate, so fragile compared to his gnarled fingers. *Lord, forgive me, I thought Edward was acting like a fool. We both just wanted to protect her. I understand why he felt the way he did.*

He stroked her fingers, praying for reconciliation. After what had happened on Pratt Street every fiber, every nerve in Sam's body pleaded for him to fight. It was not cowardice that kept him from doing so. It was the belief that God had chosen another path for him. *I cannot condone slavery. If only Julia could realize that.*

Sam had tried to explain it to her. When Edward had thumped up the staircase, muddy boots, muskets and all, Julia had turned her eyes to him. He saw the doubt in them, the fear. He knew Edward's words carried great weight.

"Julia," he said as he moved to embrace her, "You know I would give my life for you but this isn't the way—"

"Go with him, Samuel. Please."

Her request had shocked him. "Do you really want me to leave? Do you really know what war is?"

"No, of course not! I don't want you to go! I don't want any of you to go! I don't want any of this to be happening!"

"Then think about what you are saying. We must stay together! We must convince Edward not to go south."

"He won't listen! He would rather die than dishonor his state! Samuel, please! Go with him. Only you can take care of him."

"Julia, I can't willingly support the position the South is taking. I can't condone slavery."

Pure confusion filled her eyes. "But we don't even own slaves!"

"I can't support a government which allows others to do so."

As soon as the words were out of his mouth he realized how ridiculous they sounded. He had sealed his fate.

"You have supported one thus far!" she said, tears hardening into anger. "How many Maryland plantations on the eastern shore rely on slaves? You are using that as an excuse! I have never known you to march with the abolitionists! Edward is right! You are a coward!"

She ripped the engagement ring from her finger. "I will not marry you!"

Sitting beside her now, he continued to hold her hand as Reverend Perry prayed. Sam knew Julia had begged him to join Edward not because she wished for war but because she feared for her brother's safety—and for their own. He had no quarrel with her brother. He would give anything to see their relationship restored, their family reunited.

Lord, I believe that slavery is wrong but my own state supports it! And what of Dr. Carter and his abolitionist friends? What if they are radicals? What if they advocate the methods of John Brown?

The newspapers had been full of stories just a few months ago concerning the raid on Harper's Ferry. The town was held hostage. People were killed.

I don't know which position is right or which side to be on. All I know is that I love her. Show me Your will...

If Reverend Perry had meant for his prayer to be a comfort, it had just the opposite effect. When the congregation was dismissed many of the women were in tears and the men were grumbling.

Julia was pale, pensive, lost in her own private world. Sam led her from the pew, her arm through his. The air inside the church was stifling and he worried that she might faint. He steered her to the door and down the front steps. A slight breeze wafted across the church-yard. Julia seemed glad for it. Her face pinkened.

The fact that she was allowing him to lead her was a good sign. *Perhaps today we can iron out our differences. We can commit to navigating the unknown together.*

Once outside, parishioners began conversing. Reverend Perry's prayer was the subject of much of the discussion. Sam caught snatches of it as he walked Julia to the carriage.

"That man is riding the fence! Waiting to see which side prevails!"

"Praying for Lincoln! He should be praying for the souls of those on Federal Hill!"

Sam ignored their words. He waited as Dr. Stanton helped his wife inside the carriage. He studied Julia. She was still silent but her color was definitely improving with the fresh air. While they were waiting, Warren Meade, one of Dr. Stanton's patients, approached them. Julia's father had recently set his broken arm.

Sam nodded to the man and Dr. Stanton smiled when he saw him. "Warren, how's your arm today?"

"Fine," the man said gruffly.

"The pain is diminishing?"

"Yes, but I am not here to talk about that."

"Oh?" said Dr. Stanton.

"I am here to tell you that I have found a new physician."

Julia's father blinked. "Is something wrong?"

The man was obviously angry and whatever the disagreement between patient and doctor, Sam thought it best to give them privacy. He helped Julia into the carriage. His back was to the ongoing discussion. Julia had just taken a seat when all of a sudden, Warren Meade said loud enough for everyone to hear,

"Slavery is a sin! God won't protect men who fight for it!"

Sam cringed. He knew the reference was in regard to Edward. Julia knew as well. Her eyes narrowed. Her jaw stiffened.

"Don't pay any attention to that," he said to her. "He doesn't realize what he is saying." He reached for her hand.

She pulled it back. Her eyes held the same look that Edward's had the night he left for Virginia.

"Samuel," she said slowly, mouth set tight. "I must ask you not to visit my house or sit in my family pew again."

He was stunned.

Warren Meade must have stormed off after making his point, for Dr. Stanton climbed into the carriage.

"It is time to go," he said. He sounded as though there was a lot more that he wanted to say but was holding his tongue. He glanced at his wife, his daughter, then at Sam. "Son, will you be joining us for dinner?"

Sam could not get past the look of contempt in Julia's eyes. She had apparently classified him in the same category as Warren Meade. He wanted to tell her that he thought nothing of the kind about her or her father. He wanted her to know that he prayed for Edward daily, just as she.

But he could not find the words.

Dr. Stanton was waiting for an answer. Sam looked at him.

"No," he said. "Thank you, but I must tend to some things at home."

Dr. Stanton nodded. He gave his horse a click. "Then soon," he said and the carriage rolled away.

The carriage rocked back and forth as the wheels rolled over the cobblestone. No one said a word. They traveled in silence toward Monument Square. Federal soldiers were stationed periodically throughout the public gardens. Hands shaking, Julia closed her eyes. She did not want to see them. The sight of the men was nauseating.

She tried to think of happier times as she wobbled in her seat. She remembered how, as a child, she and Edward would ride to church. Julia would be dressed in her finest laces. Edward would purposefully tug at her skirts, trying to wrinkle them. He would knock into her as they turned corners, overexaggerating the carriage's motion.

"Edward!" she would whine.

"Julia!" he would answer back.

They would fuss. They would argue. Their mother would scold them into silent submission but they could never remain quiet or still for very long.

She then thought of her first carriage ride with Samuel, their first outing as a courting couple. Edward was chosen as the chaperone. Planted squarely in the front bench seat, he purposefully sped through the streets of Baltimore. He'd taken corners with lightning speed and had managed to find every bump in the road.

Samuel had only laughed, and slapped Edward on the shoulder. "Drive faster!" He'd slid his arm around her. Shocked, Julia looked at him.

He'd grinned innocently. "I am just making certain that you don't fall out of the carriage."

She couldn't help but laugh. Samuel had done the same.

Friends and coconspirators, she thought. *Now they are on opposite sides.*

A family must stick together. A church should stick together.

She had seen the flash in Samuel's eyes when Warren Meade made his vehement declaration. She knew it had angered him. He knew it had angered her.

But he did nothing. He didn't even turn around and face the man. He just stood there! He let the man condemn my brother, my family!

Her anger swelled.

Samuel isn't the least bit interested in defending Edward's name, or any of the rest of my family. For all I know, he agrees with Warren Meade.

She crossed her arms in front of her, mind certain. *I have made the right decision.*

Chapter Three

On Monday morning, Julia and her mother set about their regular routine. They prepared breakfast then moved on to the tasks of laundry and housekeeping.

The foyer floor still showed signs of mud from the night of Edward's departure, so Julia readied the linseed oil and hot water to give it a good scrubbing. While she worked, she prayed for her brother and all the other men who had traveled south.

Bless them, Lord, and keep them safe. May they all return home soon.

As heartsick as she was, Julia moved about the house at a productive pace. Everywhere were signs of Edward; a book in the parlor, his work boots at the back door. She returned all the items to their proper places. Then she aired his linens and beat his rugs. She wanted his room fresh and ready for his return.

When it was time to begin midday meal preparations, she noticed the kindling box was once again running low. She went to the lean-to and gathered up as much wood as she could carry. She was painfully aware of who had split the logs but she did her best to ignore the fact.

I now know what kind of man Samuel is. Edward's enlistment, as awful as it is, in a small way is a blessing. At least the relationship was severed while it still could be. If I had married Samuel Ward, goodness knows how my life would have turned out.

She carried the wood across the yard and then into the kitchen.

"Thank you, dear," her mother said as she laid it in the box. "You should hurry now and change."

Julia wiped the front of her dress. Wood was wood, yes, but her yellow day dress wasn't that dirty. "Why?" She asked.

"For the prayer meeting, of course."

Julia had no idea what her mother was talking about. "What prayer meeting?"

Esther gave her a quizzical expression. "Reverend Perry called for a prayer meeting today at noon. He announced it yesterday at the end of the service." She paused, the corner of her mouth revealing just the hint of a smile. "Weren't you listening?"

Julia could tell by the look on her mother's face that she did not need to answer that question. Her embarrassment for not giving her full attention to the Lord was only surpassed by the humiliation that her mother knew exactly why she hadn't been listening.

Samuel had been distracting her.

All that she could fully remember of the worship service was that Reverend Perry's prayers were not well received.

"The congregation is so divided," Julia said. "After yesterday it is a wonder that he would even call such a meeting."

"That is exactly why he is doing so. Hurry now. Change your dress. Your father will be home shortly."

Julia went upstairs to make herself ready. She wondered what this meeting today would involve. One thing she was certain of, she would not be distracted by Samuel Ward this time.

By scheduling the event during the noon hour the Reverend surely hoped to draw folks on their lunch break. Samuel would never be able to make it from the seminary in Rolland Park all the way to the church on Charles Street and back in one hour.

I will be free to pray for my brother's safety and for the concerns of my city without his disapproving eye.

Her father returned from his morning rounds and the family started off. Julia rode mostly in silence, eyes drifting from one house to the next. There were no visible markers but she knew many of these homes had a son or brother who had chosen to fight.

Bless them, Lord. Bring them home soon.

When the carriage rolled past one of the local taverns, several Federal soldiers were standing outside. Julia made the mistake of looking at them. One man had the audacity to wink at her. Clutching her Bible tightly, she focused her eyes on her father's stovepipe hat.

Her hands were trembling. All she could think of was that day at the train station, when Federal gunfire nearly led to her being trampled and sent eleven of her fellow citizens off into eternity.

The bell chimed the hour as Dr. Stanton brought their carriage to rest in front of the church.

"Come now," he said as he helped Julia and her mother to the street. "We mustn't be late."

As eager as she was to be safely inside, Julia was not ready to endure divided seating arrangements and political barricades. When she stepped into the sanctuary, however, only Reverend Perry was present.

"Thomas!" the man said, immediately coming up the aisle to greet her father. "And ladies...how good of you to come."

"I had several visits to make this morning," Dr. Stanton said. "I feared we would be the last to arrive."

"On the contrary," Reverend Perry said. "You are the first."

Julia glanced around. Though grateful there were no icy glares or judgmental remarks, her heart still sank. *Will we be the only ones? Isn't there anyone else who will pray for this city? For our brave men?*

She brushed away the discouraging thoughts and lifted her chin with determination. *I will do so. I will pray for Edward and for Baltimore.*

If Reverend Perry was disheartened by the lack of attendance, he did not reveal it. He quickly led Julia's family to the front pew and started the service.

"Let's begin with a hymn."

Without the benefit of pipe organ or additional singers, the four of them joined in singing, "How Firm a Foundation."

The meager voices barely filled the space between the walls but Julia reminded herself that where two or three were gathered, God himself was in attendance.

They finished the hymn and sat down.

Reverend Perry then prayed. He did exactly as he had done before, praying for the safety of the city and for the protection of all soldiers involved in the war. When he fell silent, Julia's father carried on. With heartfelt sincerity he prayed for the congregation. He asked that they would be able to put their political differences aside in order to present the gospel of Christ.

Though he did not mention the man by name, Julia wondered if he was not thinking of Warren Meade. Her nerves bristled as she remembered his words. She stiffened even further when she thought of Samuel's clear unwillingness to defend her brother's good name.

Edward seeks to protect us from danger, from the tyranny of those Federal soldiers. Samuel would simply let them have their way.

Julia did not lift her voice in public but she did pray silently for Edward's swift return. She then remembered the citizens who had been injured on Pratt Street.

And for them and their families, Lord...please comfort them. Please don't let such a thing happen again!

She heard her mother's voice. Somewhere near the end of the prayer, the back door opened. Footsteps quietly, rhythmically came down the aisle. They stopped midway. A pew then creaked.

Someone else has joined us! Oh thank You, Lord!

Her faith stirred and hope soared until she recognized the petitioner's voice.

"Lord, Almighty, thank You for hearing our prayers..."

Samuel! She clenched the lace handkerchief in her lap. *How dare he come!*

Any spiritual comfort she had previously felt evaporated. All she could think of was the man sitting just a few rows back; the one who had promised to love and protect her, yet, hadn't the courage to do so.

He is probably here to wish for Edward's destruction, to condemn all those who support States' Rights!

She was so busy imagining what he was praying for that she failed to hear what he was actually saying.

"My sins, Lord... Forgive me for my sins."

Though Sam had intended on coming to this meeting to pray for Edward, he could not get past the need to confess his own faults to God. For too long he had simply gone about his life with his plans for the future, Julia, his teaching position, an honest but comfortable life here in Baltimore.

He had never once considered God may have other things in mind.

Frederick Douglass's experiences flooded his thoughts.

The man in his autobiography had shown owners whipping and cursing their slaves while simultaneously quoting Scripture to them. He also told of plantation owners who bowed their heads each night at supper to thank God for their food only to then turn around and starve the very hands that had farmed it.

The former slave explained that he loved the Christianity that Christ had preached, the message of love, peace and purity. Yet, in America, Christ's message had become polluted. Those who called themselves followers yet whipped women and stole babies from their mothers' arms were corrupt and hypocritical.

Where am I in all of this? Sam wondered. *What form of Christianity do I cling to?*

Sam had never owned another human being. He had never beaten or cursed any man. He attended church each week, read his Bible daily. He prayed faithfully yet he couldn't help but sense there was more to it.

Does Jesus expect more from His followers? Does His sacrificial love demand it?

Sam had always sought to live a life of peace, to show others the love of Christ.

...As ye have done it unto one of the least of these my brethren, ye have done it unto Me...

The Savior's words pricked his heart. *One of the least of these...* who were the very least? Who did society, the law and government itself claim as the least?

Sam knew full well the answer to his own question.

Simply refusing to join those who supported slavery, or at the very least allowed it, was no longer enough. He knew that now. He would attend Dr. Carter's meeting. He did not know what else may be involved but he sensed the Lord was urging him to find out.

"I will do Your will, Lord."

And following God's will, Sam realized, meant placing Julia in His hands. Sam could not continue to spend his strength worrying and planning how to win her back.

He had to focus on being obedient. He had to trust.

What was happening, Julia could not fully explain. The Reverend and even her own father were now in tears. A shiver ran through her for she could sense the Almighty's presence in the place.

Oh, Lord, thank You for hearing our prayers. Thank You for what You will do here in this city.

After a few moments, eyes opened, heads raised. Reverend Perry concluded the meeting by extending an invitation.

"I ask you to join me tomorrow and each day thereafter at noon."

Her father quickly said they would. When the Reverend looked to Samuel, Julia bristled.

He explained it was impossible to reach the church at noon but, "I will gladly give what time I can."

Wonderful, Julia thought sarcastically. *I suppose I will have to get used to him.*

When the service was over her mother and father continued to speak with Reverend Perry. Julia waited a step away, discreetly eyeing Samuel from the safety of her lace trimmed bonnet.

He approached her slowly.

"I wanted to offer my apologies," he said before she could speak first.

She was taken aback. "For?"

"For pressing you. For not honoring your wishes."

His brown eyes were fixed on hers. Julia couldn't help but think of the love that had filled them the night he'd asked for her hand, of the ardor with which he had kissed her.

Heat flooded her face. Her skin was tingling and her mind churning.

"It was wrong of me to visit the house and to sit in your family pew," he said. "It will not happen again."

She opened her fan, hoping her voice was smooth and calm. "Thank you, Samuel."

"You are welcome. Good day, Julia."

He turned and walked up the aisle, through the doors and out into the warm May sunshine.

After he had gone, her parents were ready to depart as well. Julia followed them to the carriage. A chill had now settled over her.

"Did you bring your sewing basket, dear?" her mother asked. "We can drop by Sally's on the way home."

"Oh," Julia said absentmindedly. "No. I did not. I completely forgot about the sewing circle."

She was still mulling over what Samuel had said. Part of her felt relieved, the other struggled with the finality of it all. Why did she suddenly feel so guilty?

This is what I wanted. I will not marry a man like him.

"Well, then," she heard her mother say. "We will just drive home. You can walk back to Sally's after you gather your things."

"Perhaps I will stay home this week," Julia said.

"Why is that?"

"I don't feel much like visiting."

Every week, she and her neighborhood friends met together for conversation and needlework. The real reason she did not wish to attend today was that the girls were scheduled to begin the lace for her wedding gown. The white dress had already been sewn. All that was needed to complete it was the finishing trim. Julia had not yet told any of them about the broken engagement.

She dreaded doing so.

Some of them, like her closest friend Sally Hastings, would understand. Her brother Stephen had left for Virginia the same time Edward did. Sally had even at one time had eyes for Edward. The woman could sympathize with Julia's pain.

Prissy, opinionated, Rebekah Van der Geld would not. Rebekah had recently expressed disdain for the growing secessionist movement.

"It is treason," she'd said flatly, "and anyone who fights for the Confederacy deserves to be hanged."

Julia sighed. She had once considered Rebekah a friend but did not any longer. She wondered how the girl continued to come to their group when she clearly held such an opposing view.

Why must politics invade every aspect of life? Why can't we just go on living?

Her mother spoke. "I talked with Sally briefly yesterday at church. She told me she was hoping you would come today. I think she misses Stephen terribly."

Julia's agitation was replaced with concern for her friend. She knew what Sally was feeling. She wanted to comfort her and perhaps, if they had a moment in private, she could tell her about Samuel. It would help to have a friend's blessing when her guilt over the broken engagement came calling.

"Perhaps I will go," she said to her mother, "but are you sure you want me to?"

"Life must continue, Julia, despite hardship, despite grief. The best thing we can do for Edward, for all of us, is to pray and then go on living."

When Julia arrived at the Hastings home, Sally met her at the front door. She gave her a hug.

"I am so pleased that you came," she said. "We must catch up when the others have gone."

"Yes," Julia said. "I would like to."

Sally took her hand and ushered her into the parlor. The other girls were all there, sisters Trudy and Elizabeth Martin, Emily Davis and sour-looking Rebekah Van der Geld.

The girls smiled. Rebekah stared. She sat with her back straight and rigid as though she was ready to pounce on any subversive political idea. The black bonnet she wore was too big for her head. Julia thought she looked ridiculous.

"We weren't certain that you would come," Trudy said. "We heard about Edward." Her voice was sweet and genuine.

Julia liked her and her twin sister. Their older brother George was considering enlistment. She sat down next to them. "Has George decided?"

"He wants to go," Trudy said, "but fears what it will mean for Mother."

Elizabeth leaned forward. She looked exactly like her sister but for a few freckles on her nose. "George has been the man of the house ever since Father passed away. He feels torn between two duties."

"Both honorable," Julia said.

Rebekah huffed.

Julia shot her a look. Sally stepped between them with a tray of cold tea. She smiled.

"It is warm this afternoon, isn't it?"

Sally Hastings had a peaceful presence that could stabilize almost any situation. Julia envied her friend's ability to do so. She wished she were more like her.

"Thank you," Julia said as she took a glass.

"There are tea cakes as well," Sally said. "Rebekah, will you serve them?"

Rebekah got up from her seat and did as Sally asked, though not as graciously as her host. Julia took an orange-glazed tea cake from her tray if only to be polite.

"How is your father feeling?" she asked, knowing he had been ill with stomach pains.

Rebekah's face softened but only a bit. "Much better, thank you."

When the refreshments had been served, the young ladies got down to business.

"Well," Sally said. "We have finished our other projects and given what has been happening these last few weeks, I thought that perhaps we might do something different today." She paused, eyes sweeping the room. "We all know at least one man who has gone to serve. Perhaps we could take on a project for the regiment."

Elizabeth looked delighted by the suggestion. "I have heard that there is a group of ladies in Carroll County who are at this very moment sewing a coat for General Lee."

Trudy nodded enthusiastically. "Yes. Yes. Let's do something of that sort."

"Why?" Rebekah grumbled. "Your men left in full uniform."

Emily Davis was an only child and had no relatives

serving as of yet but she liked Sally's suggestion as well. "What about sashes?"

Sally nodded, though hesitantly. "Yes, but wouldn't that be only for officers?" She looked about the circle.

The women had no idea.

"What about a regimental flag?" Elizabeth suggested.

"That could get you arrested," Rebekah announced. "Haven't you read the paper? No displays of Confederate regalia, no Confederate music... Why I even read a notice concerning red-and-white-striped stockings."

"For goodness' sake, what is wrong with striped stockings?" Sally asked.

"Red and white have been deemed pro-secessionist colors. Anyone found wearing such could be arrested."

Sally blew out her breath and Julia's face heated as she thought of her own red and white stockings which were tucked beneath her hoop and petticoats. Part of her feared catching the attention of some impudent Yankee rascal on the way home. The defiant streak in her wished to display the stockings proudly.

"Well," Elizabeth said. "If they insist on spying on our ankles then I suppose we will have to wear extra petticoats to hide them."

"Indeed," Emily said.

"Speaking of stockings," Trudy said. "What about socks for our men?"

"You mean ordinary, plain ones?" Sally asked.

"Yes. Of course. Surely no one, even Yankees, could object to sending our men socks. They will need them for winter."

The thought of Edward still on the battlefield come Christmas time was too much to bear. Julia looked at Sally. She must have been thinking the same about Stephen. Her chin quivered.

"Let's hope it doesn't last that long," she said.

"Why are we so concerned with the soldiers?" Rebekah asked. "Aren't we supposed to be making lace?"

The women stopped. They quickly looked at Julia.

"Oh, my dear, I am so sorry," said Sally. "Forgive me. I can't believe I forgot."

Julia felt incredibly uneasy but it had nothing to do with Sally's forgetfulness. "It is all right," she said. "We have all had other things on our mind."

A heaviness blanketed the room. No one seemed to know what to say and Julia had no idea where to begin.

"Dear me," Emily said at last. "Samuel hasn't gone, has he?"

"No," Julia said, feeling the color creep up her neck.

"Finally, a wise man," said Rebekah.

All eyes were on Julia. The knot in her stomach tightened. She couldn't bring herself to say what she knew she must. She didn't want her friends to know that her fiancé had refused to join her brother. She also couldn't stand to hear Rebekah sing Samuel's praises for doing so.

"The wedding," she said weakly, "has been *postponed*."

A collective sigh went about the room. Even Rebekah looked concerned.

"Edward was to be Samuel's best man, wasn't he?" Sally said, obviously thinking that was the reason.

"Yes."

Julia's friend tried to smile, to sound hopeful. "I am certain he will be home soon."

"Yes," Elizabeth said. "They all will."

The women dabbed their eyes with their handkerchiefs. Emily then spoke. "I think we should continue with our original plan and work on Julia's lace. That way everything will be ready when the time comes."

The others nodded in agreement.

Julia tried to object. "That is very kind of you but it isn't necessary."

"Nonsense," Sally said. "I would rather look ahead to happier times."

"So would I," Trudy said.

Julia could hardly argue with that. If looking forward to a wedding that would never actually take place was what it took to lift her friends' spirits, then Julia would not interfere. Not today, when she was already uncomfortable and upset over her encounter with Samuel at the prayer meeting.

"Thank you," she said meekly.

"Now," Sally said, eager to begin, "which pattern did you choose?"

When the hall clock chimed four, they put their newly constructed lace in their baskets and agreed to meet again the following week. Julia was slow in packing up her supplies. She put away the dining room chairs while Sally bid her other guests goodbye. When she came back into the room, she spoke softly.

"I wanted to tell you something," she said, "but I didn't want to say it in front of the others, especially not Rebekah."

"What is it?" Julia asked.

"My father will be handling the mail."

Julia did not understand. Mr. Hastings was a member of the city council. "He has taken a new job?"

"No. The Confederate mail."

"Oh."

"When our brothers are able to write, the letters will

come through special channels, not the regular post," Sally explained. "Bring your letters here to mail them. It will be safer that way."

Julia nodded. She hadn't thought about how to mail letters to an opposing army but she was glad someone else did. "I hope we hear from them soon," she said.

"So do I. Now...what is bothering you? I know it is more than Edward. You barely mentioned Sam at all today. That's not like you."

Julia sighed, hoping the others hadn't noticed. "I was going to tell you. I just didn't know how."

"Tell me what? Did he do something to upset you?"

"It's more what he didn't do."

"I don't understand."

Julia motioned to a chair. "Perhaps we should sit. This may take a while."

Sally did so and as Julia spilled the entire story she listened most sympathetically. "Oh, Julia. I am so sorry. I didn't know he held abolitionist views."

"Neither did I, until recently. What do you think?"

"About Sam or slavery?"

"Both."

Sally shrugged. "Slavery is legal but..."

"But what?"

"My father says there are some who abuse the law. That they treat their slaves as though they were subhuman. That's not right."

"I don't think so either and I can understand why Samuel would be angry about that."

"But?"

"But look at what has happened in our city. This has nothing to do with slaves. To say he will not fight because the Confederacy supports slavery sounds like an excuse to me. There is an army outside with guns. They are telling us what music we can and cannot sing, how we may dress. They opened fire on my family right in the middle of Pratt Street!"

"I know," Sally said. "That's why Stephen enlisted." She paused. "And you're angry with Sam because he didn't."

Julia looked at her. There was no need to reply to the last statement. Sally already knew her thoughts.

"You still have feelings for him, don't you?"

Julia sighed heavily. To deny it would be a lie but to acknowledge them was to deny her brother's honor.

"I can understand your dilemma," Sally said.

"You can?"

"Certainly. If my fiancé refused to defend our city I would feel the same."

She saw doubt in Sally's eyes and she knew she was keeping something back. "But?" Julia encouraged.

Sally shrugged. "Perhaps it isn't cowardice."

"What do you mean?"

"Well, Sam is a man of conviction. Although it may not be the same conviction you share. It takes courage to stand up for what you believe when no one else believes the same."

Julia sighed once more. "He came to the prayer meeting today."

"What prayer meeting?"

"The one at the church."

Sally looked embarrassed. "I forgot about that. Father must have as well. He said yesterday that we would attend."

"It was only my family, Reverend Perry and Samuel."

"Did he sit with you?"

Julia shook her head. She explained what happened after the service had ended.

Sally's eyes widened. "He said he would honor your wishes?"

"Yes."

"I see."

Finality hit Julia with a thud. The engagement had been severed. Samuel Ward would not be her husband.

"I should have been more open with the others," she said. "I should have told them everything."

"Well," Sally said slowly, "there is no need for gossip, especially from Rebekah." She squeezed Julia's hand. "Things will sort out in time."

She knew Sally was right.

But how much time would have to pass before Julia knew happiness again?

Chapter Four

The following morning, Sam finished his first class and walked to the third-floor faculty room for a meeting. The assembly had been called unexpectedly and all were eager to learn why. He took a seat amidst his fellow history and rhetoric professors. The discussion of war was already churning.

"It is no wonder that attendance is falling," one man said. "An invading army will do such a thing."

"It will keep many a young man hiding in his root cellar."

"Only because by hiding there he has an excuse not to finish his assignments."

Several of the teachers laughed and the conversation continued to swirl. The staff shared their opinions and concerns of what the coming weeks may hold. Sam did not add to the discussion. His mind kept drifting in and out of focus, somewhere between God and Julia much of the time.

He could not forget the look on her face yesterday as he'd approached her, eyes hesitant and suspicious. Her dark hair had been covered by a butternut bonnet. Sam couldn't help but wonder if she had chosen the color on purpose, as a statement of her political position. Edward and his fellow Maryland Guard members had left town in uniforms of the same color.

More than anything, Sam hoped that in time Julia would see he was not against her or her family. He wished for an opportunity to speak with her, to reaffirm his love. He prayed they could reconcile their differences.

But he had promised God he would follow His path wherever it led, whether Julia joined him or not. It appeared that path meant traveling the antislavery route.

Sam had not yet spoken to Dr. Carter about his plan to attend the abolitionist meeting. He intended to do so upon the first opportunity.

The conversation around him still buzzed, though it had shifted from the Federal occupation to the question of slavery. His ears perked when mathematics department chair, David Longsworth, spoke his mind. "I fail to see what all the division is about. Property is property. As an owner of such I have full authority over what belongs to me."

The word "property" when referring to a human being was nauseating to Sam.

If men were created in God's image how could the color of one's skin change such? Men were men. In Sam's mind there was no question.

Longsworth shifted to the economic benefits of slavery. "How are we going to produce goods in this country without slaves? On my word, without them the economy would collapse overnight."

Money, Sam thought. *It is all that some seem to be concerned with. What about the suffering of our fellow man? What about the God-given thirst for freedom deep inside us all?* He drew in a deep breath, ready to express such.

At that very moment, Dr. Carter entered the room. He called for everyone's attention.

"Gentlemen," he said. "I am afraid that I have some disturbing news."

Silence covered the room like a shroud. Sam's heart immediately began to pound. *What has happened? Has there been further bloodshed? Is Julia safe?*

"I was approached by one of General Butler's aides this morning," Dr. Carter said. "I have been told that the Federal Army is in need of our facilities."

Wordless, worried expressions showed upon each faculty member's face. Sam looked the same.

"Therefore, effective immediately, our classes will be suspended. We will resume teaching when the seminary can secure a new location." Dr. Carter paused. "You are dismissed, gentlemen."

The dean of students walked to the door and exited the room. The rest of the faculty, Sam included, sat in stunned silence.

"So the Yankees have commandeered the school," Longsworth said finally.

"And put us all out of work," said another.

A sickening feeling washed over him as Sam sank back in his chair. *My best friend, my fiancée, my teaching position...* Air slowly escaped his lungs. *Lord, I want to believe You have everything under control, that You are working these things for our ultimate good.*

Help me trust You.

Julia had been at the market since it first opened that morning. She had bought flour, two cones of sugar, eggs and a host of other necessities. She was just about to return home, when she spied her favorite delicacy.

Strawberries! They have strawberries.

Her basket was already heavy. Besides that, her reticule was running low on coins but the longer she stared at the red, ripe fruit, the more she wanted them. She couldn't resist purchasing a quart. *I love strawberries. I look forward to them every year. Samuel loves them as well. They are his favorite fruit.*

She smiled to herself as a plan formulated in her mind. *I know what I will do; I will make shortcake and then when he—* She came to her senses. There was no reason to bake shortcake. Samuel wouldn't be dining with them anymore.

Her heart sank a little deeper in her chest as she stared at the berries. They didn't look quite as red or luscious as they had just a moment ago.

"A quart, miss?" the vendor asked.

Still, she wanted them. "Yes. Please."

She shifted her basket to the other arm and counted out the coins in her reticule. She had just enough so she handed the vendor the money. It was then out of the corner of her eye that she noticed a blue uniform. The man was standing straight and tall, just a few steps from her. A large, brass buckle with the letters U. S. wrapped his waist. He appeared to be watching her.

Images of Pratt Street raced through her mind. Her mouth went dry. She desperately tried to remember what color stockings she had put on before leaving the house.

Are they white? Yes. Simply white.

She tightened her grip on her basket and stared straight at the vendor. *If I don't get in the soldier's way then he won't bother me.*

The man handed her the quart of berries. Julia put

them in her basket. She stole a peek in the soldier's direction. He was still watching her. A shiver ran through her. Her heart began to pound. She looked back at the vendor. She tried to smile.

"These berries will be delicious."

The man tipped his slouch hat. "Enjoy them, miss."

Julia dropped her reticule in the basket. She hoisted the heavy parcel higher on her arm. She turned.

The blue uniform stepped forward. Julia swallowed. Ears thudding, she took another step. He came up along side her.

The Federal soldier smiled at her. "Help you with that, miss?"

Julia did not smile back. By now, her heart was racing. "Thank you, no," she said. She hurried away from him, walking as fast as the heavy basket would allow.

The *pop, pop, pop* of musket fire echoed in her ears as she mentally replayed that dreadful day at the station. The sight of blood-splattered cobblestones filled her memory. A thousand terrible images raced through Julia's mind and just as many petitions for protection.

Lord, please don't let that soldier follow me. Please don't let him!

She hurried on.

The market was crowded with people and items. It was difficult to get back to the street. A barrel of pickles with children clustered about it blocked the easiest route. Moving opposite, Julia rounded the corner where the chickens were sold. Their featherless bodies hung limply from a line strung across the stall. She peeked through them to see if the Federal soldier was following her.

He was coming in her direction.

Julia hoisted the basket and took off once more,

only to run directly into the chest of another uniformed soldier.

"Excuse me!" she gasped, nearly dropping the basket.

He took hold of it. "Help you with that, miss?"

She could barely breathe. *Lord, help me!* "No. No, thank you."

He turned her basket loose and tipped his kepi as he stepped out of her path. "Good day."

The way to the street was clear. Julia walked as quickly as she could. The basket was cutting into her arm but she did not stop to shift its weight. All she wanted to do was get away from there.

Once she passed the market's perimeter she took off running, caring not by now if her petticoats or her stockings were showing. She kept running but the yards of dress fabric and her hoop made it impossible to keep up the pace for very long. Out of breath, arms and legs aching, she stopped in front of a ladies hat store. She glanced backward.

Neither of the soldiers had followed her.

She set the basket down taking a moment to rest. As the panic faded, the thought struck her that perhaps the men were only trying to be kind. Feeling foolish yet not wanting to take any chances, she picked up the basket. It was then that she noticed her prized strawberries had gotten crushed beneath a jar of honey. To make matters worse, the sticky red juice now stained Julia's dress.

Oh, no...

Feeling deflated, she trudged for home. She had just enough time to put away the groceries and set her dress to soaking before the prayer meeting.

The Federal soldiers were already setting up camp as Samuel left the seminary's main gate. Their canvas tents covered the center green and supply wagons choked the road all the way back to Mount Vernon.

Sam tried to think charitable thoughts concerning the men but it was difficult. Though his tenure here at Rolland Park was short, he had grown to love the place. He did not enjoy being driven from the grounds.

When he would return to pursue his life's vocation, he did not know. The only way he could console himself was the thought that at least now he could attend the prayer meetings on time.

He walked back home and deposited his books on the parlor table. After eating a quick meal of cornbread and buttermilk, he started off. He would be early for the meeting but Reverend Perry might have need of assistance in some way or another. Goodness knows Sam needed something to do.

As he passed by the Stanton home, Sam couldn't help but wonder what Julia was doing at the moment. He had given his word to the Lord that he would follow Him regardless of the cost but that promise didn't quell the ache in his heart. Julia was the only woman he had ever loved. He prayed for her unceasingly. He missed her even more.

He arrived at the church well before noon. Reverend Perry was happy to see him.

"Samuel, welcome! I thought you would not be able to join us until later."

He explained what had happened at the school.

"Dear me," Reverend Perry said. "I am sorry to hear that."

Sam knew it would do no good to dwell on the issue so he moved the conversation forward. "I would like to be of assistance if I may," he said. "I think the prayer meeting is a noble idea."

"Thank you, but I cannot take credit for it."

Reverend Perry explained that the idea for the noon meeting came from an event in New York City four years earlier. During a financial crisis, the city had experienced a laymen's revival.

"It was an interdenominational event," he said. "The churches were filled to capacity for months. Thousands came to know Christ."

"Do you believe such a thing could happen here in Baltimore?" Sam asked.

The Reverend's eyes were full of compassion. "For eternity's sake, I do hope so."

Sam's heart went out to the minister. The kindhearted man was trying his best to shepherd a divided flock where each side claimed to be the true sheep and the other, the goats.

"Where do we begin?" he asked.

"Your attendance and prayers are the most important," Reverend Perry said, "but there are a few other areas where I could use your help."

"Such as?"

"I have sent word to the other ministers of the city. Most seemed to appreciate the invitation. I am hoping for a higher attendance today, therefore, I had a bill of direction printed. Would you be kind enough to hand them out?"

"Of course."

"Would you be interested perhaps in doing something to engage our citizens outside of the church?"

"Certainly."

The Reverend smiled. "Thank you. I will speak more to you about that later."

Reverend Perry went to retrieve his handbills and Sam eagerly took his place in the foyer. It wasn't long before Julia arrived. She was wearing a yellow silk dress, trimmed in ribbons and lace. Sam thought she looked like a ray of sunshine. He couldn't help but smile.

"What are you doing here?" she asked, eyes wide with surprise. "Shouldn't you be at the seminary?"

The remark was not made because she felt pleasure at seeing him. "The Federal Army has need of our facilities."

Her jaw dropped. "They closed the school?"

"This morning."

"Oh, Samuel..."

She laid her hand gently on his forearm. Sam willed his heart to beat a normal rhythm.

"I am so sorry."

Concern laced her voice and compassion showed on her face. Sam appreciated the emotion but he did not want her to worry.

"We will relocate. It will just take a little time."

She evidently mistook his words for indifference and the warmth fled from her eyes. "Is there nothing they can do to offend you?" She asked.

"They haven't closed us down. They only want the building."

"And what else will they want, Samuel?"

Before he could answer she turned on her heel, her hoop and skirts swishing like a giant bell as she strode away.

She walked to her family pew. Inside she was fuming. *The Federal Army has commandeered his school, effectively ending the work he loves and all he can do is smile and hand out prayer bulletins?*

She wondered what he would have said if she had told him about the soldiers at the market this morning. Would he have been concerned for her safety or would he have simply smiled and acted as though nothing was wrong?

I don't understand him at all! Slavery doesn't even concern us! The real trouble is right outside our door.

She took a seat beside her mother and father and waited. The room was hushed with reverent stillness. She tried to use the time to rein in her focus, to think about what she was really here for.

After a few moments her emotions stilled. As the hands on her father's pocket watch neared twelve, Julia heard the sounds of footsteps and polite whispers. Curious, she discreetly glanced about.

To her surprise, the attendance was growing. There were people seated that she did not know. Sally and her father were there as well.

She smiled at Julia.

More people have come! Oh, thank You, Lord.

Reverend Perry stepped to the pulpit and began the service. "Please turn to hymn number sixty in your *Christian Songster.*"

Julia stood with the others. A gentleman that she did not recognize readied the pipe organ and the singing began.

I want to have wisdom that comes from above,
I want my heart filled with the purest of love;
I want my faith stronger, my anchor hope sure,
And like a good soldier, all hardness endure.

As the lines from the stanza passed out of her mouth she thought of Edward. What hardness was he now enduring? She prayed God would give him strength.

I want to be stripped of all human pride,
All malice and anger, I would lay aside;
From sin and from bondage I want to be free,
And live, my dear Savior, live only to Thee.

Julia meant the words she sang. Truly she did. But how to go about implementing them, she was not sure.

Lord, help me act in a way that pleases You. I want to do Your will.

When the hymn was over Reverend Perry read a few requests. There were several members who wished to pray for the salvation of their loved ones. As Julia listened to the heartfelt pleas ascending around her, both her heart and conscience were stirred. She, too, wanted to show Christian love, concern for her fellow countrymen.

Show me what to do. Show me how I may honor and serve You.

The congregation prayed for about an hour. When the meeting concluded the members broke into groups, visiting momentarily before departing. Sally came to see her.

"Julia, will you come? The Reverend wishes to speak with us."

"Oh? What about?"

"I don't know. He only said it was important."

Julia followed her to the front of the church where Reverend Perry was waiting. He smiled broadly.

"Ladies, thank you for coming. The service is growing."

"Indeed," Sally remarked.

"I was reminded today, though, that there are others who may wish to join and yet cannot do so. Others still who may be afraid of entering the church. I wondered if you would be interested in an avenue of service."

"Certainly," Julia said. The Lord was obviously answering her prayer. She just didn't know yet where He was leading.

The Reverend explained that he wished to demonstrate Christ's love to the citizens of Baltimore in a simple, practical way. "To those who pass by on the street."

"You mean like a cup of cold water?" Sally asked.

"Yes!" he said enthusiastically. "Or perhaps a slice of bread and jam? I know for a fact that each of you bakes wonderful bread."

The women looked at each other and smiled.

"We can set up a table by the sidewalk and distribute the items. Hopefully we can draw people inside the church. And you ladies would not be unattended. You would be properly chaperoned. Can I count on your assistance?"

It sounded like everything she was looking for. It was a simple way to show kindness to the people of her city, to help brighten the darkness this war had brought.

And if we are to be chaperoned I need not worry about Federal soldiers.

"Of course," Julia said. Sally pledged to serve, as well.

"Wonderful," said Reverend Perry. "Here is what we will do."

He determined a time to meet and the ladies decided what baked goods they would bring. "I will have one of our gentlemen furnish a table and fill the water barrels."

Julia was pleased. If there was one thing she could do well, it was bake bread and make jam. No politics or disagreements could invade.

Chapter Five

Sam had promised Julia that he would not visit her home or sit in her family pew, but that would not keep him from serving the Lord. When Reverend Perry asked for his assistance with the bread table, he could hardly say no.

He had found a table in the cellar, then carried it to the edge of the churchyard. He gathered the water barrels and filled them high.

While he worked, he prayed. He prayed for his city, his seminary and his best friend. But, above all, he prayed for Julia.

Lord, You know I love her and I still believe You mean for us to be together. I want to do Your will. I want Julia to find Your will for her life. But if that means we must go our separate ways, then please give me the strength to accept Your plan.

He wondered how she would respond when she found out they would be working together. He hoped the interaction would lead to opportunities to prove that his intentions were good.

Give me the words to say to her, Lord, and the grace to respond as You would.

* * *

Julia had baked two loaves of bread and turned the mashed strawberries from the market into mouthwatering jam. As she prepared for the prayer meeting that day, an excitement pulsed through her veins. It was a feeling she had not experienced since before the beginning of the war.

Lord, thank You for this opportunity. Thank You for giving me a way to make a difference.

She arrived at church well before noon. The table was ready and the water barrels were waiting.

"It appears everything has been prepared," her father said.

"Indeed." With eagerness, Julia set her tray of bread and jam on the table.

Her father peered into one of the barrels. "They are filled to the brim."

"That is good."

They would need to be. The day was going to be warm. The late May sunshine was strong. Already heat rose in ripples from the cobblestone.

Sally and her father pulled up in their surrey at that moment. She hurried to where Julia was waiting. She, too, looked eager to begin.

"I made lemon tea bread," she said.

"Wonderful!" said Julia. "Everyone that passes by will want a slice."

"I do hope so."

The traffic on the street, both foot and carriage, was light, yet the women knew it would increase once the noon bell rang.

"Julia, you have no cups or ladles," Mrs. Stanton noticed. "I'll fetch them."

"And I'll see to it that the gentleman scheduled to assist you knows that you both have arrived," her father said.

"Thank you."

Her parents climbed the church steps. The moment the front door shut, Sally reached into her pocket.

"Before someone else joins us…I have news. Stephen sent a letter."

Julia gasped, immediately abandoning the bread and jam. It was the first communication that they'd had with their loved ones since their departure. "When did it arrive?"

Sally handed it over. "This morning. They are in Virginia, although he did not say exactly where."

"They don't want to take any chances on the information falling into the wrong hands." Julia unfolded the letter carefully. Stephen wrote of regimental drilling and of Virginia farmland hospitality. Her heart then soared. "He is with Edward!"

"Yes," Sally said happily. "Tent mates. Isn't that wonderful?"

"Indeed."

When Stephen mentioned chess matches and Edward's snoring, Julia had to laugh. "I am so pleased that they are together."

"Yes. They can look out for one another. Oh, Julia, I was so relieved to hear from him. I pray that you will hear from Edward soon."

"You must promise to bring the letter to me as soon as it arrives."

"I will. You have my word."

Julia smiled. "I cannot wait to tell Mother and Father."

The church door creaked. She quickly gave back the precious news and Sally slipped it in her pocket.

My brother is safe, Julia thought. *Thank You, Lord.*

* * *

Sam drew in a deep breath and started down the steps. Sally saw him before Julia did.

"Samuel!" she said, smiling with pleasant surprise. "Are you assisting us today?"

"I am."

Julia turned, her face draining of all color. He wanted to laugh. He couldn't help it. She looked as though she had just been caught in a traitorous act. Sam decided to make it known that he had seen the letter. After all, he too was eager for news.

"Have you heard from Edward?" he asked casually as he placed the box of tin cups on the table.

She blinked, blue eyes wide and uncertain. "Yes. Well, from Stephen. Sally did, that is."

He wondered why she felt it necessary to state Stephen Hastings had not written her *personally*. He took it as a hopeful sign.

"Are they both well?" He asked.

"Yes."

"Good. I am pleased to hear that."

Sam wanted to act as if there was no division between them, as if Edward and Stephen had simply gone on a fishing trip and would return in a matter of days. He smiled at her.

Julia's face was still as pale as a winter moon.

Sally, on the other hand, was grinning, a conniving expression at that. Sam figured she knew all that had taken place. Julia always told her everything. By the look on her face, Sam guessed Sally was still on his side.

"What kind of bread did you bring?" he asked evenly.

Julia gestured toward the loaf on the table and absent-mindedly mentioned strawberry jam.

"She made it yesterday," Sally added.

"Fresh jam," he said. "That will bring the people in droves."

"That is what we are hoping for, isn't it, Julia?"

She nodded politely then gracefully moved to the far end of the table, placing Sally between them.

The noon bells chimed and as anticipated, the street traffic increased. Many people stopped by the church table out of curiosity.

It was a wonderful sight to see—yet Julia moved about in a daze, feeling out of place and ineffective.

Samuel ladled out the water and Sally smiled sweetly as she offered each person something to eat. The pair invited everyone to join those in the sanctuary for prayer.

Most declined.

"Oh, I'm on my way to such and such," they would say, "but thank you."

Undaunted, Sally responded politely in kind, promising to pray for the person's well-being. No one chaffed at her promise. They thanked her for her kindness.

Julia envied her. Sally was lifting heavy spirits, showing God's love. She was doing what Julia longed to do.

As for Samuel, a smile filled his face and his voice held its usual warmth. Little children giggled at the jokes he made. Laborers going about their tasks stopped to ask him to pray for specific requests.

"My cousin's joined up. Pray he will come home safe when all is said and done."

He would do so on the spot. Samuel never mentioned politics; he just offered a simple prayer for the one in need or the loved one they had mentioned. The person then usually went away with a smile.

A cloudless sky stretched over them. His hair shone reddish-brown in the midday sun. Julia marveled at the effect he was having on others until she thought better of it. *More is needed than prayer. Even Jesus told his disciples at one point if they didn't have a sword to sell their cloaks and buy one.*

Time marched on. The bonnet covering her head was beginning to feel like a bread oven. Though the emerald green dress she wore was made of light silk, the fabric clung to her uncomfortably. She took out her lace handkerchief and blotted her face. There was a lull in the traffic and Samuel mentioned Edward.

"Did your brothers say where they are camping?" he asked.

"Indirectly," Sally innocently answered. "They are in—"

Julia quickly caught her best friend's arm. What was Sally thinking; ready to report Edward and Stephen's activities to him?

"They have gone south," Julia said.

"Yes," he chuckled. "I suppose they would."

His lightheartedness was infuriating. "What do you find so amusing?" she asked.

"Forgive me," he said, though still chuckling. "It was the look on your face, just now. Don't worry, Julia, I have no intention of reporting your letters or your brother's activities to the Provost Marshal."

His promise gave little comfort. "Then what are your intentions?" she wanted to know.

"The same as yours. I would like to send Edward a letter."

Her anger brewed. Her head felt even hotter. "And just what would you say to him, Samuel? Would you condemn his actions? Would you argue your so-called abolitionist views?"

Her emotions had gotten the better of her. She had

raised her voice. Samuel looked embarrassed. Sally did, as well. Her face was three shades of red.

A woman with a baby carriage and two small youngsters had approached the table. Julia felt her own embarrassment rising. She tried to remember why she was here, the mission of kindness she had undertaken. But as Samuel took her hand and steered her to the nearby maple tree, all thoughts of Christian charity evaporated.

"Julia, I have nothing against your brother. I pray daily for his safety."

"But not his victory," she said.

"I pray that God's will, that right, will prevail."

"Right will prevail? I suppose that means the Federal Army?"

"I didn't say that."

"You have by your actions."

"You have misinterpreted them."

"Have I?"

He stepped closer, his brown eyes full of intensity. "I would give my life for you, for your family if necessary."

"Would you?" she scoffed. "Where were you the night my brother tried to keep the army from invading this city? Where were you when those soldiers approached me yesterday at the market?"

Sam's heart filled his throat and the hair on the back of his neck stood up. Julia's jaw was clenched but the emotion in her eyes had shifted from anger to fear.

"What soldiers? What happened to you?"

"They were watching me as I was shopping. They asked if I needed help with my basket."

It was obvious that she thought the men had been insincere in their offers of assistance. She looked him full in the face. All her anxieties were openly displayed. His heart ached for her and without thinking, he took her hand in his.

"What did you say to them?"

Her fingers were trembling. Her voice was, as well. "I told them no thank you and then I ran away as quickly as I could."

"Did they follow you home?"

"No. I made certain of that."

He had feared such things from the Federal occupation and much worse. The troops were here to keep the peace, to preserve the Union. But at what cost? The memory of what they had done on Pratt Street still made his blood boil, and the thought of one of them harming Julia—or any lady of this city—made him want to pick up a musket and join the Confederate ranks.

But Sam knew that wasn't the way. "My sabbatical from teaching is a blessing," he said. "Next time I will go with you to the market. That way there won't be any trouble."

He lost her on the word *blessing*. She pulled back her hand.

"The Federal Army is in no way, shape or form a blessing, Samuel. And do not bother to grace me with your presence. My brother will see to it that those soldiers are removed from Baltimore."

She whirled about on her heel and hurried for the front steps. Sam started to go after her but the church doors had opened and people were exiting the building.

The hour for prayer and reconciliation had ended.

Julia got as far as the back pew and then froze. She knew she had behaved horribly. Her guilt came crashing over her in suffocating waves the moment she saw Reverend Perry.

He smiled at her then immediately strode up the aisle.

"Julia, my dear, did you have many visitors to the table?"

His hope-filled tone heaped burning coals upon her head. The purpose of the day was to show compassion to lost and burdened souls, not to argue with Samuel.

Oh, Lord, forgive me. Had it not been for Sally, not a single passerby would have received a kind word. She did not let herself think of the kindness Sam had shown to passersby, as well.

"Sally spoke with many people today," Julia told the Reverend. "And many asked for prayer."

Reverend Perry's smile broadened. "Wonderful! I knew I could count on the two of you. Will you serve again tomorrow?"

Julia could feel the heat in her cheeks. She wasn't worthy to attend to the duty but she felt she had to make up for the disaster of today. "I will serve graciously," she promised. "You have my word."

He patted her arm in a fatherly way, then moved on to speak with another member of the congregation.

Julia sighed. Turning for the front door, she knew exactly what she must do. She had to apologize to Sally.

Her best friend stepped into the foyer at that very moment.

"I am sorry," Julia blurted out immediately. "Please forgive me."

Sally pulled her toward the belfry. Once inside, she shut the door behind them. Gold dust rays shone through cracks and crevices above them.

"I forgive you," Sally said, "but I must tell you that I believe you are making a mistake with Sam."

Julia's back stiffened. She wanted to make things right for her unchristian behavior but she did not wish to discuss what had driven her to such in the first place. "Sally…"

"He loves you. It is written all over his face. Despite your differences I believe he is willing to compromise, to work things out."

Julia shook her head. Compromise wasn't possible. "He says he would give his life for me but I don't believe him."

"If I were you, I would be thankful he hasn't proven that."

"What?"

Sally's hands moved to her narrow, drawn-in waist. "What would you really do if Samuel enlisted? You don't know what it is like to have the man you love more than life itself serving on some unknown battlefield. To know not whether he will live or die."

Julia's jaw dropped. Sally had never talked this way before. *The man you love more than life itself? She can't mean Stephen.* Then it hit her. *Edward.* Sally Hastings had never gotten over her brother.

Shame and sympathy flooded Julia's veins. How foolish she had been ranting on about Samuel when Sally felt this way. "Oh, Sally, I am so sorry. I didn't realize. I thought that ended long ago."

Tears squeezed past her friend's golden eyelashes. Her cheeks were flushed. "Edward never showed any interest in me when he was home. I have tried to forget him but I…" Her voice cracked.

"You can't."

Sally shook her head then offered a pitiful smile. "Forgetfulness it seems is in short supply these days."

Julia handed her a clean handkerchief.

"Please forgive me," she said, "for everything. I am so sorry. If I had known how you felt, I never would have complained so."

Sally wiped her eyes. She chuckled softly. "Of course I forgive you. You are my dearest friend."

"And you are mine," Julia said as they hugged each other. "Listen, when Edward writes, I want you to open the letter first."

"No. That would not be right."

"Then I will give you the letter as soon as I read it."

Sally stepped back. Her countenance had lifted. "You had better."

They both laughed then Julia turned serious.

"Reverend Perry asked if we would continue sharing our bread."

"What did you tell him?"

"I told him yes."

Sally's left eyebrow arched.

"I promise you," Julia said, "I won't let my anger get the best of me again."

"I believe you but what will you do about Sam? He told me that so far he is the only man willing to help."

Julia sighed heavily. Like it or not, she knew what she was going to have to do. She would have to make peace with him. A greater purpose depended on it.

"I will apologize for my behavior today."

Sally gave her hand a squeeze. "God bless you, Julia."

"No. God bless you. You are always my example. You are the lady I want to be."

Sally waved her off with a smile. Her face then darkened with worry. "You won't tell your mother or Edward, will you?"

"Of course not. But I will spend a little extra time in prayer tonight."

Sally giggled slightly. Julia considered it a victory.

"I would appreciate your prayers," she said. "But consider what I said about Sam. He does love you. When it comes down to it, that is really all that matters in this life, to love and be loved in return."

"I didn't know you were such a philosopher," Julia quipped.

"Perhaps I read too much poetry," Sally mused, "but in times like these… Well, consider what I said. Will you?"

Her words carried weight. Part of Julia wanted to find Samuel at that moment. The other part had no idea what to say to him.

"I will consider it well," Julia promised, "and perhaps you could spend a little time in prayer for me."

Sally smiled. "You have my promise."

Sam put away the water barrels and washed the tin cups. Then he promptly left the building. He tried not to think about what had happened between him and Julia. He just wanted to keep moving.

He walked up Charles Street deciding to pay a visit to his old employer, Collin O'Hara, a local blacksmith. Sam had no idea how long it would be before classes would resume. He could not sit home and wait. Neither his wallet nor his mind would allow it.

Mr. O'Hara was delighted to see him. His bushy, red mustache rose with a smile. Though when Sam asked about possible work, the man's face fell.

"I thought you would be teaching by now."

"I am. Or at least, I was." Sam explained what had happened with the school. "I thought that perhaps with all of the soldiers in town, you may need a little extra help."

"Sorry, boy. Business isn't that good. Many of my regular customers left for the war and as for the soldiers, well, they have their own smiths."

"I see."

Mr. O'Hara must have sensed his discouragement. "Tell you what," he said, "if business does pick up I will be sure to take you on. You were always a hard worker, trustworthy, as well."

"Thank you, sir. I appreciate that."

They shook hands and Sam turned to go, mentally going through his list of where else he might find temporary work.

Maybe tutoring, though it's unlikely anyone would want to hire me on a short-term basis. I suppose I could always chop firewood. A sad smile moved across his face. *What would she do if I just showed up?* The thought was tempting but his honor kept him from doing so. *I promised her that I would respect her wishes. Perhaps I should speak to Reverend Perry and ask him to find someone else to look after the bread table.*

The thought of not seeing Julia filled his heart with a pain he could not bear and the thought of her in danger by Federal soldiers made his stomach roll.

Oh, Lord, why can't there be peace? Why can't life be as it was before?

His mind drifted back to a day last summer on Chesapeake Bay. He and Edward had taken a few days to go fishing.

"Why do you want to marry my sister?" Edward had asked.

At first Sam hadn't been certain if the question was one of curiosity or brotherly inquisition. Knowing Edward, it was probably a little of both. He'd answered honestly, "Because I love her."

The corner of Edward's mouth lifted with a smile. "I knew you would say that. I just hope you realize what you are getting yourself into."

Sam chuckled and tugged at his line. Neither of them had caught anything yet. "What is that supposed to mean?"

Edward looked at him incredulously. "Have you ever seen her get angry?"

"A time or two," Sam said. "It is usually directed at you."

The boat rocked slightly as Edward let out a hearty laugh.

The water rippled beneath them. The fish hadn't been biting but neither of them seemed to care.

"Jesting aside," Edward had then said. "My sister is a good woman. Stubborn but faithful. She will do anything to care for those she loves."

"I know that." It was one of the qualities that had drawn Sam to her in the first place.

Edward pulled his eyes from the blue-gray water. "I am glad it is you," he said. "I don't think I could let my sister marry anybody else."

Remembering, Sam sighed. The sincerity in Edward's voice that day was a far cry from the night of the Pratt Street riot.

When the city leaders learned that additional Northern troops were en route to Washington via Baltimore, they had sent a telegram to President Lincoln. They'd told of the attack and had advised him to send no more troops through Baltimore.

When Washington failed to comply, Mayor Brown and the police commissioners took matters into their own hands. They'd decided to burn the railroad bridges north of the city. Local militia had been pouring into

Baltimore all day. Everyone feared further confrontation with Federal soldiers.

Sam had followed Edward to the armory that night. Members of the Maryland Guard, police officers and volunteers had gathered. The air was charged. A frenzied excitement filled men's faces.

Instructions were given. The group would be divided into two forces. One would burn bridges on the Philadelphia rail line, the other on the North Central Railroad.

"No Yankee will step foot in Baltimore under our watch," one of the police officials had shouted.

Cheers radiated from the volunteers and many of the Guard. Slurs on the Northern troops spilled out. Listening, Sam had an uneasy feeling in the pit of his stomach. The impulsive, protective spirit that had caused him to follow Edward to this place was waning. Reason was taking its place.

The argument for burning the bridges was a matter of safety. "We have seen what the Massachusetts troops have done," voices cried. "If we don't protect this city it will be on our heads!"

But the air was just as hot with talk of secession. "They trample our rights! Let us follow Virginia and South Carolina!"

Sam had begun to seriously wonder if the men swarming around him had Baltimore's best interest at heart, or if they were simply championing their own banner. He was no military strategist but he had enough sense to know that secession would not fare well for Maryland. The Union would not suffer its capital in Confederate hands. A bloodbath would ensue.

The planning had continued. The longer he'd stood there, the more certain he'd become that burning the railroad bridges would be one step closer to secession, one step closer to the Federal Government's retaliation.

He tugged at Edward's sleeve. "This is wrong."

Edward nodded. "Yes. Yes," he'd said with enthusiasm, hearing nothing but the cheering crowd.

Sam caught him by the shoulder. Edward turned, a questioning look on his face.

"This is a mistake," Sam had said. "We should let the soldiers pass through."

Edward's eyes widened. "Pass through?"

"Yes, to Washington. Let them go on their way."

A hush had fallen over the tumultuous crowd. Those around him fixed their attention solely on Sam. Speaking to Edward yet knowing others were listening, he'd drawn in a quick breath and plunged forward.

"Burning the bridges will only invite trouble. We should let the soldiers continue to Washington."

"So they can raise arms against one of our sister states?" Someone shouted.

Sam shook his head. "So they can put an end to this matter before any more are killed."

The comment had brought a fury of disagreement. Faces twisted in disgust. Anger permeated the building.

The police commissioner on the platform had said, "It is not open for debate, young man. The decision has already been made. If you don't agree with it, you should leave."

Sam looked at Edward. "Surely you see what I am talking about."

Edward's eyes narrowed to dark slits. His jaw was clenched. "I asked you here because I thought you were with us."

"Edward, I am with you. With all of you. Think of Julia."

"I am thinking of her!"

"Don't you see? This will bring war!"

"We are already at war!"

The crowd pressed in around him and a dozen hands seized him. The next thing Sam had known, he was face down in the spring mud. The armory door shut behind him.

And from that moment on we were at odds.

When Julia learned that Sam had not participated in the defense of the city she had been greatly distressed.

"You left Edward and the others?"

That was the beginning of her doubts. That is when her opinion of me began to change.

Sam tugged at his topper then thrust his hands deep into his pockets and kept walking. He believed in freedom, justice and good for all mankind. He was no coward.

But how was he going to prove that to Julia?

How could he make Edward understand?

Now *was* the time for action, the time to stand up for liberty. But obtaining freedom for some meant limiting the rights of others. If Sam fully embraced the abolitionist cause, would Julia and Edward ever be able to forgive him?

Chapter Six

Julia swallowed back the lump in her throat as she approached the table. Samuel was already there. Sally was nowhere to be found. Julia wondered if her best friend would purposefully arrive late today so that Julia would be forced to interact privately with Samuel. Knowing Sally, she probably would.

Samuel was dressed in a black cutaway coat and was wearing the red-and-gold-silk vest she had sewn for him last Christmas. As was his custom, his gold watch chain was looped through one of the button holes. Julia couldn't help but wonder if her picture was still tucked safely inside the heirloom timepiece.

"Good day, Julia." Samuel's smile reached all the way to his eyes.

She tried to ignore the effect it had on her. "Good day, Samuel."

She had considered what Sally had said earlier concerning him. He did care for her. That was still obvious. His contrary political convictions may mean she could not marry him but it did not give her the right to remain angry with him.

She realized although their engagement had been

broken, that did not mean Samuel was going to disappear from her life. They lived in the same city, shopped at the same market and worshiped in the same church. She was going to have to set her disappointment aside in order to interact with him. She must be civil. He was still her Christian brother and God's word commanded that they bear one another.

She set her tray on the table and removed the cloth covering the bread. She thought her parents would stop by the table to talk with Samuel but they simply waved and walked up the church steps.

"I am pleased to see that your mother and father are well," he said. His tone was pleasant and even, the same way he always spoke to her. "I was worried about them."

"I appreciate your concern." She was putting off the inevitable and she knew it. She took a deep breath and turned to face him.

"Samuel, I must apologize for yesterday. I shouldn't have spoken in such a way, especially with visitors nearby…"

She made the mistake of looking into his face. His brown eyes cut her to the core, not with condemnation but with love. Julia promptly lost her voice and all coherent thought.

"Think no more of it," he said. "I understand that Edward—"

That snapped her back into reality. She held up her hand. "Please." If there was one thing she could not discuss, it was her brother. Too many emotions churned. "We are here to serve our fellow citizens. Let's just leave our conversation to that."

He studied her, face full of concern. Silent seconds passed. Julia could feel her chin begin to quiver.

"If that is what you wish," he said.

It wasn't what she wished for but it would have to do. She wanted to step into his arms and feel the warmth of his embrace. She wanted him to comfort her, to tell her everything would be all right.

But it isn't all right and it won't be, at least not until this war is over and Edward returns safely home.

Her eyes were watering. It was all Sam could do to resist pulling her into his arms. She was close enough to smell her rose water perfume, close enough to kiss; but he held back, for the sake of honor.

"What kind of bread did you bring today?" he asked.

She drew in a quick breath and for an instant he thought he saw a hint of a smile. She turned for the table and adjusted the tray.

"I brought boiled milk rolls and cornbread with jam."

He smiled at her then asked about Sally.

"I am not certain she will join us today," she said.

He started to ask why but figured Julia would have told him so if she wanted him to know. "Well, then," he said. "I suppose we will have to manage without her."

"Indeed."

The noon hour approached. So did the people. Carriages clustered about the church and Sam noted that there were several in attendance today who were not members of the congregation.

Julia noticed, as well. "Word is spreading," she said. "Father told me that Reverend Perry extended an invitation to all of the ministers in the city, even churches outside our denomination."

He told her about the meetings in New York. "Reverend Perry said that one of the reasons the event was successful was that people were willing to steer clear of politics and controversial issues. They simply came to seek God's will."

She nodded slowly. "Perhaps when all is said and done the churches here will find more common ground."

It was the cry of his heart, not only for the Christian community but for the two of them, as well. *One can serve Christ alone but so much more can be completed when two are equally yoked together.*

Tensions between them relaxed somewhat as Julia settled into a productive pace. Sam doled out the cold water and she the smiles and bread.

"Would you care for a bite to eat, sir? God bless you."

The sound of her voice, the rustle of her petticoats as she moved about the table kept a smile on his face. Simply being near her made his head spin. He longed to tell her how often he thought of her, how much he missed her but he reminded himself to tread lightly.

Her manner toward him was cautiously guarded. All was not mended between them but at least they were together, interacting civilly.

A steady stream of citizens passed before their table—shoppers, police officers, laborers. One gentleman, a banker on his lunch break, inquired as to the reason for the church's hospitality.

Sam explained. "We wish to show kindness to our fellow citizens."

The banker squinted shrewdly, mistrust evident in his eyes. "Are you pro-Union or secessionist?"

Sam hesitated, unsure how to answer. In Julia's mind he was certain the response would be, "Both."

She surprised him.

"We aren't doing this for political reasons, sir. We are here to extend God's love."

She handed the man a milk roll then moved away

from the table. Sam's heart swelled so that he thought he would lose the buttons on his vest.

Julia had seen the two Negro children before, watching wistfully from the far side of the street. They had passed by about a half hour ago, struggling to carry a large sack of grain. They were barefoot, clothes in tatters. She could tell by their thin faces that they were hungry.

While Samuel spoke with the banker, she chose two slices of cornbread, ones loaded heavily with jam, and made her way across the street. The children's eyes widened when they saw her coming.

The older boy poked the younger on the shoulder. They quickly turned away from her.

"Wait!" she called out.

Immediately they stopped, turning to face her. Their faces were even thinner up close. Their eyes showed fear.

Julia tried to put them at ease. "You both look hungry. Would you like some bread and jam?"

Fear melted into smiles as she knelt to hand them each a slice.

"Thanky ma'am," the older one said.

The younger boy grinned, busily enjoying the jam.

"Are you brothers?"

"Yes'um. We is."

"What are your names?"

"I'm Elijah and this here's Elisha."

Julia grinned. "Well Elijah and Elisha, it is such a warm day, would you like a cup of cold water? We have plenty at the table."

"Thanky ma'am but no. We gotta be off. Our master be 'spectin' us."

She stood fully erect, not wanting them to be late. "All right then, run along—but I will be in the church-yard each day at noon. Come back and see me."

They nodded enthusiastically. "Oh, yes'um. We'z will. Thanky."

They scampered off, jam staining their dark faces. Julia chuckled to herself and once again crossed the street. She sensed somehow, God was smiling.

Sam had been watching her from the corner of his eye but the moment the banker walked into the church, he gave his full attention to Julia and the children.

They were slaves. He could tell by looking at them. His heart ached at the prospect of the young lads spending the rest of their lives in backbreaking bondage. More and more, he was looking forward to the meeting he planned to attend. He prayed that he might indeed be able to do "fine work" to help boys like these. For the moment, though, he chose to focus on the smiles Julia was coaxing, the bellies she was filling.

When the two boys ran off, Julia crossed the street. On her face was that innocent, sweet expression that he found so irresistible.

"You did a very good thing, just now," he said.

She blinked, her long dark lashes fluttering. "How so?"

"They are slave children, Julia. Most people wouldn't even notice them much less go out of their way to give them something to eat."

"They were hungry," she said.

"Yes. I am certain that they were. You made a difference in their life today."

"It was nothing."

"Yes, it was. Most people don't realize how hard life is for them. If they did, things would be a lot different."

Her eyes shrank suspiciously. "You mean the war?"

"I mean life."

He realized he was treading on dangerous ground. The last thing he wanted to do was start an argument. The day had been so pleasant. He wanted to keep it that way.

She studied him for a moment, her dark curls framed by that butternut bonnet. "Samuel," she suddenly asked him, "what exactly are your intentions concerning the abolitionist viewpoint? Do you advocate the methods of men like John Brown?"

He was caught off guard by her directness. He wondered for a moment if she somehow knew of Dr. Carter's friends. Did she know something of their history? Were they indeed radicals?

Deciding that couldn't possibly be so, he answered honestly, "I don't know what my intentions are at this moment, Julia, but I do know that holding people hostage, slave or free, is wrong."

She nodded slowly, contemplatively.

He was encouraged by the silence.

"Is that what has been bothering you?" he dared to ask. "Do you think I am going to run off with radicals and start my own war? That I would be willing to shoot other men to make my own point?"

"No," she said. "I know you would not do such. You don't want to fight."

His shoulders slumped. She knew him better than anyone yet when it came to this issue, she simply did not understand.

"Julia, it isn't that. I—"

Something over his shoulder captured her attention.

Her face blanched and her eyes immediately widened in fear. Sam turned to see what she was looking at.

Two Federal soldiers were approaching.

Julia's knees were wobbly beneath her petticoats and her hands were shaking. She tried to breathe normally but the best she could do was grab small snatches of air. The soldiers approached the table. Their muskets glinted in the afternoon sun.

"What's in your barrel?" one of them asked.

"Cold water," Samuel replied. "Would you gentlemen care for a drink?"

They nodded gruffly.

Julia watched as he ladled out a cupful for them both. One drank readily. The other surveyed the table.

She wondered if the man somehow knew who was pro-Union and who was not. She was thankful Sally was not there. She feared what might happen if Stephen's letter was still in her pocket.

"We have bread, as well," Samuel said, "if you are hungry."

They helped themselves, dirty hands and all. One of the men grinned at her. Samuel either did not notice or did not care. He started conversing.

"Where are you gentlemen from?"

"Pennsylvania."

"Is that so? I went to school in Philadelphia."

Samuel may feel comfortable speaking with such men but she certainly did not. Their language was coarse. She did not like the way their eyes kept scouring the table, the way they kept looking at her.

Lord, help me.

One of the water barrels, the smaller of the two, was empty. As discreetly as she could, Julia picked it up and started for the church side door. She rounded the building, then stole a quick glance back.

The blue uniforms were still there.

The hour was almost through and the prayer meeting would dismiss at any moment. Julia decided to put away the one barrel then wait safely in the foyer for her parents.

She realized she had left her serving tray at the table but did not return to fetch it. When her father's carriage rolled from the churchyard, Samuel was still conversing with the soldiers.

What can he possibly be talking about? Her suspicions grew. She feared somehow he was revealing details from Stephen's letter and that the soldiers would soon descend upon an unsuspecting Confederate Army.

Returning home, Julia was in a fretful state. She took care of her afternoon chores then hurried to Sally's for the sewing circle.

Her friend was waiting for her at the front door.

"And how was the prayer meeting?" she asked.

"Fine, I suppose, but where were you?"

"Father had a council meeting and I though it best to remain at home." She grinned slyly. "Did you speak with Sam?"

"I did and I apologized."

Her grin widened.

"Don't get your hopes up," Julia said. "I will not change my mind. Not when he is so friendly with the Federal Army."

"What do you mean?"

Julia told her about the soldiers. "Watch what you say around him, Sally."

"Sam would never betray our confidences."

"Perhaps not intentionally but what if the soldiers press him for information?"

Sally bit her lip, considering the thought. She then tugged at Julia's sleeve.

"Come help me serve the cold tea."

They stepped into the parlor. The girls were all in attendance except for Rebekah. Julia wondered if she'd had enough of rebel traitors and decided not to come back. Sally made no mention of her. As she filled up the glasses with the sweet liquid Julia whispered, "Why don't we work on socks today, like Trudy suggested before."

Sally gave her a measured look. "No more lace?"

Julia shook her head. "I'll tell them what happened."

She nodded without question. "Julia has suggested that we return to Trudy's idea and make socks for our soldiers," she said.

The girls all looked at Julia.

"Are you sure?" Emily asked.

"Yes." A lump was growing in the back of her throat. She tried to swallow it back. "Our men need our support. It is the least we can do."

Trudy nodded gravely. "Our brother George left last night for Virginia. I want him to know that we are thinking of him." Her eyes teared up.

Everyone in the room felt the emotion.

Elizabeth shook her head in agreement. "And today is a good day to do so. Rebekah isn't here and we don't have to hear her complain."

"Do you think she will come back?" Emily asked.

Sally shrugged. "I don't know. Time will tell."

"But Julia," Trudy said. "What about your lace?"

Julia drew in a deep breath and pressed forward.

"There isn't a need for it now because there isn't going to be a wedding."

A gasp went up around the room.

She hastened to explain. Though disappointed, the others offered their sympathy and support.

"I would never have guessed Samuel would side with the Federal Army, not after you were attacked on Pratt Street," Emily said.

"You are a good sister," Trudy said, "standing by your brother. I would be honored to knit socks for his regiment."

"Thank you."

The subject closed and the ladies went to work. Knitting needles clicked all afternoon long. Julia counted every stitch as a prayer for Edward's victory and for Stephen and George, as well.

Watch over them, Lord and please bring them home soon.

Chapter Seven

Sam stared at the address in his hand then at the small, unimpressive building across the street. It was red brick with crooked black shutters, not much different than the rest of the buildings on the street. Fell's Point was a working class district, full of shipyards and factories. Frederick Douglass himself had once worked in this part of town. Sam thought about how the man had compared his city enslavement with his experiences on the eastern shore plantations. He had said that a slave's life in Baltimore was much improved. That they were almost freemen.

Almost, Sam thought. *And yet, still slaves for life.*

Though he had read of the horrors of field life, he still could not fully grasp the hardship of why someone would say city enslavement was the better of the two. The workers who passed Sam on the street, both white and Negro looked weary and worn out from their labors.

Sam crossed the street, not knowing what or whom he would find in the dilapidated structure before him. He knocked on the front door. After a moment it opened partially.

An old woman, dressed fully in black, stared shrewdly

at him. The doorway offered her a measure of protection from the stranger who had knocked upon it.

Sam hadn't exactly expected a warm welcome but neither had he expected such suspicion.

"I am a friend of Dr. Carter," he hastened to say.

A smile broke on her lined face and immediately her tone changed. "The young man from the seminary!"

He tipped his hat. "Yes, ma'am."

She pulled back the door, wide. "Come. Thee are welcome inside."

He knew immediately by her words that she was a Quaker.

Once inside the parlor she introduced herself as Mrs. Eli Jordan and said that her husband was a minister.

"It is a pleasure to meet you," Sam said.

"It is a pleasure to meet thee."

Sam followed Mrs. Jordan through the house to the kitchen. It was there that Dr. Carter and a handful of others were gathered. Excluding Mrs. Jordan there was one woman and three men. Sam stared at the grim-faced lot. They brightened only when Dr. Carter assured them he had invited Sam to join them.

Dr. Carter turned back to Sam. "I am so pleased that you have decided to join us. You must forgive our rather cold reception. We must be careful of strangers."

"I understand," Sam said, though he was still wondering what he had gotten himself into.

"Please," said Dr. Carter. "Have a seat." He turned to the white-haired gentleman at the head of the table. "Eli, will you give dear Samuel an idea of what our purpose is?"

Eli was none other than the minister husband of Mrs. Jordan. Sam took a seat next to the man.

"Our purpose here," the minister said, "is to bring glory to God."

Sam was taken aback slightly. He had expected, "abolish slavery, educate others on its evil" but the answer the preacher had given was unexpectedly simple.

"God created all men in His image," Eli said. "It is our duty as His servants to declare His message of love."

Sam liked what he was hearing and his fear of associating with harsh temperaments like Warren Meade or radicals such as John Brown was quickly fading.

"If I may ask, sir," he said. "How do you go about spreading this message of love?"

The old preacher smiled kindly, his face a roadmap of miles and years of service for his Lord. "Perhaps I should defer to Mr. Phillips here." He motioned to the man on his right. Sam learned that this man was a city lawyer.

"There are many ways to spread God's message," Mr. Phillips said, "and many avenues of service to choose. We are not all represented here today. There are many of us."

"There are?" Sam said, wondering just how large this group was.

The lady beside him smiled. She was dressed a bit more colorfully than Mrs. Jordan. Her name was Grace Wilkerson.

"We are, as you may wish to call us, a confederation of servants," she said.

"All with the same goal," Phillips said. "There are those who pray. Those who write articles, who speak out publicly against the injustices of slavery. There are those who petition our government for change."

The old preacher leaned forward in his chair. "And then there are those who answer but to God's authority."

"What do you mean?" Sam asked.

Dr. Carter explained. "He means that there are many legal ways in which one can assist in the dismantling of slavery and then there are ways that are not legal according to the law of the land."

Sam was familiar with the Underground Railroad. He had met those in Philadelphia who had assisted in the escape of slaves.

"You mean conductors and station masters?"

Dr. Carter smiled. "You are familiar with the terms."

"Somewhat," Sam said.

"Then you know what difficulties those assisting runaways may face."

"Difficulties now made even more so by the presence of so many soldiers in our city," Grace added.

"You understand," Mr. Phillips said, "that these soldiers *must* enforce the state and local laws."

Sam knew what he was getting at. Slavery was legal in Maryland. Until that law was changed, the Federal soldiers were obligated to protect slaveholders' rights.

Anyone violating such would face the army's wrath.

"I understand, sir."

Julia's face, pale and frightened when the soldiers approached the table, flashed through his mind. Sam pushed the thought away. God's path had led him thus far to this meeting. He would give these people his undivided attention.

"There are other needs, as well," Phillips pointed out, just in case the prospect of sneaking slaves into Pennsylvania was too much for Sam to consider. "Many that we meet are dreadfully malnourished, sick, beaten. They need the attention of a caring physician. One who could be trusted. They need food to sustain them."

"Our station masters share what they have, of course," Eli said, "but extra food would go a long way."

"Yes," Mrs. Wilkerson said. "We can do more *with* more."

Sam thought of Julia again, of her need to bake. Shared bread could mean the difference between life and death for a runaway.

"You have certainly given me much to consider," he said to those gathered around the table.

Eli nodded. "Consider well thy service for the Lord. Follow the path that He has chosen only for thee."

The path God has chosen. Sam inwardly sighed. He appreciated the fact that those around the table did not try to persuade him into taking actions that the present law deemed illegal.

He couldn't help but wonder how many in this room had actual contact with runaways. Had they personally stared into the dark eyes of a trembling slave and offered God's comfort and love? Did he have the courage to do the same?

"Come then," Eli said. "Let us pray for this young man and for countless others like him."

They clasped hands. The old man looked at Sam.

"Fear not," he said. "The Lord Almighty will guide your footsteps."

Sam left the meeting that day without clear direction for his course but he had the faith that God would soon reveal his part in all of it.

And as for Julia and her part, he would continue to pray.

I should be happy, she told herself yet Julia walked home from the sewing circle that day with a great heaviness in her heart. *I am doing what I wished. I am serving my city and my brother at the same time.*

Yet the bread for the prayer meeting and the knitting for Edward's regiment weren't enough. She didn't understand why. She told herself it was because she missed her brother and that was all.

I will write him tonight and tell him about the prayer meeting, of the news from the sewing circle.

She told her parents, as well, when they sat down to supper that evening.

"We are making socks for Edward's regiment," Julia explained.

They both smiled.

"You girls are performing a wonderful service," her mother said.

"Yes." Her father then added, "Useful, too. It is important that soldiers keep their feet dry."

"Keeping busy will help pass the time until he returns," her mother said.

Julia was determined to do just that. When they had finished the meal she cleared away the dishes. When all the evening tasks were complete, Julia went to the study. She sat down at the desk and took out several sheets of paper from the drawer. She dipped her pen in ink and began to write.

Dear Edward...

She wrote of how she missed him but also told him how proud she was of his enlistment. *You are standing up for what you believe. Your actions give the rest of us courage.*

She told him that their parents were well and that the weather had been warm. She told him about the prayer meeting.

Each day someone is praying for you.

Samuel's words drifted through her mind. *I pray daily for his safety.*

She pushed the thought away. She did not tell her brother about that conversation. In fact, she had not written anything about Samuel at all. She did not know how to express all she was feeling in just a few lines.

When Edward writes, if he asks about him, then I will try and explain.

She closed her letter with a prayer then sealed the envelope. She placed it in the desk drawer along with the others she had written. Even if Edward was unable to write for several days, Julia could send hers. She would take her letters to Sally's house in the morning.

Saturday was Julia's favorite day of the week. The family rose later than usual and enjoyed a leisurely breakfast. All but the necessary housework was saved for Monday. Unless there was an emergency, her father was home. He often took the family on an outing. Since there was no prayer meeting scheduled for today, they would have the entire day.

Over a plate of eggs and ham, Dr. Stanton decided to take Julia and her mother shopping.

"I was thinking we would go down to Madam Fontine's and see about a new ball gown."

Julia was excited. She could tell her mother was, as well; but did not wish to be as free with the finances as her husband.

"Oh, I don't really need a new dress, Thomas, but thank you. My plum-colored gown is just fine." She smiled. "I am sure Julia would like to have one though."

He looked at his daughter. "Would you now?"

"Oh, yes! Thank you!"

He winked at her and his gray-streaked mustache

lifted with a smile. "Perhaps we can talk your mother into picking out a new bonnet."

"Yes," Julia added. "You can wear it to the train station when Edward returns home."

"That's a wonderful idea," he said. "Don't you think so, Esther?"

With a fond smile she took away her husband's empty plate. "I pray that day will come soon."

"Speaking of Edward," said Julia. "I have some letters for him. May we stop at Sally's house on our way shopping?"

"Of course."

She hurried to dress and twist up her hair. Then they started off.

Overcast skies covered the city but it did not spoil Julia's mood. Her parents waited in the carriage as she opened the front gate to the Hastings's home. A warm breeze caused the garden flowers to nod, so much so that it appeared the irises were bowing as she passed by.

You are the Belle of Mount Vernon, she remembered Samuel saying once, *and the queen of my heart.*

She brushed the memory aside as a housewife would a pesky fly then walked toward the front porch. The imminent shopping trip and the letters she carried in her dress pocket put a spring in her step. One letter in particular quickened her walk.

She had promised Sally that she would not mention a word of her true feelings for Edward but that wouldn't keep Julia from writing about her. She had written about the latest news of hearth and home but then took great care in describing the new dress that Sally was working on.

She told Edward how beautiful her friend was going to

look in it and how all of the eligible beaux of Baltimore would be clamoring to dance with her at the next ball.

If I can provoke a jealous thought or two in Edward's brain then perhaps it will encourage a little romance when he returns.

Sally would be mortified if she knew she was the main subject of the letter but if Julia's ploy worked, she would thank her in the end. The result would be worth the risk.

Absorbed in her plot, she bounced up the front steps. Before Julia could knock on the door, however, it swung open wide. There stood Sally, an uncomfortable expression on her face. For a split second, Julia couldn't help but wonder if her friend knew the extent of her secret mission.

"Good afternoon," Julia said slowly.

"Good afternoon." Sally craned her neck, glancing up the street as though she were searching for someone.

"Is something wrong?" Julia asked.

"No. You just missed him, that's all."

She didn't need to ask who, she already knew. Samuel had been here. Julia heaved a sigh. For a split second, she felt a small measure of disappointment.

Sally motioned her inside then shut the door behind them. "He brought a letter for Edward."

Her disappointment immediately dispersed and the lightheartedness she felt carrying Edward's letters grew into a fierce protectiveness. What had Samuel written? How would Edward respond when he received it?

Julia scolded herself, her anger building. *I should have explained to Edward about our broken engagement. I don't want to give him any reason for questioning my loyalty. I must write and explain fully at the first opportunity.*

"He also brought your bread tray," Sally said, breaking into her thoughts. "He said you left it at church."

"I did."

"That was thoughtful of him to return it so I could give it to you."

"Yes. It was." Julia knew what Sally was doing. She was pointing out Samuel's good qualities, hoping to change her mind. She would not be persuaded. Anyone conversing freely with Federal soldiers had no business courting her or writing her brother.

"Did you bring a letter?" Sally asked.

"Yes. Several, in fact." She pulled the small stack from her pocket.

"I will tell Father right away," Sally said.

"Thank you."

The tray was lying on the foyer table. Sally exchanged the letters for it. "Will you stay for tea?"

"Thank you but Father and Mother are waiting. We are going shopping."

"That's nice. Then I will see you tomorrow in church?"

"See you then."

Julia stewed about the letter for the entire day. When it was time for church on Sunday she was still thinking about it. Samuel was seated in a back pew when she arrived. He smiled at her. She nodded as she passed by but only for the sake of being polite.

By now word had gotten around about their relationship and in a congregation divided by political lines, no one seemed surprised. Julia took a seat beside her parents in their family pew. The tone of the room was a far cry different than that of the noon prayer meetings. The small weekday group had set aside their differences for a higher purpose. Such was not the case for the Sunday morning crowd. If anything, tensions were getting worse.

Julia noticed several families were absent this morning—most notably, Rebekah's family and also the Meades. She could not say she was unhappy about that. Her family had suffered through enough of their icy, judgmental stares.

At least Samuel smiles when he speaks to me.

She wondered what Monday's meeting would bring. She had promised Sally and Reverend Perry that she would serve with a charitable attitude.

But if he continues to befriend Federal soldiers then I shall have to think otherwise. After all, the Reverend would not want Sally or me in harm's way.

Sam bowed his head to pray. He had made his peace with Edward, at least as far as it depended on him. The letter he had written was not a long one but he felt a great weight had been lifted from his chest the moment he placed it in Sally's hands.

"Bless you, Samuel," she had said. "If more men of this city showed your spirit of reconciliation, I believe this war would end without further injury."

He appreciated her kind words as well as the prayers he knew she was offering on his and Julia's behalf.

Goodness knows, he needed all the prayers he could garner. The pull on his heart to become further involved with Dr. Carter's abolitionist friends was growing stronger every day. He prayed for them and for the runaways they were assisting. He had already given money from his meager savings for food and whatever other expenses they may incur.

But he could not help but believe he was called to do more.

Still, he hesitated. Actively assisting runaway slaves was against the law. Sam did not fear his own arrest, for he firmly believed God's law superseded any written by man. But he could not bear the thought of those he cared for being implicated in such so-called crimes.

What if my activities somehow endanger Julia and her family? The suspicion against those in the Mount Vernon district grows stronger every day. The Federal Army needs no further excuse for badgering them.

He had wanted to speak with Dr. Stanton about the issue from the beginning. The man had expressed interest in Sam's antislavery discussions ever since his first semesters in Philadelphia. Dr. Stanton had even recently asked to borrow his narrative of Frederick Douglass, saying he would like to learn more on the subject.

Perhaps I should just speak straightforwardly. I know that even if Julia's father believes my actions are foolish, he would never report me to those in authority.

Sam made up his mind. He would approach Dr. Stanton after the service and ask for a time to meet with him.

Chapter Eight

Finally, the service drew to a close. Reverend Perry concluded his sermon, then a hymn was sung and the congregation was dismissed with a prayer. Sam then approached Dr. Stanton. The man smiled pleasantly as always.

"Sir, I was wondering if perhaps there would be a time that I may speak with you this week? There is something I would like to discuss with you."

From the corner of his eye he saw Julia. She was watching him. Before she could become a distraction to him, Sam focused his full attention on her father.

"I am available to meet with you now," Dr. Stanton said.

Sam was delightfully surprised yet hesitant. As eager as he was for the man's advice, he suddenly felt unprepared to share all he had been thinking.

"Unless of course this is a private matter," Dr. Stanton said.

Julia turned away, moving to visit with a friend in another pew. Sam's thoughts cleared somewhat upon her departure.

"I am in need of some advice," he told Dr. Stanton.

The man stroked the ends of his mustache. "Well,

perhaps it is best not to delay. We could speak now. Esther and Julia can visit with their friends."

"That would not be an inconvenience?"

Dr. Stanton grinned and shook his head. "Of course not. They always accuse me of leaving church too quickly."

He spoke to his wife briefly and Mrs. Stanton nodded. She smiled at Sam then sought out Reverend Perry's wife for conversation.

Dr. Stanton asked the minister if he could borrow his ready room. He and Sam walked to the front of the church and opened the small door to the left of the pulpit. The room was crowded with hymn books and Bibles. A clerical robe hung from one of the peg racks.

Dr. Stanton took a seat at a small table in the corner of the room. "Now, son, what's on your mind?"

Sam made certain that the door was shut tight before claiming the second chair at the table. He whispered a quick prayer and plunged forward.

"Well, sir, it concerns my antislavery convictions."

"I see. What about them?"

He told him of Dr. Carter and of the meeting he had attended. Dr. Stanton listened patiently, with great interest.

"I have been praying for the end of slavery for sometime now and you of course know my position concerning the war."

Dr. Stanton nodded. "But you sense the time has come to do more than pray."

"Yes, sir."

"After reading your book, I can't say I am surprised."

Sam's heart quickened with excitement. He respected the man as much as he had his own father. He hoped Dr. Stanton would say more but when he didn't, Sam decided to ask plainly, "What do you think I should do, sir?"

Julia's father was quiet for a moment. He tugged at his spectacles before speaking. "That is not for me to say, son. That is between you and the Lord."

Sam's heart sank. He knew the man was right, of course. He supposed what he had really been looking for was Dr. Stanton's blessing. It shouldn't have mattered so; but it did.

"Yes, sir, well, I thank you for listening. I would appreciate your prayers."

"I have been praying for you," the man said, "about a good many things and I will continue to do so."

Sam shook his hand. "Thank you, sir." He stood. Just as he was about to move to the door, Dr. Stanton spoke again.

"I will say this."

Sam stopped.

"Should you decide that the Lord is leading you to take such action..." He paused. "Should you ever have need of a physician, well, you know where to find me."

A peace immediately washed over Sam. Julia's father had given him the blessing he had hoped for. His faith was strengthened by Dr. Stanton's offer to help. It further encouraged Sam that his course of action was the right one. He prayed that wherever this road was leading, Julia would eventually travel alongside him.

She arrived before noon on Monday with her tray full of bread. Her manner was guarded. Whether that had to do with Federal soldiers, his conversation with her father or his letter to Edward, he wasn't sure. He was certain Sally had told her that he had written him. Sam wondered what she thought about that but he did not ask.

"Thank you for returning my tray," she said to him.

"You are welcome. I was going to bring it by the

house but—" He caught himself. There was no point reminding her that she had asked him not to call. She knew that already.

There was an awkward pause. He offered a smile and asked, "What kind of bread did you bring today?"

"Barley loaves and apple butter."

His mouth watered and a delightful memory stirred. "Is that the apple butter from last fall?"

"It is."

He had been home from school on a semester break. They had gone to the Hastings family farm north of Baltimore. He and Edward had gathered the apples. Julia and Sally had stood over the cooking pots.

Sam had carried in armful after armful of firewood to keep their warm, golden pulp at the proper temperature. It was a task he had not minded. Julia let him steal a kiss when no one was looking.

He wondered if she remembered doing so. She must have, for her face was now as red as one of those perfect apples. She drew her handkerchief from her pocket. She dabbed at her cheeks.

"It is going to be warm today," she said.

He tried not to stare but even when flustered, she was so beautiful.

"It will be," he said. "I have filled the water barrels to the brim."

"That is kind of you." She slipped the handkerchief into her pocket then began spreading the apple butter on the bread. While she worked, she studied the street. "I wonder if Elijah and Elisha will be back today."

"They will if their master sends them this way."

With Sally's arrival, Julia began to smile. The conversation between him and her, however, was still strained.

About half past noon Elijah and Elisha approached. Once again they were struggling with a sack of grain.

She scooped up two slices of barley bread and immediately started across the street. He followed after her with two cups of cold water. She glanced back at him as if he were intruding.

"They won't come to the table for a drink, Julia," he said. "We will have to go to them."

Without a word, she hurried between the carriage wheels. The boys set down the sack. Elijah lifted the tattered cap covering his head.

"Afternoon, ma'am," he said.

"Good afternoon," Julia replied. "Do you boys like apple butter?"

"Oh, yes'um!"

She handed them each a slice. Lips smacking, they practically inhaled the bread. Sam chuckled to himself then handed them each a tin cup.

"You must be thirsty," he said.

"Oh, yes, ser."

All tension had melted from her face. She smiled at the boys and then at him. Sam drank in the moment.

The two brothers had made an impression on her, apparently as much as she had on them. Julia spoke to them as she would have to any other child, lovingly, enthusiastically. Elijah and Elisha had relished the attention. She may be set in her opinions and given to temper at times but there was still no other woman Sam wanted to influence *his* children.

"That is a large sack of grain you are carrying," she said to the boys. "Where are you going?"

"We'z goin' to the blacksmith up yonder on Scott Street," Elijah said.

She looked surprised. It was a distance of another five blocks. "How far have you come?"

"From Master Wallace's dry goods store."

"And where is that?"

"On Light Street."

Sam knew the place. It was a store just before the wharf. As heavy as the grain sack was, it was a wonder their backs had not given out.

The children thanked them for the refreshment then Elijah said, "We'z best be on our way."

Sam helped them shoulder the grain and the two boys started off. He and Julia crossed back to the churchyard. Her eyes, however, continued to follow after them.

She and Sally served the bread to those who passed by. Samuel handed out the cold water. She was thankful there were no Federal soldiers at the table today; yet Julia still had a heavy heart. The two Negro children remained in her thoughts. Their bodies were thin and gaunt. How they had managed to drag such a heavy load all the way from the harbor was beyond her imagination. She wondered if they had reached their destination. Had the bread she had given them provided enough nourishment for the journey?

I should have done something more to help them, she thought.

In a small way the brothers reminded her of Edward and Samuel when they were young. One was talkative, the other quiet and observant. The two of them were always covered in dirt, as well—play clothes torn.

Perhaps that is why I feel drawn to them. They remind me of a simpler time.

She sighed. Whatever the reason, the little boys made

her smile. She prayed the Lord would allow her to see them again.

However, the following day her prayer went unanswered. Elijah and Elisha did not pass her way.

Sally left the noon meeting early because her father was hosting an event for some of his fellow city council members and she had to prepare the meal. That left Julia alone at the bread table with Samuel.

She tried to make polite, task-oriented conversation but it was difficult. The traffic on the street was light. Few visitors came. The lack of attendance set her to worrying.

Have most given up on prayer? Will Edward's regiment feel the difference?

Reverend Perry stuck his balding head out the front door as the service was dismissing.

"Sam, Julia, would you come here, please?"

Sam acknowledged the man with an affirmative nod.

"I do hope nothing is wrong," Julia said.

"I don't think anything is wrong." If anything, the preacher seemed rather excited.

They left the empty cups at the table and climbed the stairs. He kept a step behind her until she reached the front door. He then opened it for her.

"After you," he said.

"Thank you."

Reverend Perry was standing in the foyer, grinning from ear to ear. Two elderly matrons were with him. Each held a basket of baked goods in her hands.

"I believe you both know Widow Crowley," the Reverend said.

Sam did. The woman attended their congregation. She used to pinch his cheeks when he was a little boy.

"Ma'am," he and Julia both said in unison.

She nodded, the long lappets on her lace cap swaying. She then gestured toward the woman beside her. She wore an identical cap. "This is my sister-in-law, *Mrs.* Crowley. She is a Catholic."

Sam wondered what the woman's church affiliation had to do with anything but he smiled politely.

Reverend Perry explained. "These dear ladies have brought forth a wonderful gift. They have packed a basket of sweets for each of the local businesses."

"It is more than sweets, Reverend," Widow Crowley pointed out. "It is manna from heaven."

Sam and Julia exchanged quick glances. *Mrs.* Crowley then explained,

"We placed Bibles in the baskets, as well. My cousin works down at the American Bible Society and he gave me a box full of New Testaments. We baked the tea cakes last night."

"How many baskets did you make?" Julia asked, intrigued.

The Crowley women smiled proudly. "Twenty-five."

She gasped, obviously impressed. Sam couldn't help but grin. Julia had met her match in the kitchen.

"We added a notice about the prayer meeting, as well," Reverend Perry said. "I have already enlisted the help of several volunteers but would the two of you be kind enough to help deliver a basket to one of the businesses?"

"Of course," Sam said immediately. "We would be happy to."

He had not looked to Julia when he said that. He wasn't sure she would be interested in delivering anything, anywhere with him. He was fairly certain though that she would not decline a service opportunity in front of Reverend Perry and the matrons.

She surprised him, however, with her enthusiasm. "We could visit the dry goods store on Light Street."

He turned. She looked at him almost mischievously. In choosing that location he knew she was thinking of Elijah and Elisha. It pleasured Sam to share the secret.

"I think that is a wonderful idea," he said.

Julia grinned.

"So do I," said Reverend Perry. "I will see to the remaining baskets." He thanked them and then returned to the Sanctuary.

Widow Crowley handed Sam the basket she was holding. When his hands were full she reached up to pinch his cheek. For a moment he was five years old again.

"Bless you, boy," she said. "Your mother and father would be proud of you."

"Thank you, ma'am, and thank you for your service."

A delightful sound, one he had not heard in quite a while filled his ears. Julia was giggling. He glanced at her. The look on her face was worth the pain in his.

She quickly stifled her laughter. "I shall be just a moment," she said.

"I will wait outside."

He wasn't sure what she was up to, but, a few minutes later, Julia descended the front steps, carrying a second basket. She was beaming.

"I asked Widow Crowley if it would be all right with her to give two baskets to one business," she said.

"What did she say?"

"She told me to follow the Lord's leading."

Her eyes were wide with excitement. She was hatching a plan but just what kind, he could not say. Sam cocked back his topper. "What did you have in mind?"

"Perhaps we can give the tea cakes to Elijah and Elisha themselves, to their family. And the Bible—"

"They can't read," he said.

"Well, yes I know they are still young but when they get older…"

He shook his head. She had no idea what their life was like. He could not blame her for that. He had no idea, either, until recently.

"Julia, it is against the law to teach a slave to read."

Her eyes narrowed. "Truly?"

"Yes."

"That makes no sense at all," she said. "Would they not be better workers if they were literate? Could they not make deliveries with more ease if they could read the street signs and notices?"

"It isn't about *their* ease."

She looked hurt. He hadn't meant to discourage her; he simply wanted her to understand. Sam hoped to give her an idea of what life was like for Elijah and Elisha but he had to choose his examples carefully. Slavery was a brutal institution. No lady should be subjected to such horrible details.

"Your idea is a noble one," he said. "And I, more than anyone, would like to deliver the basket to them but…" He paused, searching.

"But what?"

"In all likelihood, their master won't allow it."

"Why? What harm is there in tea cakes and Scripture?"

"It is a matter of control. If a slave is kept illiterate, unable to know of the value the Savior places on his life, then that slave will never rebel."

"Rebel?"

"Freedom and for that matter, love, is an unquenchable desire. Once you have a taste of it, you thirst for more."

She suddenly looked very uncomfortable. Avoiding his eyes, she started stacking the tin cups in the box, ready to take them to the pump for a washing.

Sam hadn't intentionally meant to draw a parallel between the children's relationship with God and their engagement. It just happened.

"Try not to be discouraged," he said, steering the discussion back to its proper course. "Perhaps the Lord will give us other opportunities to show Elijah and Elisha kindness. Perhaps they will pass this way tomorrow."

She nodded contemplatively, though still avoiding his eyes. "I suppose I should return the second basket to Widow Crowley."

"Keep it," he said. "The Lord may yet have plans for it."

When the water barrels and cups had been cared for, Julia found her parents and explained where she was headed.

"And Sam will escort you?" her father asked.

"Yes."

She did not like the idea of spending so much time with Samuel. His presence confused her. His lack of support for her family still angered her but there were moments when his smile erased all memory of such things. Personal interaction aside, she wanted to deliver the basket, even if she could not minister to Elijah and Elisha directly.

Perhaps by being kind to their employer, God will pass a blessing on to them.

She rejoined Samuel on the sidewalk in front of the church. He carried a basket in each arm.

"I should have brought my carriage today," he said. "I am sorry this will be a long walk."

She had retrieved her parasol from her father's carriage before he and her mother left to make a delivery of their own.

"That is all right. It is a pleasant afternoon."

Although she was hesitant about being in Samuel's continued company, in truth, she was eager for the opportunity to stroll. She missed doing so. The occupying army had put an end to her carefree outings.

"We should pray before we start," he said.

"Indeed."

He set the baskets on the ground then reached for her hands. He had often done so when they were engaged to be married. Julia thought of the warmth in his touch but did not give in to the memory. She kept her hands tightly about her parasol. Samuel pulled back and closed his eyes.

"Lord, may we be Your ambassadors of goodwill today. May our words and deeds soften hearts in the dry goods store. May this man be sympathetic to Elijah and Elisha's needs. May his heart become in tune with that which pleases You."

She, of course, hoped for the salvation of the shopkeeper but she had trouble believing what Samuel had said earlier concerning slaves and masters. She doubted if the law excluding them from being taught to read and write was really a matter of control.

Surely his abolitionist friends are provoking hysteria. The masters probably don't want their slaves studying the alphabet during working hours. It is simply a matter of an honest day's work.

They started in the direction of the harbor. A sense of uneasiness dogged her heels. It was the first time she had traveled that way since the day of the riot. Walking along, she tried to focus her attention on the store windows and street vendors, not on the recent history of the city or the man who was escorting her.

Thankfully, Samuel kept their conversation confined to their mission.

"I believe we should tell the proprietor where we are from and then say we would like to give him a gift. What do you think?"

Truth be told, she wasn't really thinking of the impending conversational exchange. She was still hoping to catch a glimpse of Elijah and Elisha.

"Whatever you think is best," she said.

The rumble of cartwheels and clanging of ships' bells could be heard as they neared the Baltimore harbor. The smell of fish and burning coal filled the air. The dry goods store was located in the last row of shops before the wharf.

"Here now," Julia said when they reached their destination. "Let me carry the second basket while you speak with the man."

Samuel thanked her then opened the door. A bell on the back of the glass signaled their arrival. Julia closed her parasol as they stepped inside. The odor of the sea mingled with the scent of the earth. Large, open barrels of oatmeal, corn and dried beans lined the walls.

A middle-aged man wearing a sack coat and apron stood behind the counter. He smiled and addressed Samuel.

"A good afternoon to you, sir. How may I serve you?"

Samuel moved forward. Julia followed a step behind discreetly surveying her surroundings. Her heart beat with anticipation. Were the children here?

Samuel explained the reason they had come. The

merchant seemed pleasantly surprised. He nodded to Julia. She smiled in return.

"You say you are from the church on Charles Street?" the man asked Samuel.

"Yes. Just a few blocks north of here."

From the corner of her eye Julia spied movement. At the far end of the room little Elisha appeared, broom in hand. His eyes widened as he recognized her.

Julia smiled and shifted the basket from one hand to the other. *It is the perfect opportunity,* she thought. *The businessman is pleasant enough, surely he won't object to a little kindness on the children's behalf.*

She took half a step in Elisha's direction.

"Boy!" the merchant suddenly barked. "Quit gawkin' at the lady and get back to work! I ought to sell you South! You ain't worth a shoelace!"

Julia froze, the harsh, unexpected tone stinging her ears. Elisha immediately dropped his gaze. His broom began to fly. She felt so terrible for distracting him that she started to speak on his behalf. Just as she opened her mouth, Samuel clasped her elbow. He must have read her mind.

She glanced at him. The look in his eyes was an unspoken warning.

Though it pained her, she kept silent.

The man behind the counter changed his tone like a gentleman did a soiled shirt. "Well, I thank you both for the gift," he said. "That is right kind of you. Give my best to your preacher."

"You are quite welcome sir," Samuel replied. "We will. Have a pleasant day."

He nudged her gently. Julia cast a quick glance in Elisha's direction before turning to go. He was still sweeping, his eyes seemingly nailed to the floor.

They stepped outside.

A buckboard pulled in front of the store and a trio of laborers in scrap shirts jumped to the sidewalk. Julia paid them no mind. She was too busy thinking of what had just taken place in the store. The merchant had spoken quite kindly to them, so much so that she perceived him a charitable man. How could he in the same breath shout at Elisha, as though he was no better than a stray dog?

"I brought trouble upon him," she said, not really meaning to voice the thought.

Samuel took the second basket from her then remained close to her side. The sidewalk was narrow.

"Elisha knows your intentions were kind," he said.

She looked up at him. He seemed as troubled as she felt. "You knew that man would behave in such a way, didn't you?"

"No, but I assumed he would."

She sighed heavily.

"Few people show their slaves any kindness," he said. "Most see them only as a source of labor, of property."

She shook her head, disgusted by the thought. "They are children."

"Yes, they are, and God loves them."

"They need to know that," she said.

Sam agreed with her. Elisha and Elijah did need to hear of God's love. He admired her desire but as she saw for herself today, teaching a slave child about Christ was a difficult matter.

But there must be some way.

A steamboat had docked and the way was crowded and noisy. He and Julia walked in silence until reaching Charles Street. He was so lost in his own thoughts that he failed to see the opportunity God had placed before them.

Julia recognized it before he did.

A few feet ahead of them, a man in a green silk vest and stovepipe hat was just about to step into an elegant carriage.

"Samuel," she whispered. "The basket."

He quickly gave it to her, recognizing just as Julia had that the man was the banker who had stopped by the bread table a few days ago.

"Excuse me, sir," she said, going up to him.

The man turned to look at her. His expression indicated that he recognized her, as well. He tipped his hat and smiled. "You are the lady from the church, aren't you?"

"Yes, sir. Would you be so kind as to accept this gift on our behalf for you and your business associates?"

Though by all outward appearances the man had want for nothing, he seemed touched by her generosity. Sam was, as well. Julia could warm the coldest heart with her Christian charity.

"I would be honored to do so, miss," the banker said. "Thank you."

She smiled sweetly, a look which she held long after the banker's departure. As they strolled up Charles Street, Sam's heart thumped wildly. His mouth was dry.

I know You have a plan for us, Lord. And I believe You mean for us to serve You together.

"Well," she said. "I suppose the Almighty used one misfortune today for something good."

"Indeed. And I believe He often does so." Though hesitant, Sam acted upon what he was thinking. "It is near the dinner hour. Would you care to stop in one of the restaurants for a bite to eat?"

Chapter Nine

❧

Her fingers tapped her parasol as she considered the idea. Her foolish heart wished to accept his invitation. Her determined will, however, kept her on course.

Serving our community is one thing. Eating together is quite another.

Whether Samuel saw the event as simply an extension of the day's journey or an opportunity to rekindle love lost, she did not know. Thankfully the sewing circle offered her the luxury of politely declining his request.

"Thank you, but no. I must return home for the sewing circle."

His face showed his disappointment for the slightest moment but he then offered her a pleasant smile.

"Of course. I forgot. We mustn't keep the ladies waiting."

Ever the gentleman, he escorted her promptly home.

Since Sally was otherwise occupied, Julia was hosting the circle that afternoon at her house. Rebekah had still not returned. Julia, however, was not distressed. Her absence gave the other women freedom to discuss the activities of the men they each prayed for.

"Our brother George is well and eager to be in action," Trudy said, having also received a recent letter.

"Edward and Stephen are, as well," Julia said, "though I do hope the Guard will be able to put fear into those Federal soldiers without using force."

"As do I," Elizabeth said.

They tugged at their yarn and speedily completed pairs of butternut or gray socks. Yet even as Julia labored for her brother's brave men, she found her thoughts returning to Elijah and Elisha.

If anyone needs stockings it is them. They won't be able to make deliveries barefoot come autumn.

Though she would gladly knit them each a pair, she wondered how she could possibly make certain they would receive them. By his actions at the store, more than likely the man behind the counter would not allow them to keep any gift.

I should ask Samuel. Perhaps he can think of a way.

The following day the two of them were together again. Thankfully, Sally returned, as well, bringing her special spice cake for the hungry good citizens of Baltimore.

Three more visitors entered the church house and the banker they had met on the street returned. He stopped again at the table.

"I must thank you for your kindness yesterday," he told them. "The tea cakes were delicious."

"You are very welcome, sir," Julia replied. "They were made by one of our widows."

He smiled. "I must confess, I was quite hesitant to be involved with any religious gathering but I found your prayer meeting most enlightening. I would like to learn more about Christ."

Julia's heart swelled with joy. She looked to Samuel who then lovingly explained God's sacrifice for mankind.

"The Word tells us that God so loved the world that He gave His only begotten Son, that whosoever believeth in Him, should not perish but have everlasting life."

The banker was listening attentively, so Samuel continued on. Julia smiled. Samuel could articulate the truths of Scripture in a way she never could. It was a privilege to watch as he pointed the man toward a relationship with Christ.

She and Sally silently prayed. When the man went into the church house rejoicing, Julia touched Samuel's sleeve.

"God bless you," she said, tears filling her eyes. "Heaven rejoices because of what you have just done."

The look he gave her enveloped her in warmth. "It was you who gave him the basket. You are the one who told him we weren't doing this for political reasons."

Her heart swelled even further. Samuel was one of the most humble men she had ever known. He never claimed a success as his own but always chose to include others, no matter how small the role.

"I suppose we have done as Reverend Perry had hoped," she said. "We have served our community, united."

"Indeed we have. It is my hope that we will continue to do so."

"There is a city full of opportunities," Sally said.

Julia broke eye contact with him. For a moment she had forgotten that her friend was even there. Sally pointed across the street.

"Here they come," she said.

Julia looked to see Elijah and Elisha on their way up

the street. She quickly brushed the tears from her eyes, her excitement building.

"Will you help me?" she asked Samuel.

"Certainly."

She snatched two slices of Sally's spice cake and headed across the street.

"I am so pleased to see you both," Julia said. She looked then at little Elisha. The hole in the knee of his trousers was getting bigger. "And I am terribly sorry for getting you into trouble."

He looked at her with those wide brown eyes. His brother draped his arm around him. "Oh, don't you fret none, Miss Julia," Elijah said. "He's fine."

She was not convinced. What if the man had scolded him further after her departure or worse? "Is that the truth?"

"Yes'um."

Elisha nodded, as well. He smiled. Julia's heart lifted.

She handed them each a slice of cake. They devoured it in one breath.

"This here's the best bread we'z ever eaten!" Elijah proclaimed.

Julia chuckled. "I'll tell Miss Sally that you like it."

Samuel handed them each a cup of water. "You have been working so hard," he said. "How about if I deliver that grain for you? Then you can linger here with Miss Julia."

Elijah's eyes widened in shock and so did his brother's.

"Oh, no, ser. We'z can't have you doin' our work."

Around them people were passing. A few stared. Some glared. Samuel, however, was not deterred.

"Well, then, what if I carry it for the next three streets then you can finish the delivery?"

The boys started to protest but Samuel hoisted the grain on his broad shoulder. "We had better be on our way, young men. We don't want to be late."

"No, ser!"

The two children thanked Julia for the bread then hurried off. They skipped around Samuel as he walked. Before the rumble of the wagon wheels drowned out their voices she heard him ask, "Have the two of you ever heard about Jesus?"

Julia smiled to herself as she crossed back to the churchyard. A waiting Sally was grinning. "Word will get out and every hungry child in town will be on this street."

"Then that will be a good thing."

"Yes, indeed."

Julia gave Elijah and Elisha an extra slice of cake on their return route. They thanked her profusely then scampered off toward the harbor. Samuel escorted her across Charles Street.

"I heard you speak of Jesus," she said. "What exactly did you say?"

The light of God shone on his face. Julia couldn't help but stare. "I told them that God loved them," he said. "That He had sent His Son to pay the penalty for the wrongs they had done." He paused. "Do you know what they asked?"

"No. What?"

"They asked if Jesus was a white man."

She blinked. "How did you answer them?"

"I told them He was neither white nor Negro. That we were all created in God's image and therefore He looked a little something like us all."

Julia smiled. She had never given much thought before to what the Savior actually looked like. She supposed what Samuel said was true. "I think that was a wise answer."

By the time they reached the bread table the prayer meeting was ending. Julia's parents had just stepped out the church door.

"Would you allow me to walk you home today?" Samuel asked. "There is something I would like to discuss with you."

The request took her by surprise. She was eager to continue discussing Elijah and Elisha but she did not wish to make walking with him a habit. He had honored her wishes by not discussing her brother or politics thus far but what if that changed? What if as they strolled through Mount Vernon, he tried to convince her that the secessionist position was the wrong course of action?

"You wrote Edward," she said.

He blinked. "Yes. I did."

"Why?"

He blinked again, mouth shifting slightly as though he were searching for the words. "I wanted to tell him that I was sorry for the way we parted company. I wanted to tell him that I am praying for him."

"Did you tell him about us?"

He looked surprised. "I supposed you had," he said.

Heat filled her face and Julia immediately regretted the question. Samuel would think she had not told Edward because she still had hopes to be his wife.

Well, I don't. We are far too different. He may be an admirable man but I can only be yoked with someone who will support and defend my family's honor.

There was a long pause. The look in his eyes tugged at her heart.

"Will you walk with me?" he asked once more.

Though her pride and political position warned her otherwise, she agreed.

"Let me speak with Father and Mother," she said.

"Of course. I will see to it that we are finished here."

Sam hurried to return the water barrels and other items to the church cellar. Sally followed.

"Go on now," she said with a grin. "I will wash the cups."

He thanked her for her kindness then quickly went back outside.

Julia stood waiting on the front steps. With one full look at her, Sam had to catch his breath. Her blue eyes were framed by a sea-green and white bonnet. The matching dress she wore was airy and light.

He had to remind himself why she was waiting for him. She did not do so as a fiancée eager to be with her betrothed. It was simply because he had requested to speak with her further.

Have patience, he told himself, *and be thankful for small things.*

"Thank you for waiting," he said. "Shall we go?"

He offered his arm but she did not take it.

"What did you wish to discuss?" she asked. He could hear the uncertainty in her voice.

"Actually, it concerns your sewing circle, I suppose."

His own nervousness was very apparent to him. He hoped she would not notice. If she did, she did not say.

"The circle?" she asked. "What about, exactly?"

"Sally mentioned that you are knitting socks for Edward's regiment."

Her spine stiffened. The look she shot him was that of a lioness ready to defend her cub.

"I think it is commendable that you are knitting for

the men," he said quickly. "They will need the socks for winter."

The lioness transformed to a kitten before his eyes. A hint of a smile emerged. "Then I knit with your blessing?"

It encouraged him that she asked for it. "Of course. Men need to keep their feet warm."

"Thank you, Samuel. I appreciate that."

The lace trim of her pagoda sleeve was brushing the back of his hand and her rose water scent was intoxicating. He tried to keep focus.

"You are welcome. I was wondering if perhaps you might be interested in helping someone here in town. I mean, in addition to Edward and his men."

Her expression settled to a curious look. "What kind of help?" she asked.

"A few pairs of wool socks, perhaps a loaf of bread or two. It would be for a good cause."

A column of Federal soldiers rounded the corner, their boots clicking in unison step. Julia immediately went pale. She clutched his arm. Linked together they remained until the men had passed. Julia then dropped her hand.

"What cause?" she whispered. "Whom would I be helping?"

"Someone in great need. Someone hungry and cold." He stopped, turning to face her fully. He could see the questions in her eyes.

He wanted to share in detail the opportunity that Dr. Carter had presented him and tell her how, more than anything, he hoped she would join him in that cause. Though he wished to tell her everything, he knew he could not. At least not yet.

"I am sorry I cannot tell you more," he said, "but

please know that I wouldn't be asking you this if it was not of the utmost importance."

Her eyes held his as though she were searching for any hint of insincerity. "Just answer me one question," she said.

"Certainly."

"Does this have anything to do with Yankee soldiers?"

Sam let out a laugh. He couldn't help it. For once they could agree. Soldiers in blue were the last people that he wanted involved.

"Absolutely not," he promised. "Not one Federal soldier. You have my word on that."

That irresistible smile slowly filled her face. "Well, then, in that case, I suppose I could knit an extra pair this week."

"And the bread?" he dared ask.

"I could spare a loaf."

He could barely contain his happiness. "Bless you, Julia."

Her smile broadened. That mischievous glimmer danced through her eyes. "I must confess, I have wanted to knit for those in need. I just wasn't sure how to go about delivering the items."

Sam could barely believe his ears. *The Lord's hand is in this. He is preparing the way of service for the runaways.* In his enthusiasm he reached for her hands.

"Oh, sweetheart."

She pulled back and quickly looked down at the ground. Her cheeks were pink from his attention. Sam took a half step back and adjusted his hat.

"When would you need the items?" she asked.

"When could you have them ready?"

She raised her head. Her lower lip disappeared as she

calculated the time. "A day or two," she said. "It doesn't take that long to knit a pair of socks. I can bring them to the meeting."

"That would be wonderful."

They continued walking and to Sam's dismay they reached her family's front gate all too soon. He opened it slowly then tipped his hat.

"I appreciate your assistance," he said.

Julia nodded formally, almost regally, and he was completely caught up in the moment. His heartbeat quickened.

"I always thought you looked beautiful in that color."

The pink blush darkened to scarlet. There was a look in her eyes that he was certain was still love.

Chapter Ten

⮑

Julia's skin still tingled, long after Samuel's departure. Their walk had been pleasant. The scent of lilacs drifted lazily on the breeze as they passed by their neighbors' front gardens. He was kind and complimentary. War didn't seem so imminent among the vines and blooms.

He wanted to help someone in need. It wasn't her family that he wished to help but she had to stop pining over that. She was certain he would find a way to deliver her socks and bread to Elijah and Elisha. As for other items, given his interest in abolition, he would more than likely send things north to some former slave that he had met during his time in Philadelphia.

Whatever he is doing, it isn't going to cause harm to Edward or the rest of my family.

May marched into June and the presence of Federal soldiers increased in Baltimore. With the exception of the sewing circle and the prayer meeting, Julia spent the majority of her time at home with her parents. When she wasn't attending to household duties, she was knitting.

Three pairs of socks for Edward's company had already been completed. She had given a pair of gray socks and a pan of cornbread to Samuel on Tuesday.

The pair she was currently working on was also for him. Seated comfortably in her father's study, her needles clicked quickly.

Around seven o'clock, there was a knock at the front door. Julia started to rise.

"Keep your place," her father said as he laid aside a copy of *The Sun*. "You are doing important work." He smiled at her then walked into the foyer.

Julia went back to her knitting. A moment later her father came back into the room. He grabbed his medical bag.

"Thomas Wilkerson has need of my services," he told her. "Please let your mother know where I am."

He was back out the door before she could even speak.

Julia set aside her yarn and walked to the front window. She watched as her father disappeared into a closed carriage, one she did not recognize.

That must belong to one of Mr. Wilkerson's relatives, she thought. *Please Lord, let him be well.*

The carriage sped off then Julia went to find her mother.

Sam's pulse raced. Every carriage, every horse that passed the Wilkerson home set his nerves on edge. Were the approaching sounds signaling Mr. Wilkerson's return or the arrival of Federal soldiers?

The boards above him creaked. Mrs. Wilkerson moved about the upper floor trying to keep her children occupied and out of sight from their unexpected guest. The woman was huddled in the corner of the small, windowless room. Her dark, fear-filled eyes studied Sam. He had given her a cup of cold water but she was trembling so that it sloshed all over her blistered, bruised hands. His heart ached.

How could anyone survive such a beating?

He took the cool, soft cloth from the wash basin beside him. He knelt to her level and dabbed carefully at her left eye. In another few moments he was certain it would swell shut.

"Do not worry," he said softly. "Help will be here soon."

She had escaped from a house on nearby Hanover Street. How she had thought to come to the Wilkerson home, he did not know. He did not ask. The less one knew, the better.

He rinsed the cloth, wrung out the blood. "What is your name?"

"R-r-rose."

He smiled at her. "That is a beautiful name."

She winced and clutched her protruding belly. Sam's anxiety grew. He feared for the unborn child she carried.

Lord, please... He had no idea what to do. He prayed Mrs. Wilkerson would settle her children to bed and quickly return. *A woman would know better how to help her.*

A moment later, to his great relief, the door opened. Mr. Wilkerson had returned. Dr. Stanton followed close behind. A weak, kittenlike cry escaped Rose's injured lips when she saw Julia's father.

"There is nothing to fear," Sam told her. "He is a friend. He is a doctor and you can trust him."

Sam moved back to give Dr. Stanton room. He heard him sigh pitifully as he removed his hat and knelt before the trembling runaway.

"Sam." Thomas Wilkerson motioned for him. He followed him out of the room.

Worry darkened the man's face. "She cannot stay here," he whispered. "It is too close. Her master is only one street over. If he gets word that she is here…" He did not finish the rest of his sentence.

Sam knew the man was fearful for the sake of his wife, his children. He understood.

"Would the Jordans' home be a better choice?" he asked. "Will they receive her?"

"Yes. But how will we see to her?"

Fear peppered his mind but Sam squared his shoulders. He knew what he had to do. "As soon as Dr. Stanton says Rose can travel, I will see to her."

The lines on Mr. Wilkerson's face eased somewhat. "Thank you. How will you go about it? You may use my carriage if you wish."

Sam had no idea how he should transport the injured, expectant mother but he knew who he should ask. "Before we make any plans," he said, "let's spend some time in prayer."

By the following day Julia had finished her second pair of socks and carried them to the church. Samuel was already there, water barrels filled, tin cups waiting.

"Good day, Samuel."

His face was practically aglow. She imagined the look of peace, of quiet strength on Samuel's face at present must resemble that of a heavenly messenger.

"Yes, indeed," he said. "It is a good day. I must tell you, God is simply amazing."

Her Christian upbringing testified to that fact but she wondered what specifically he was referring to. Had some special blessing occurred this morning? As far as she knew a Northern army was still camped on Federal Hill.

"And how is that?" she asked as she handed him his package. He slid it beneath the table for safekeeping.

"His timing," he said. "You agreed to knit and bake and He supplied the person in need."

Samuel's simple faith warmed her heart. She wondered if Elijah and Elisha would be sporting stockings next time she saw them. She smiled, a genuine expression of Christian love.

"I am pleased to be of service."

He took her hand in his and gave it a squeeze. Julia was struck by the familiarity, the comfort of his grasp but she did not allow herself to dwell on it.

One should feel a closeness, a kinship when serving the Lord together.

"Thank you," he said. "From the bottom of my heart, thank you."

"You are quite welcome."

He let go of her hand then busied himself with the water barrels. She unwrapped her bread.

By noon the usual congregates had gathered inside the church. They were nowhere near the attendance of the New York meetings, but every petitioner was a welcomed encouragement. Every day that passed peacefully in Baltimore and without report of a distant battle was a blessing.

The banker who had recently joined them was approaching. This time he had brought one of his fellow business associates. Julia recognized him from the day she had delivered the basket. Both men stayed for the prayer meeting.

"Isn't it wonderful," Sally remarked. "People from all across the city are coming."

"It is wonderful," Julia said, "and I do hope it continues."

She sliced her bread, spread the jam, all the while keeping a lookout for the boys. Their milk-white smiles brightened her day and the sound of their giggling tugged at her heart. She could not wait to see them.

In addition to her bread she had brought two rolls of Necco Candy Wafers. They were her favorite sweet. She was certain Elijah and Elisha would like them as much.

At fifteen till one o'clock she spied them. She had to wait for several wagons to pass before she could cross the street. Samuel followed after her, once again ready to help carry the heavy grain sack.

Today Elijah and Elisha were struggling with an even heavier load. They stopped to catch their breath as she approached.

"A good day to ya, Miss Julia," Elijah said.

She returned the smile. "And a good day to you both. I have a surprise for each of you. Hold out your hands."

They did as instructed and Julia promptly dropped the small roll of candy into each of their palms. Their eyes widened. Their mouths gaped.

"Oh, thanky!" Elijah said. "We ain't never had no candy before."

She should have guessed that would be the case. By the looks of them they barely had enough clothing and necessary food. Knobby knees poked through their threadbare trousers.

Perhaps if I sew them each a new set, Samuel can figure out a way to convince their employer to let them keep them.

She handed them each a slice of bread. Samuel stepped up beside her.

"So where are we going today, gentlemen?" Samuel asked.

They both giggled.

"Aw, we ain't no gentlemen, Mr. Sam," Elijah said. "We'z slaves."

"In my eyes you are fine gentlemen."

Julia watched as the two boys stood a little taller. Her heart swelled with admiration. Samuel never hesitated to pass on an encouraging word.

He handed them each a tin cup then bent down to lift the grain sack.

"You there!" someone shouted. "Halt!"

Tin cups clattered to the sidewalk. Water splashed her shoes. Julia turned in the direction of the angry voice.

She gasped.

A blue uniformed officer was marching toward them, his forehead lined in a scrutinizing glare. Julia immediately stepped in front of Elijah and Elisha, her bell-shaped skirt hiding them from the soldier's view.

"Citizens are not to interfere in any matter with persons of servitude!" the man barked.

Her heart was thumping wildly. Julia gulped back fear and prayed her knees would hold. A sword was fastened to the officer's waist. His gloved hand rested upon it.

Samuel stepped between her and the man. "We are not interfering, Captain. We are simply extending a kindness, a cup of cold water in the name of Christ."

The soldier obviously held no regard for the Savior's name. He cursed. "Abolitionists! I know what you are up to."

Julia cringed and backed closer to the boys. They, too, were trembling.

"Captain," Samuel said, his voice louder, "may I remind you, a lady is present."

He cared not and he shoved Samuel out of the way. Julia froze as he then pointed at the children.

"Both of you," he ordered. "Be gone!"

God himself must have helped lift the grain sack, for the boys quickly shouldered the load and hurried up the street. They did not look back.

The Federal officer then turned to her and Samuel. He gripped his sword. "I strongly suggest that the two of you remain in the churchyard from now on."

Satisfied that the implied threat was enough, he turned on his heel and marched up Charles Street. Samuel turned to her immediately.

"Are you all right?"

She couldn't stop trembling. Cold chills ran through her. "Will h-he follow them?"

"It doesn't appear so. Look. He is turning toward Howard Street."

"M-may God k-keep them safe."

Not knowing what else to do, she bent to pick up the tin cups. The sidewalk suddenly seemed lopsided. She felt lightheaded. Pins prickled her skin.

The next thing she knew Samuel's arms were around her, steadying her.

"Breathe deeply," he said. "Slowly."

She tried but it was difficult. Her corset, once comfortably drawn, now felt painfully restrictive. Her lungs ached for air.

"Look at me," she heard him say. His voice was calm but firm, his gaze fixed. "That man is gone. He isn't coming back. Elijah and Elisha are making their delivery."

She felt his arms tighten around her, could smell the warm scent of his shaving balm. Giving in to weakness, Julia leaned into him, surrendering fully to his embrace.

Sam's heart was pounding. She was shaking all over, even more so than that day on Pratt Street.

"W-what a h-horrible man," she stammered.

His mouth soured at the way the soldier had spoken in front of her, at the way he had frightened Elijah and Elisha. He was coarse and arrogant, obviously more concerned about showing his power then safeguarding the city.

She lifted her head from his chest. Her blue eyes were wide and wet with tears. "Th-thank you for b-being here, S-Samuel. If I h-had been alone—"

"Hush now," he said, tenderly tracing the outline of her face with his fingers. "Don't be frightened. It is over and done with."

He wanted to heed his own words but he shuddered to think of what could have happened. He wanted to hold her tightly, to shelter her but the soldier's warning still pounded in his brain. The street was no place to stand. He needed to get her back to the churchyard as quickly as possible.

"Take my arm."

She did so though her movement was unsteady.

Sally must have gone to fetch Dr. Stanton for he was descending the church steps. Sam led Julia to her father and explained what had happened. His face drained of all natural color but the predominant emotion in his eyes was one of disgust. Sam understood. He felt exactly the same thing.

"Thank you, son, for looking after her," Dr. Stanton said. "Come, child. Let's get you home."

Her hand brushed his arm as she slipped away. Sam stood where he was, torn between keeping the promise he had made not to visit her home and following after her to make sure she was safe.

He was certain that would be the end of their working together—sure that after today's confrontation, Julia would withdraw from service. He understood why she would do so but his heart selfishly ached at the thought of her absence.

He wanted her beside him now and always, serving the Lord together. Her smile buoyed his courage and brought a light to this otherwise dark world.

But Your will, Lord, not mine. I want to do Your will.

His faith, however, was again strengthened when Julia returned the very next day with a basket full of bread on her arm.

"I wasn't certain you would come," he said. "But I am pleased that you have."

"I had to," she said. "I had to make certain that Elijah and Elisha are safe."

He wasn't sure the slave children were ever safe but he didn't tell her that. Julia's focus concerned the incident from yesterday. He didn't want to give her anything else to worry about.

"I have been praying for them," she said.

"So have I."

She offered him a tender smile. It was all he could do not to reach for her. She had felt so good in his arms.

From her basket she drew a small, brown paper package. She handed it to him. He peeked through the paper and twine. It was two pairs of gray stockings and boiled milk rolls.

"I hope that will be acceptable," she said. "Father asked for them with supper tonight and the recipe makes so many."

"It is perfectly acceptable, although I must confess that I will have a difficult time not eating them myself." He loved her milk rolls.

Again, she smiled.

He set the package beneath the table. She then placed

a linen cloth, long and full, over where they were stand-ing. He wondered if it was her way of hiding the extra socks and rolls from prying eyes. He supposed in this case caution was wise.

Sally came up beside them with the set of cups.

"Oh, that looks pretty," she said.

"Thank you," Julia replied.

The three of them filled cups, sliced bread and of-fered it to those who passed along the way. Julia engaged in polite conversation with the visitors but Sam could tell her heart was not fully in it. She was worried about Elijah and Elisha.

"They should have been here by now," she whispered to him at one point.

"They may have taken a different route or perhaps they had other work today."

"Perhaps," she said softly but he knew she did not believe that was the case. In truth, he was just as con-cerned. Had his eagerness to show God's kindness caused the children harm? Had their master learned of Sam's assistance? Was he punishing them because Sam had carried the grain?

"God knows where they are," he said, more for his benefit than hers. "Just keep praying."

She nodded. "I will."

About half past noon they spied them, coming south on Charles without any grain. Julia quickly collected two slices of tea bread. He stopped her. The Federal captain's warning to remain in the churchyard rang through his mind. Sam didn't want Julia to be in danger but he, in good conscience, could not ignore the children.

"Wait here," he said.

"I brought them candy."

"I will take it."

She handed him two rolls of candy wafers which he promptly dropped in the left pocket of his frock coat. He gathered the bread and cups then started across the street.

Midway across he glanced back at her. Julia's eyes were sweeping the area, searching for any hint of Union blue.

Oh, Lord, he prayed, *please don't let any soldiers come today.*

He met the two boys on the far sidewalk. Their conversation was a quick one, just long enough to exchange the bread, water and candy and a few words. Elijah and Elisha then hurried on their way.

Sam turned back to cross the street. Julia's eyes were on him. She was standing at the churchyard's perimeter, a look of eagerness and concern on her face.

"Are they well?" she asked as soon as he joined her.

As well as a slave can be, he thought. "They are fine. They traveled up Hanover Street today to make their delivery. They didn't want to get us into any trouble."

Her shoulders fell with a grateful sigh and her countenance immediately settled into a smile. "Bless their hearts," she said.

"They said to thank you."

"Thank *you,* Samuel."

"It is my pleasure."

Knowing the boys had escaped the clutches of that surly Federal soldier now put her in a happy mood. She returned to her bread. After a moment or two she was humming.

The hour passed all too soon. Sam did not want Julia to leave. He debated over asking her to walk with him again. Sally carried off the tin cups for a good scrubbing as Julia shook the bread crumbs from the tablecloth. She packed it in her basket.

"Is there any word yet when your classes will resume?" she asked.

"Not yet, but I have found temporary work."

"Oh! That is wonderful. Where?"

"Tutoring my colleague's relative for a few hours each week. A young lad who is having trouble with his history." The pay wasn't much but it was enough to get by. For that, he was thankful.

She rocked back and forth on her feet, her skirt and petticoats rustling. Her blue eyes were full of encouragement.

His heart beat a little faster.

"Well, I am certain the boy will be a scholar in no time at all," she said.

"Thank you. Do you have a busy afternoon?"

"Oh, yes. Father is taking me to Madam Fontine's for a dress fitting."

His balloon of buoyancy burst and a lump lodged in his throat. If she was going to Madam Fontine's then it was for a new ball gown. There was an upcoming party. It stung to realize he would not be her escort.

Whether the emotion showed on his face or Julia herself regretted sharing such information, he wasn't sure. She bit her lip then hastened to explain,

"It is for Dolly Moffit's coming-out party. I really don't want to go. She is so high society but Father says that since we were invited it would be rude to decline."

"Yes," he said, absentmindedly.

She looked at him. He looked at her. Neither seemed to know what to say to the other. Sam cleared his throat.

"Well, I hope you have an enjoyable time," he managed. "Thank you again for the socks and bread."

There was another awkward silence. It was Julia who finally broke it.

"I thank you, Samuel."

"For what?"

"For being such a gentleman."

Sam nodded to her then picked up the empty water barrels. He walked to the cellar as her words repeated over and over in his mind.

Such a gentleman.

It was an improvement over the word *coward* yet it still stung.

The pale green silk rustled as Julia turned in front of the large looking glass. The ball gown fit but it didn't feel right.

Madam Fontine fluffed Julia's crinoline and underskirts. "You look exquisite in the gown," she said. "Although the purpose of this ball is mademoiselle Moffit's debut, I have no doubt that the gentlemen's attention will be on you."

Julia flushed, embarrassed by the proclamation but further embarrassed that she had mentioned the ball to Samuel in the first place. She had seen the hurt in his eyes and regretted her words immediately. They both realized what the ball meant.

It was the first social event Julia would attend without him.

True, she had attended other balls while he was away at school, but only to dance with her brother, sample the sweets and socialize with her friends. Never to dance and converse with other men.

She knew this day would come. She just didn't understand why it was so hard. She stared into the looking glass while the dressmaker continued to primp her skirts. Julia did not want to dance with other men. Could it be because deep down she secretly hoped things would work out between her and Samuel?

Could he come to realize that their convictions were one and the same? He liked the Federal Army no more than she did and if the abolition of slavery meant that much to him, couldn't he let the individual states decide that themselves?

That was all Edward wanted. That was all she wanted.

She looked into her own face. *No. That isn't what I want. I don't care who chooses what. I only want my family to be whole.*

Her mind drifted back to several years ago, to a cold, snowy February day, one more bitter than usual. Samuel's parents had both taken sick with the typhoid fever. Julia and her mother were in the kitchen making soup to send to them when Samuel had knocked on the door, snow dusting his hair.

They could tell immediately by the look on his face that the worst had happened. Julia's mother had hugged him.

"Oh, my boy, I am so sorry."

He hadn't cried but neither could he speak. He simply sat down at the kitchen table, a lost look in his eyes. Not knowing what else to do, Julia had ladled out a bowl of soup then cut a slice of cornbread, which she set before him.

"Thank you," he'd said simply. Then he bowed his head to pray.

Julia had stared at him, her own heart aching. *Sixteen and all alone,* she had thought. *What will happen to him now?*

By God's grace, Samuel had pressed on. He'd worked. He'd finished school. He'd become part of Julia's family.

Standing in front of the dressing mirror, she realized that she still considered him so. For the first time since Edward's enlistment, Julia entertained the thought of compromise. Samuel said he could accept her support for Edward. He had given his word that he would not report the sewing circle's activities or her letters to the Federal Army.

Wasn't that enough?

I don't know. I just don't know. It isn't as if Samuel has chosen to wear a blue uniform. He isn't actively endangering Edward or the rest of my family.

Madam Fontine's heavy French accent pulled Julia from her thoughts.

"The new corset is comfortable. *Oui?*"

Julia stared at her hourglass figure. The gown bodice was shapely and snug, just as it should be. "Yes. Thank you."

The woman then held up a length of delicate white lace. "Now this is the finishing you have chosen."

"Yes. That is correct."

"Then I will add it to the edges of your sleeves, along with the contrasting piping…then I will add two rows to your skirt."

"Yes," Julia said.

"I will have the gown delivered to your house on Tuesday. *Oui?*"

"Tuesday, yes. Thank you."

"It is my pleasure, mademoiselle."

Julia stepped from the looking glass, melancholy and deep in thought. She wished she could make decisions about her life as easily as she could choose the trimmings for her ball gowns.

Chapter Eleven

Julia changed back into her rust-colored taffeta tea bodice and skirt and walked to the front of the store. Her father was waiting for her.

"All finished?" he asked.

"Yes."

His mustache drooped. He could tell something wasn't right. "Weren't you pleased with the gown?"

She took his arm. She tried to sound a little more enthusiastic. "Oh, yes. It is beautiful. The color reminds me of the first leaves of spring. Thank you for buying it for me."

He patted her hand. "It has been a while since you have had a new one."

They had just stepped out onto the sidewalk when Thomas Wilkerson came hurrying up to meet them. Julia was pleased to see he was feeling better.

"How are you, Mr. Wilkerson?"

"Fine. Thank you, miss." He then looked straight at her father. "We are concerned."

Dr. Stanton let go of his daughter's arm and stepped a few paces from her. Julia stayed where he had left her but was most curious to know what or whom the men were whispering about. At one point, her father looked at her. An uncertain expression covered his face. He then looked back at Mr. Wilkerson.

"I will come immediately," he said.

Mr. Wilkerson expressed his thanks, then hurried off in the direction from which he had come. Thomas Stanton turned to his daughter.

"They have need of my services. You will have to come with me."

"Of course," Julia said. It wasn't the first time an outing with her father had been extended due to a medical emergency. She was prepared. She always kept a small carpetbag in the carriage filled with embroidery or other handy projects. "I have my knitting."

He didn't respond. Whoever was ill must have been seriously so for her father's usually happy face was lined with concern.

Julia climbed into the carriage and her father then sped off in the direction of Fell's Point. She prayed while the wheels wobbled. *Lord, I don't know who needs You but please help them. Please let my father be an instrument of Your healing.*

The carriage stopped in front of a factory worker's house with sagging shutters. Julia quickly gathered up her ruffled skirt and her father helped her out.

"Hurry," he urged.

With carpetbag in hand, she followed him to the front door.

"I want you to wait in the parlor," he said, "and under no circumstances are you to come upstairs."

"Yes, sir," she said.

An eerie feeling washed over her. Who was so ill that she had been warned not to intrude? Was it so contagious that her father should be concerned for his own well-being?

An old woman dressed in black answered the door. She quickly motioned them inside.

"This is my daughter," Dr. Stanton explained.

The woman did not give her name but gestured to the parlor.

"Please," she said, inviting Julia to sit.

Before Julia could even thank her, the woman ascended the staircase. Dr. Stanton followed close behind.

Julia removed her bonnet. Stepping into the tiny sitting room she glanced around. The parlor was furnished with only the bare necessities. There were four wooden chairs, a small table and a lamp. Faded paper covered the walls. In one corner it was peeling.

She assumed the closed door at the end of the room led to the kitchen. She could hear the sound of muffled voices coming from that direction. Above her was the sound of her father's heavy feet.

Whose home is this? she wondered. *And how does Mr. Wilkerson know them?*

With answers unavailable and not knowing how long she would be waiting, Julia sat down in one of the chairs. She took out her knitting needles and yarn. Since she had already begun another pair at home for Edward's men, she decided to make this new set for Samuel. The soft white yarn would be more suitable for a young child or lady.

Within a moment she was well into her first row. Her fingers raced as quickly as her mind. *Who is upstairs? Who is in the kitchen and why are they whispering so?* Again Julia prayed for her father and for this family that was obviously so in need.

She tugged at her ball of yarn. It wasn't long before her thoughts once again settled on Samuel.

I never should have mentioned Dolly Moffit's party. I wasn't thinking clearly. I can never think clearly when he looks at me that way.

Samuel looked at her as if she were the most beautiful woman in the world. Despite all that had happened in the recent weeks, it was obvious that his love had not faded.

When it comes down to it, that is really all that matters in this life, to love and be loved in return.

Sally's words echoed in her mind and Julia couldn't help but think about whoever was ill upstairs. *If that was me, who would I want beside me?*

Her heart told her the answer.

He had stood between the soldier and her, a shield of protection. He had held her in his arms, a comfort she did not wish to leave. She knew it as surely as the sun would tomorrow rise.

She loved him still.

The kitchen door opened. Julia looked up to see Samuel and another man stepping into the room. Shock rippled through her and heat immediately crept into her face. For a moment she thought he had surely read her previous thoughts.

He, however, looked just as surprised to see her. His eyes widened.

"Julia," he said, quickly coming toward her. "I didn't know you were here."

"I didn't know you were, either."

The other gentleman, an older one, nodded to her. Samuel introduced them. "This is Dr. Carter, my friend and colleague."

The man smiled knowingly. "Ah, so you are Thomas's daughter."

"Yes," she said.

"It is a pleasure to meet you."

"A pleasure to meet you, sir." She was dying to ask what they were doing and how this man knew her father but she didn't question for fear of being rude.

Dr. Carter did not offer any further clues nor did he stay to converse. He made his excuse saying he was in a hurry, then he climbed the staircase.

What is going on up there? she wondered.

"For Edward?"

She turned her attention from the stairs back to Samuel. He smiled and pointed to the yarn in her lap.

"Oh," she said. "No. I thought that perhaps you might be in need of another pair."

He smiled at her and drew up a chair. Everything Julia had been thinking about since Madam Fontine's came flooding back. *Oh, Lord, is compromise possible? What should I do? I don't know what is right. Please tell me.*

Sam could see the questions in her eyes.

"Mr. Wilkerson met my father on the street in front of the dress shop," Julia said. "He said he needed his help. That it was urgent."

"It is. That is why we sent for him."

"We?" she asked in a whispered tone. "Samuel, who are these people? How do you know them?"

"I met them by way of Dr. Carter. He is a professor at the seminary."

"Oh," she said slowly.

"They are good people, Julia. They aren't radicals."

Her blue eyes blinked inquisitively. "They are abolitionists?"

"Yes."

She leaned slightly back in her chair, as though she were trying to put a measure of distance between them until she could determine whether he was safe or not.

After a moment or two of hesitancy, she relaxed somewhat. Her face took on an expression that he had not seen in quite a while.

"Well, I suppose there is nothing wrong with expressing one's personal views," she said. "You didn't stop me from knitting socks for a Confederate regiment. I suppose if you wish to write pamphlets or distribute bread, it is of no consequence to Edward."

His heart began to race and his ears were thudding. Julia's words were full of promise. On impulse, Sam reached for her hand. He was thrilled beyond words when she allowed him to take it.

"Tell me," she said, "my bread, the socks that I knitted, are they now benefiting some former slave?"

Her directness stunned him but he realized it was better to have the subject out in the open at last. "Yes," he said. "They are."

She did not look surprised. In fact, a smile tugged at the corners of her mouth. "I figured as much, especially when you acted so secretly about who it was for."

He couldn't help but smile.

"Will you do the same for Elijah and Elisha?"

It was as though the Almighty had revealed to her the subject of his prayers. "God willing," he said. "Somehow."

Their eyes were locked and the intimacy of the moment made his heart pound.

"Your teachers," she said, "your friends in Philadelphia, I am certain are grateful for your assistance. Are there many more up north that you wish to help?"

Sam balked. *Up north?*

His heart sank like a stone to the bottom of the Chesapeake. She thought he had sent the items to Philadelphia. She had no idea what he was really involved in.

Decision time was at hand. He would not lie to her but this wasn't where or how he had intended to tell her. Although her words up to now were charitable, he feared what she would say if she knew the full truth.

But I must tell her and then leave the rest in God's hands, he told himself.

"Julia," he said slowly. "The bread did not go to Philadelphia. It was for someone here in Baltimore."

"Oh?"

"In fact, that is why your father is here now."

"Is the woman's husband ill?"

"No."

"One of her grandchildren?"

His chest was tightening. "It isn't anyone in her family. It is a young Negro woman. She hadn't eaten in days and she was beaten severely."

Julia's fingers turned to ice and her face immediately drained of all color. "What are you saying?"

"She is a runaway," he whispered. "We are helping her get to freedom."

She ripped back her hand and she stood quickly to her feet. Her ball of yarn fell from her lap. Sam's chair raked across the floor as he also stood.

"Julia—"

"Oh, Samuel! How could you? How could you?"

"Julia, if you only knew what she has been through—"

"You are breaking the law!"

"Sometimes laws made by men are unjust."

"But the soldiers! After that captain's warning? Giving bread on the street is one thing, but this! Samuel, how could you?"

He watched fear give way to anger as she realized the full implications of his actions. "I am an accomplice to your crimes! And my father...now you have dragged him into it, as well!"

"No one dragged him, Julia. He came willingly."

"He came because someone needed his help. He didn't know—"

"Yes, he did. I spoke with him several weeks ago, when I was trying to make my own decision on whether or not to be part of this."

"Am I to believe he gave you his blessing to break the law?"

"He told me that the decision was between me and The Lord but that if his service as a physician was ever needed, he would be available."

She couldn't believe what she was hearing. Didn't he understand what would happen if they were caught? Didn't he understand what those soldiers would do? Julia was so angry that she could barely get the words out.

"Samuel, are you purposefully seeking to destroy my family...or are you simply doing so in ignorance?"

"Julia, I would never let anything—"

"I don't believe you!"

She had raised her voice so loudly that her father had come into the room. Shirtsleeves rolled up, red faced, he looked as angry as she felt.

"That is enough, Julia!"

His tone was so firm, so uncharacteristic that she was shocked into silence.

"We will discuss this later," he said. He then looked at Samuel. The color slowly faded from his face. "It pains me to ask this, son, but would you be so kind as to escort my daughter home?"

"Certainly, sir."

No! Julia thought. *I won't go with him! Father, why are you doing this? Don't you realize what is happening here? Don't you realize what is at stake?*

Dr. Stanton turned for the staircase. Julia glanced at Samuel. He was busy gathering up her yarn and stuffing it in her carpetbag. It was clear that there would be no discussion. He handed her the bag. Julia snatched it from him then walked to the door.

It was a cold carriage ride. Sam held his tongue for the course of six blocks, then he spoke.

"I am sorry that you had to find out this way. It was not my intention to deceive you."

He stole a glance at her. She was staring at the back of the mare. She said nothing. She refused to even look at him.

"I had planned to tell you everything when the time was right."

They stopped at an intersection. When a group of soldiers crossed the street in front of them, Julia gripped the bag on her lap. Her knuckles turned white with fear.

"I can see how frightened you are," he said when the soldiers were a safe distance from them. "And I am sorry that I am the cause of that. But believe me, Julia, I would not be involved in such things if I wasn't absolutely convinced that this was the right course of action to take."

Silence still. Complete, lonely silence.

For a moment he was tempted to tell her everything, to give her details he had learned. He wanted to tell her how the poor runaway in the Jordan's attic had come to be in such desperate conditions, how the child she carried was not the result of a loving, marital union.

But he could not bring himself to do so. Julia had already seen enough hatred and horror of war so that it filled her with fear every time she saw a blue uniform. What would she think if she knew what slave-holding men of this city were capable of?

The carriage wobbled repetitively over the uneven stones. She firmly held her bag and her place, as far away from Sam as possible. He pulled to a stop in front of the gate. Before he could secure the reins, Julia stepped from the carriage, her hoop swaying as she hurried to the front door.

"I love you," Sam said as the door shut solidly behind her. He couldn't help but think he had just seen her for the very last time.

Julia scurried up the front walk and bolted the door behind her. Heart racing, she leaned back against the secure frame in order to catch her breath. A cold sweat made her shiver. What had happened today was the final straw. There was no hope of compromise. Samuel was harboring fugitive slaves! It wasn't the charity given to the poor souls that troubled her. It was doing so illegally that was so terrifying.

To make matters worse, her own father was assisting! Soldiers already patrolled her neighborhood looking for traitors. What would they do if they knew her father was actively undermining Maryland state law?

Instinct told her to shutter the windows and search Edward's room in the event that he had indeed left a musket behind to defend them. Her heart told her to pray but for whom and what outcome, she had no idea. She despised Samuel for involving her in such a conspiracy.

While Edward defends our liberty, Samuel actively seeks our downfall. How could I ever have considered marrying a man like him?

She passed the next two hours monitoring the windows and pacing across the parlor. When her father finally arrived home, Julia begged him for an explanation. He offered very little.

"Her name is Rose," he said. "She is about your age and she is carrying a child."

He then went into his study and retrieved a small book. He handed it to her.

"Samuel didn't want you to read this because he didn't want to expose you to such terrible things. But I think the time for protecting is past. You are old enough to know that this life does not consist of society balls and beauty for everyone."

Julia glanced at the book in her hand. *Narrative of the Life of Frederick Douglass, an American Slave.* The last thing she felt like doing at this point was reading a book. She looked back at her father.

"Does Mother know about all this?"

"Of course," he said. "We have no secrets from each other. A marriage cannot survive without both parties united in purpose and love."

Well said, she thought. *Which is exactly why it won't work with me and Samuel.*

"I want you to read that. Afterward, if you still consider Sam's actions and mine foolhardy, then so be it." He studied her for a moment; his spectacles perched upon the end of his nose. "But I trust that whatever you decide, you will keep what you know of our activities to yourself."

"Of course I will," she promised. *I would never betray my family.*

Sam had hoped to assist Dr. Carter in making certain that Rose safely reached Pennsylvania. But given what had taken place in the Jordan's parlor, it was rather obvious to the man that Sam's fiancée did not support his endeavors. When questioned out of concern, he was compelled to explain what had happened.

"I see," Dr. Carter said thoughtfully. "You need time to pray, young man, and so does she."

Sam was thankful that the man did not speak unkindly of Julia or dismiss her altogether. He wondered how much more time he would have to spend in prayer before he saw a change for the better. Things had not gone as he had imagined. He didn't understand why. Hadn't he done his best to follow God's will? Hadn't he prayed each step of the way? Why wasn't Julia more receptive?

Lord, don't You promise if we delight in You then You will give us the desires of our heart?

Struck by the self-centeredness of the thought, Sam searched his motives. Had he served Rose only for his own gain? Had he become involved in something that was never God's plan for him? *Have I misread Your instructions, Lord?*

He then was reminded of the look in Rose's eyes when he helped to clean her wounds. He remembered how her unborn child was spared early delivery because of Dr. Stanton's expertise.

God gave him the knowledge to save the child. A

lesser physician could not have managed it. And his patient demeanor helped calm the distraught woman.

Sam drew in a deep breath. In his heart he knew he was exactly where he should be. He had hoped that Julia would walk this path with him. But even if she would not, he couldn't allow her anger or fear to sway him from doing what he knew was right. *I must stay the course... trust God.*

"Let the Almighty do his work," Dr. Carter said to Sam. "And guard yourself against doubt. For it will certainly come."

Sam nodded slowly. It was as if the man had read his mind. "It already has," he confessed.

Dr. Carter gave him a grandfatherly smile. "Then seek God's strength. Why don't you come to church with me this Sunday?"

Sam accepted the invitation. He wished to worship but he did not want to be a distraction to Julia nor allow her to be one for him.

Sunday came and Julia joined her family for worship. Thankfully, Samuel did not show. To say that she worshipped, however, would be a lie. She spent the hour thinking more about soldiers, slaves and Southern rights than anything else. She had tried to pray but she couldn't seem to focus her thoughts on anything but her own family's safety.

Oh, Lord, if Father feels he must do this...please don't let the soldiers catch him. Please.

Sally stopped her on the church steps after the service had ended.

"I have had you on my mind almost constantly for the last two days," she whispered. "Is everything all right?"

Julia drew in a deep breath. She could not tell her best

friend all the things she was thinking. She had promised her father that she would remain silent.

Sally somehow must have sensed the issue was a confidential matter. "I have been praying for you," she said. "And I will keep on doing so."

So touched she was by Sally's perceptiveness and concern that Julia felt her chin begin to quiver. "Thank you," she whispered. "Keep praying for Edward and Father, especially."

Sally nodded. "And for Sam?"

Julia shook her head. "It is over," she said. "There is no hope of compromise."

Sally's face registered pain. Julia still felt the same inside but for the sake of being perceived resilient, she lifted her chin.

"I am going to go to Dolly Moffit's party and dance with every eligible young man who isn't wearing a blue uniform."

Sally gave Julia's arm a squeeze but she didn't say anything.

Word came from Edward the next day. Sally brought the letter as soon as it was daylight. When she arrived Julia was in her bedroom, still in her gown and morning robe, her hair about her shoulders.

"I knew you would want to read it privately," she said, "and not at the church."

"Thank you." Julia quickly tore into the envelope. "He says he is well."

She and Sally both breathed a great sigh of relief.

Thank you for your letters, Edward wrote. *It is good to know that Mother and Father are doing well.*

Edward stated that he and most of his fellow Baltimoreans had been placed under Corp Commander General Ewell. He went on to tell that he respected the

Confederate man greatly. *He is disciplined but fair and I am convinced that all of this drilling we are doing will make us seasoned soldiers for battle.*

Julia gulped, still hoping such a day would never really come. She prayed that the Confederate show of might would be enough to make the Northern soldiers back down. She remembered Edward's promise of how he would see to it personally that the Yankees were thrown out of Baltimore. Though she longed for the day when she could walk down the street without glares from men in blue, she still prayed the soldiers would withdraw peacefully, not at the expense of further Maryland blood.

"What else does he say?" Sally asked.

Edward then moved his pen to the happier thoughts of camp life, playing chess with Stephen and writing of a recent promotion.

"They have made him a captain," Julia said with delight.

"Oh, how wonderful! Won't he look handsome in an officer's uniform?"

She grinned. "I suspect you would find him handsome in any type of clothing."

Sally only blushed.

You cannot imagine how much I miss each of you yet I am willing to spend my life for the cause of Liberty. Continue to pray for me and the rest of our men.

He closed, *Your loving brother, Edward.*

Sighing, she handed the letter to an eagerly waiting Sally. While her brother's words brought joy, they made Julia miss him all the more. Searching for something to occupy her mind while Sally read, she reached for the skein of wool tucked in the basket beside her bed.

She only had a few more rows to go and another pair

of stockings would be complete. After Samuel's plot had been revealed, Julia doubled her knitting efforts for the Maryland Guard.

She finished the new pair by the time Sally completed the letter.

"At the pace you are going you will have the entire regiment outfitted by October," Sally said.

"Isn't that our goal?"

They smiled at each other then Sally folded Edward's letter into thirds. She handed it to Julia.

"Thank you for allowing me to read it. That was sweet of you."

"You would do the same for me." Julia slid the letter back into its envelope then tucked it safely in the pocket of her morning robe. "Will you stay for breakfast? I know Mother won't mind."

"Thank you, but no. I have much to do today at home, especially if I am going to match your pace of knitting. Will you come to the prayer meeting?"

"Yes, but I will speak to Reverend Perry about finding someone else to serve the bread."

Sally's face fell. "You can't mean that. What about the little boys?"

A lump lodged like a stone in the back of Julia's throat. She longed more than anything to see Elijah and Elisha's sweet faces, to fatten them up with food, clothe their hardworking bodies.

But the risk was just too great.

"Sally, I fear if I see them again I will put them in grave danger."

"Is this because of that nasty soldier?"

"Yes, but even more so than you realize. That soldier believes we are abolitionists. Therefore, anything that happens in this city because of *them* will be blamed on *us*."

Sally chewed on her lower lip, considering such implications.

"I wouldn't dream of telling you what you should or shouldn't do—" Julia said.

"But?"

"Be careful. Those soldiers mean business. If you continue to serve with Samuel, don't leave the church-yard."

Chapter Twelve

Although already one of the grandest homes in Baltimore, the Moffit house was decorated even more beautifully on the night of the ball. Crystal-cut chandeliers reflected sparkling candlelight as endless arrangements of pink and white roses perfumed the early June air.

Dressed in her new green silk gown, Julia was as radiant as the rest of Maryland high society. Although she was not particularly close to Dolly Moffit, she was determined to enjoy the girl's social debut. She carried a dance card for the first time since she could remember and there was no shortage in supply of young men eager to partner with her.

She danced the opening reel with Dolly Moffit's brother David and then the Snowball reel with his cousin Charles, who was visiting from Annapolis. There were plenty of other requests, as well. Her only respite came during the orchestra's midway break.

Sally, who also carried a full dance card, motioned for Julia to join her. Leaving the ballroom behind, they escaped to the topiary garden for a breath of fresh air.

"I see you have been waltzing all night," Julia said to her.

"Yes," Sally sighed, "but only because George Meriwether asked for five places on my dance card."

Julia could tell Sally was not pleased about the matter. She could not blame her. The city council member's son talked incessantly and was known for treading on a lady's slippers.

"George is a handsome man," she teased.

Sally rolled her eyes.

"Well, all right. Perhaps he is not as handsome as my brother."

That got a smile. "No one is as handsome as Edward," Sally said dramatically. "No one at all."

The air was just as warm and still as it had been in the ballroom. They sat down on a wrought iron bench and opened their fans, hoping to coax a breeze. Laughter was heard coming from the house yet neither of the women felt its comfort.

Sally sighed wistfully. "It isn't the same tonight. Is it?"

Julia flushed and it was not because of the heat. She knew exactly what Sally was referring to and it was more than just her brother's absence. As determined as she was to forget Samuel, she had to admit how strange it felt to be at a social gathering without him.

A feeling of guilt rose from the pit of her stomach but Julia refused to give in to it. Forcing herself to smile, she said as lightheartedly as possible, "Your gown turned out beautifully, Sally. If Edward could only see you in it…well, he would surely be the one claiming five dances."

It was the very dress that Julia had spent so much time describing to her brother in her last letter. Sally ran her hand over her yellow silk bodice, trimmed in lace and faux pearls. She started to say something in reply but George Meriwether caught her attention.

"Oh, no."

Julia looked toward the house.

The love-struck suitor was standing in the doorway, craning his neck for a view of the garden. In his hands he held two glasses of peach punch. Sally sighed once more, this time in agitation.

"He is looking for me."

"Another dance?"

"No. He has already exceeded his limit."

"Did you tell him that?"

"Of course not. That would be rude. I told him politely with my fan."

Julia smiled. Sally could be polite almost to a fault. "You should be a bit more forceful."

"I was." Sally placed her fan on her left ear. In the language of Belle and Beau it meant, *I wish to be rid of you!*

Julia couldn't help but giggle. "And he *still* didn't take the hint?"

"Somehow I don't believe Mr. Meriwether understands hints."

They watched the man's smile broaden. He had spied her.

"I had better go," Sally said, "lest he think I planned to meet him in the garden."

"Be charming," Julia teased.

Sally let out a sarcastic laugh then started up the gravel path, a rustle of silk and lace.

"Miss Hastings!" Julia heard George Meriwether call. "I brought you a glass of punch."

She laughed to herself. *Oh, poor Sally. This will be a long evening.*

Julia waited an appropriate distance then also started for the house. The orchestra was playing a Carolina Promenade as she stepped into the grand foyer. Charles Moffit was waiting for her.

"Oh, Mr. Moffit, forgive me. I had forgotten that you asked for a second dance."

"That's quite all right, Miss Stanton. You must be tired. Would you care to sit?"

Since her feet were sore anyway, she agreed.

"Would you care for some refreshment?" he asked. "A glass of punch or a chocolate caramel, perhaps?"

"No, thank you."

The chairs and sofas were all occupied so he led her to the staircase. Julia smoothed out her skirt and sat down.

"Have you been to Baltimore before, Mr. Moffit?"

"Yes," he said, "but I find the city much changed since my last visit."

"Indeed," was all Julia could think to say.

"Annapolis is much the same," he said.

"Has there been trouble?"

"You mean Northern soldiers firing upon civilians? Goodness no, but the Federal Army's presence is just as strong."

"Is that affecting your commerce?" Julia knew that Charles Moffit was a planter with heavy ties to Richmond.

"Unfortunately, yes," he said. "As the aggression continues it is becoming increasingly difficult to manage our holdings, especially points south."

He then smiled. Julia couldn't help but notice that his teeth were straight and white.

"I understand that your brother has chosen to fight," he said.

"Yes. He serves under General Ewell."

"Capable man," Charles said. "As is your brother, I am certain."

Julia appreciated the compliment on Edward's behalf. It made her feel proud to know that someone was grateful for his service.

"We are in good hands with men like that," he assured her. "Do not worry. This business will be over soon and Lincoln and the rest of his overreaching supporters will be licking their wounds."

Oh, how I like the sounds of that!

"But enough about the war," he said. "Do tell me about yourself."

She blushed and smiled coyly. "What exactly do you wish to know?"

"You can begin by explaining why a beautiful woman like yourself is attending this ball alone."

Her cheeks further reddened. That was one subject she was not about to discuss. She opened her fan, covering her face in an intriguing manner.

Charles Moffit, more perceptive than George Meriweather took the hint. "Annapolis has a fine harbor," he said. "Have you ever seen it?"

Julia relaxed somewhat. "No. I have not. Are there many ships?"

"Yes, indeed."

They talked for over an hour about life in their respective cities. Only once during that time did she think of Samuel. It was when Charles was describing his two hundred acre plantation on the Severn River. Julia wondered how many slaves he owned and just what Samuel would think if he knew she was talking to such a man.

Would he be angry? Would it rouse a jealous fury in

him or would he simply focus on the way Charles Moffit has chosen to work his family land?

Sam eased his horse up Charles Street. The last remaining rays of sunlight painted the western horizon in reddish-gold hues. Another work week had come and gone.

The afternoons with Dr. Carter's nephew were enjoyable. The boy put forth good effort in his studies. Sam was thankful for the rewarding work, even if it was only temporary. It gave him something to focus his thoughts on, something he could pour his heart into without fear of circumventing current law.

Perhaps if young men like Mr. Carter fully grasp the precious gift God has given us in this country, the great responsibilities that come with such freedom, then the future generations will not be so quick to hold others captive, whether by servile chains or weaponry.

The noontime prayer meetings however, were a different story. As Sam feared, Julia had given up her position at the bread table. Her mother had taken her place. As grateful as he was for Mrs. Stanton's kind assistance, her presence was simply one more reminder of his failure.

I should have told her straightaway what I was involved in. I should have been honest from the beginning.

He plodded along, his horse's shoes click-clacking along the paving stones. The road ahead was clogged with buggies. Sam immediately realized why. He was approaching the Moffit home and tonight was their daughter's debutant ball.

Some of the finest carriages in all of Baltimore were lined in front of the stately stone house. White-gloved coachmen, many of them Negro, scurried about. They

opened doors and assisted their well-to-do passengers
as they stepped from their carriages.

Sam's heart sank a little deeper in his chest as he
stared toward the large, light-filled windows. Music
drifted past his ears. He knew Julia was attending this
ball with her family. Was she now dancing about the
ballroom? Were her fingers entwined with some dash-
ing partner as he led her about the floor?

Resisting the urge to move closer to the windows,
he looked the other way. Though he longed to catch a
glimpse of her, he could not bear the view if she were
smiling at some other man.

He pulled his topper a little farther over his forehead. He urged the horse to move quicker. The beautiful summer sunset had been swallowed up by the bare
blackness of night.

Charles went to fetch her a glass of punch. Julia
waited for him on the staircase, toes tapping beneath her
skirts as the couples in the ballroom danced Nine Pins.
Watching, she smothered a laugh. A grinning George
Meriwether stood in the center of Sally's circle as the
ninth pin. Julia was certain he would make an immedi-
ate dash to claim her the moment the dance caller permitted it.

A thud in the foyer below turned her attention. A
young slave boy lay sprawled on his back, eyes staring
at the painted ceiling. A silver tray and a passel of soiled
napkins were scattered randomly about him.

Julia knew the freshly polished floor was slippery.
Poor thing, she thought. *His feet must have gone out
from under him.*

He couldn't have been any older than Elisha, though
he was dressed quite dapperly in a dark coat and trou-

sers. White gloves covered his small hands. Julia watched as he quickly rolled to his side and got to his feet. He reached back for a moment to touch his hair.

He has hit his head. He will surely have a pump knot come morning.

Injured or not, the child scrambled to retrieve the napkins and tray. The guests around him paid little mind. Only one glanced in his direction with a look of concern. Others didn't even notice him at all.

To Julia's dismay, several guests stood, feet planted. Their own conversations were apparently more important than the courtesy of allowing the boy the room to gather the spilled items. The child had to wait at the feet of one well-dressed city official until the man finished his glass of brandy, stepped off a napkin and moved aside.

Julia was irked by the man's pompous attitude. She descended the staircase, intent on helping the little boy finish the task.

And perhaps I should get Father, she thought, *let him see to his head.*

Before she reached the foyer floor, however, the child had scooped up the remaining napkins. He moved quickly to the servants' staircase and disappeared as though he had never existed.

Charles returned.

"Your punch, Miss Stanton," he said as he handed her a cut-crystal glass. "I apologize for the delay." He nodded in a gentlemanly way.

Torn between two worlds of thought, Julia forced herself to smile.

"Thank you, Mr. Moffit." *I suppose Father and I would never be able to find the little boy now, anyway. Lord, please let one of the other slaves see to his injury.*

The evening was winding down. Overall, it had been a pleasant time. To her surprise, Charles asked for the Farewell Waltz. When it was time to leave he asked for permission to see her again.

"I will be in town for another week," he said.

Though flattered, she hesitated. She was not interested in obtaining a new beau.

But Charles is likeable and a strong supporter of the Confederacy, Julia told herself. *What harm is there in tea? Besides, he will only be in Baltimore for another week. Then he will return to his own home.*

She agreed to his request.

Charles Moffit bowed formally and kissed her hand. "I shall look forward to it," he said.

Sam did the best he could to keep images of Julia floating about the dance floor far from his mind. The week's end passed quietly and when Sunday morning came he prepared for worship. A blanket of quiet covered the city as Sam walked to his own church.

As the worship hour neared he took a place in the back corner, a spot where Julia would not necessarily notice him.

Lord, if we meet today, please give me the right words. Please don't let me say or do anything contrary to Your plan.

The bell chimed the hour and the worshippers began to enter. Sam watched covertly as Julia arrived with her parents. She was wearing a white summer dress with sheer sleeves. On her head was a bonnet trimmed with daisies. She walked quietly to her family pew.

As Sam hoped, she did not see him. Sally spied him, however, when she arrived a few moments later. The smile she offered encouraged Sam that his attendance, however clandestine, was the right course of action.

The membership had dwindled further just in a week's time. Those who faithfully attended the prayer meetings had returned to their original family pews, regardless of political lines. The remaining congregants, however, scowled at one another from across the aisle.

Heart heavy, Sam spent the hour praying for the reconciliation of his fellow church members. When he wasn't doing that he was stealing glances at Julia. He had intended upon leaving unseen but she caught sight of him the moment the service dismissed.

Across the room she held him with her eyes. The look in them was a mixture of fear and something else he could not recognize. Though his heart was aching, he managed to nod.

Julia smiled cordially as she would to any stranger. That was the extent of interaction. She then turned for the door, taking his heart with her.

Give the Almighty time to work, he remembered Dr. Carter saying.

He left the church that morning promising himself that he would do just that.

However long it takes, Lord, help me to remain faithful to Your plan.

"Is that young man coming for tea this evening?" Dr. Stanton asked Julia late that afternoon.

Julia knew her father was not happy about Charles Moffit's visit and she knew exactly why. He would much rather be in his study reading *The Sun* with Samuel than entertaining a relative stranger in the parlor. She was surprised that after seeing her former fiancé in church this morning that he didn't ask him over to do just that.

"Yes, Father," she said. "Charles will be here at seven."
He grunted.

Her mother, thankfully, was more charitable. "It is only polite to have the young man visit, Thomas. The Moffits were kind enough to invite us to Dolly's party."

"Yes, I know," he said, "but I do hope he is careful about the time. I do not wish to have a late evening."

Julia didn't, either, nor could she possibly imagine it turning into one. Charles's visit was purely a polite social call. There was no need to speculate of anything further.

It is simply good manners, she told herself.

Yet as the appointed hour approached, she grew increasingly nervous. She changed her dress twice.

How long has it been since I have entertained a gentleman caller in the parlor? I hope I will remember the proper etiquette.

She hoped her father would, as well. He had been used to Samuel for so long that he had become accustomed to burying his nose in whatever he was studying then periodically reading its contents aloud for all to hear.

That is all fine and good in relaxed informality but not for a new guest, especially one with such high station as Charles Moffit.

Her fingers trembled as she tried to fasten the pins in her hair. Finally satisfied with the braided bun, she cast one last glance in the looking glass, then went downstairs. It was half past six, so she fluffed the parlor pillows while her mother placed finger sandwiches and glazed tea cakes on a tray in the center of the room. At fifteen till, she put the water on to boil. Ten minutes later, Julia was fidgeting with her gold earbobs while she waited for the doorbell to ring.

Charles Moffit arrived precisely at seven and her father showed him to the parlor.

"Miss Stanton," Charles said with a pleasant smile. "You look lovely this evening."

He kissed her hand and Julia's nervousness now mingled with intrigue. The man was handsome, undeniably so. Any woman would testify to that.

"How very kind of you, Mr. Moffit."

He stood tall and smiled, his sandy-colored hair impeccably in place. "I brought you a gift."

The intrigue was growing. He presented her a hat-size box wrapped in pink paper and tied with white ribbon. The packaging alone was beautiful.

"Oh," Julia said, trying to mask her eagerness with proper decorum. "How thoughtful of you. Won't you sit down?"

Charles nodded pleasantly and sat down on the sofa. Julia moved to a chair beside the tea table while her mother and father claimed positions on the opposite side of the parlor.

"Have you had a pleasant stay here in Baltimore?" Dr. Stanton asked his guest.

"Yes, indeed," Charles answered. "I would like to stay longer but I am afraid that my plantation won't allow it."

"I see," Dr. Stanton said.

By now Julia had unwrapped the paper. Inside the box were twelve perfectly formed, deliciously yellow lemons. "Oh," she gasped, breathing in the citrusy scent. "Mother, look."

She held out the package. Esther was just as delighted. Fresh fruit was always a welcomed gift.

"You are very kind, Mr. Moffit," she said.

"Yes," Julia added. "Thank you."

Charles smiled rather proudly. "They are from our winter conservatory."

"You have an orangery?"

"Yes," he said, still smiling at her. "Rather large, actually."

Julia was impressed. While a few families she knew had small greenhouses, no one had an entire conservatory.

Imagine, she thought, *fresh fruit all winter. You could pick whatever you wanted, whenever you wanted it.*

"My mother adores lemons," Charles said. "Why, last year, we had lemon trees lining the main staircase for our New Year's Eve ball."

"Is that so?"

"Indeed."

Julia listened with great interest as he told of a gala which made his cousin Dolly's debut pale in comparison.

Plantation owners of southern Maryland as well as statesmen dined, danced and ushered in 1861 with affluence and elegance. The Governor of Maryland and his wife had attended along with the first family of Virginia and several Federal congressmen. One could speculate that Charles Moffit's wealth carried great influence in Annapolis and beyond.

It is not a wealthy profession but it is an honorable one. Samuel's words concerning his teaching ambitions suddenly passed through her mind.

As Charles continued to talk of tobacco holdings and the price of cotton, Julia couldn't help but remember all the evenings spent in this same room with Samuel. Never once was money a subject of discussion. Although her former fiancé was of modest means he was unfailingly generous to everyone they knew.

I would not be surprised if he personally paid for the expenses of that runaway slave.

Her thoughts unnerved her. Here she was visiting with a gentleman and yet she was thinking of Samuel. *And thinking of runaways nonetheless! Why, if Charles Moffit knew what I, what my father has been involved in...*

She could feel the blood draining from her face as a cold wave of fear washed over her. Her father noticed immediately.

"Are you all right, child? You look rather pale."

"It is warm in here," her mother noted. The curtains hung straight and stiff with no breeze to sway them.

Heat now danced across her face. "Yes," Julia said. "I am fine." She tried to hide what she was feeling, doing her best to put on a cheerful face. She opened her fan.

Her father was not convinced. "Do you have a headache?"

"No," she said. "I am fine." The meager breeze generated from her fan was not helping. Julia thought of fanning rapidly but feared it would only draw further attention. Her cheeks were tingling.

Charles was staring at her.

"Your father is right," he said. "You do look pale. Perhaps I should go. I fear I have bored you enough already."

"Of course not," Julia said. She chuckled pleasantly though it was not without effort. Her fears told her that he was leaving because he knew of the abolitionist bent of the household and he planned to report them to the proper authorities.

"I have enjoyed your visit."

Charles smiled. "I have, as well."

From the corner of her eye she saw her father rise to

his feet, an unspoken indication that the evening should indeed end.

Julia stood. So did Charles. He thanked her parents for their hospitality.

"I do hope that the next time you are in Annapolis you will pay me a visit."

"Thank you," Dr. Stanton said. "Please give our regards to your family."

"I will be happy to do so."

Julia walked with Charles to the foyer. She thanked him again for the lemons.

"They will make a wonderful supply of lemonade," she said.

He smiled at her, a look that told her reporting her family was the last thing on his mind. Her nervousness eased somewhat.

"I hope you will enjoy them and I do hope you feel better."

"Thank you."

He shifted his topper from one hand to another. "Perhaps I am bold in asking this so soon," he said, "but may I have your permission to write?"

Julia was completely surprised. Charles was making his intentions known and they went far beyond polite social calls. Part of her was delighted by the request. The other part was downright scared.

"I shall have to consider that," she said guardedly.

He smiled once more. "I would appreciate it if you would."

He had apparently taken her answer as a challenge and looked as though he would enjoy such a thing. He placed his hat on his head.

"Good night, then," he said.

"Good night."

Julia shut the door behind him, her face still afire from the evening's conversation. *Gracious sakes! What am I to do now?*

Chapter Thirteen

"He asked for permission to write you?"

Sally's eyes were wide with surprise as Julia detailed the previous evening's social call while they visited in the kitchen. The beautiful lemons lay scattered across the table.

"Yes," Julia said. "He is returning to Annapolis tomorrow or perhaps the following day. I don't remember exactly."

"What did you say to him?"

"I told him that I would consider it."

"You aren't serious about that, are you?"

Julia laid aside the lemon she was slicing and looked at Sally. There was no question where her friend stood on this issue. Sally still held hope that Samuel would win out, apparently as strongly as she prayed Edward would return from the war to claim her.

"Sally, I told you before. It isn't going to work with me and Samuel."

Her face showed her disappointment. "I know but I had hoped you would change your mind. He is a good man, Julia."

"No. He is a dangerous one."

"What?"

Julia immediately regretted the comment. It would lead to questions she could not or promised she *would not* explain. "Just forget I said that."

Sally stared at Julia for a few seconds, her silence an invitation to further explain. Her confused expression then shifted to a knowing one.

"He has joined the abolitionists, hasn't he?"

Julia looked at her but still said nothing.

"I knew there was something that you weren't telling me. I could see it in your eyes every time his name came up."

"I am sorry. It isn't as though I am intentionally keeping something from you. I would tell you if I could but—"

"Say no more. If you are bound by a confidence then I understand."

Julia sighed. "Thank you." She went back to the lemons.

"Let me ask you this, though. How difficult is it going to be guarding one man's secrets while corresponding with another?"

Gracious. She laid aside her knife. *If Sally doesn't have the gift of coming right to the point then I don't know who does.* Julia had considered that very same argument herself, which was the exact reason she had not given Charles Moffit permission to write when he asked her.

There was already a risk to her family because of Edward's enlistment. Every day Baltimore's leadership moved closer to the ranks of Federal support, at least in name. If the measures continued, entire neighborhoods, including her own, could be rounded up and charged with treason.

Then there was Samuel, who held to the Union but decided which laws he would and would not obey. She could add her father to that list, as well, now *and if I were to add a slave-holding planter with powerful friends into the mix...*

Julia shuddered.

"I am not certain I intend on corresponding with him," she told Sally. "At least not at this point."

"You don't like him?" Sally said. The hopeful tone in her voice was quite obvious.

Julia had to be completely honest. "In some ways I do."

"Well," Sally conceded. "I can understand that. He is handsome, at least when compared to Mr. Meriwether."

"At least we agree on that."

They both laughed.

"In all seriousness, though," Sally then said. "I know you well enough to know that you wouldn't be happy with a man like that."

"You say that because you are still voting for Samuel."

Sally grinned. "Call me a fool."

"Or the friend of one," Julia quipped. She tossed the lemons into a pot of hot water then reached for a cone of sugar. "Will you continue to serve at the bread table?"

"Do you mind?"

"Of course not. I only want you to be safe."

"I don't leave the churchyard," Sally promised, "and neither does your mother."

Julia breathed deeply. She then asked what she desperately longed to know. "Have you seen Elijah and Elisha?"

"From a distance. Sam still takes them a slice of bread each afternoon."

A smile tugged at the corners of her mouth but Julia

kept it from showing. "Have there been any more soldiers?"

"None whatsoever."

Oh Lord, thank You, Julia prayed. *Please let it continue this way. Please keep Elijah and Elisha safe. Watch over us all.*

By that evening Julia was seated in her father's study with her needles clicking. Her mother was playing hymns on the piano in the parlor and her father was reading one of his medical journals. About eight or so a knock sounded at the front door. Julia glanced up as her father went to answer it. She continued with her yarn.

I wonder just how many pairs of socks we have finished. I shall have to ask the girls.

Men's voices caught her attention. They were unfamiliar and harsh. She put down her knitting and peeked into the foyer. She couldn't see who her father was speaking to but she could tell by his tone that he was clearly agitated.

"What on earth for?" she heard him ask.

Who is at the door?

Curiosity got the better of her and she stepped into the foyer. To her horror there were four Federal soldiers standing on her doorstep. Each was carrying a weapon. One of them, a young corporal, was holding a pair of handcuffs.

Just then, her mother walked in from the parlor. "Thomas, what is it?" Her face drained of all color as soon as she saw the men in blue.

"It is all right, Esther," her husband said. "There has been a misunderstanding, that's all."

He looked back at the corporal. "And what are you charging me with?"

"With all due respect, sir, I do not have to present that information to you at this time."

"Oh, yes you do, young man. This is the United States of America and here we have such a thing as *habeas corpus.*"

"Sir, the writ of *habeas corpus* has been suspended within the state of Maryland."

"What?"

"Now if you'll come with me…"

Julia was lost on the legal formalities but she knew wrong when she saw it. The men were arresting her father without formal charges. A mixture of shock and rage emboldened her. "Father, no! Don't go with them. They can't do this! It's wrong!"

The corporal puffed out his chest like a redheaded rooster. "Sir, I advise you to come peacefully."

Dr. Stanton turned to look at his daughter. "Stay where you are." He laid his hands behind his back. The corporal immediately snapped on the cuffs.

Anger gave way to fear. "No!" Julia and her mother screamed at the same time.

Her thoughts flew as fast as her heart. *They know about the runaway slave. That is why they are arresting him!*

She was unable to move but her mother ran toward her father. She threw her arms around him.

"Thomas! Thomas!"

"It is all right, Esther," he said calmly. "This is just a misunderstanding. I will be home soon. Don't worry."

Julia watched in horror as one of the soldiers tore her mother away from him. The remaining men in blue led her father down the front steps. Knees shaking, heart quaking, Julia moved to the doorway. Neighbors were peering from their windows to see what was going on.

Do something! she wanted to scream. *Where are all your guns now? Where is all your talk of honor?*

A black carriage was waiting on the street. Two more soldiers stood sentry with the horses. Julia stared at them. Her eyesight was getting fuzzy. She feared she was going to faint so she steadied herself against the door frame.

Her father called back over his shoulder. "Find Mr. Davis. Tell him what has happened. He will straighten things out."

William Davis was Emily's father. He was a lawyer. Julia promised she would find him. "We'll go straightaway."

By now her mother was in tears. She, too, stood in the doorway, calling out to the corporal. "Where are you taking him?"

The man at least had the decency to answer. "All political prisoners are held at Fort McHenry until further notice."

The soldiers opened the carriage door. They forced Thomas Stanton inside. He stuck his head back out at the last second. "I will be home soon," he promised.

The corporal shut the carriage door. The horses scurried off at command, leaving Julia and her mother alone on the front porch.

"Lord, help us," Esther said.

Lost in disbelief, Julia raked her fingers through her hair. She stood there for several seconds, staring after the carriage until her mother brought her to her senses.

"Go find Lewis!" she said. "Ask him to find Mr. Davis."

"Yes, of course!"

Julia ran to the stable. "Lewis! Lewis!" *Where is he?* "Lewis! It's important!"

Lewis was nowhere to be found. The carriage and mare were both gone.

Her mind was racing, her hands trembling. *Did he get scared? Did he run off when he saw the soldiers? Will he come back?*

She knew she couldn't waste time wondering. She had to find another way. Immediately she thought of Samuel. Her pride slammed the door on that idea.

No. I won't go to him. This is all his fault. If he hadn't involved us in his scheme, none of this would be happening.

She ran back to the house. Her mother was standing in the foyer, a lost look on her face.

"Lewis isn't in the stable," Julia told her.

"Where is he?"

"I don't know!" She grabbed her shawl from the peg rack and threw it around her shoulders. "I'll fetch Mr. Davis."

Her mother shook her head. "It is getting dark and it isn't safe to be out on the streets come nightfall."

Especially not with all the soldiers, Julia thought. A wave of nausea rolled through her. Fear or not, she knew she had to go. She had promised her father that she would.

"I will be back as quickly as I can. If Lewis comes back, ask him to find me."

"I will."

Before her fears could get the best of her, Julia hurried out the door. Her skirt caught on the door frame. It ripped when she tugged it free. She wanted to cry, not over the torn fabric but because of the way her father had been ripped from their home. She could not, however, allow herself the luxury of tears. There wasn't time.

She hurried down the street. The gas lamps were already being lit. Mr. Davis lived ten blocks away. She prayed she would reach his door before nightfall.

Sam was sitting in the rocking chair, a copy of Julius Caesar's *Gallic Wars* in his hand. Though classes had been suspended, he felt it necessary to keep up with his reading. It was a habit, discipline; besides, the reading kept his mind off Julia.

The lamp on the table was dimming. He reached over and turned up the wick. A golden glow warmed the room. He had often imagined the parlor in the soft light of a summer's evening, he with his books, Julia in the chair across from him, knitting, smiling. Their children would be playing between them.

He shut the book and pinched the bridge of his nose. He wasn't able to concentrate as well as he thought. He stood. He stretched. He walked a circle about his chair but the movement did little to lighten his spirit.

A fist suddenly pounded the front door. Sam hurried to open it.

"Lewis!" he said, surprised to find the young man on his doorstep. "Are you all right?"

"You have got to come with me, sir," he said, gasping for breath. "They have taken Dr. Stanton."

Sam's heart went to his throat. "Who? Who has taken him?"

"Federal soldiers. They arrested him."

Immediately, Sam was swallowed up by guilt. *Someone knows the role we played in assisting Rose. I should never have gotten Dr. Stanton involved in such.* "What did they charge him with?" he dared to ask.

"I don't know but I did hear one of the soldiers say something about the bridge burnings."

Sam shut his eyes. He was thankful it had nothing to

do with runaway slaves yet he was still just as worried. The night of the bridge burnings continued to haunt his family. "Where did they take him?"

"To the fort."

"Where is Julia?"

"She was at home with Mrs. Stanton when I left. Both of them were crying." Lewis was frantic. "Please, sir, I didn't know what else to do."

"I am glad that you came, Lewis. Go back to the carriage. I will come directly."

Lewis did as he suggested. Sam ran back to the parlor. He grabbed his coat then put out the light. He climbed into the front seat with Lewis.

"Are we going to the fort, sir?"

"Yes." He had no idea what he would say or do when he got there but if it were within his power, Sam would not allow Julia's father to spend one night in confinement.

Help me, Lord, he prayed. *Show me what to do.*

Julia pounded frantically upon William Davis's door. When the man finally answered he was in his shirt-sleeves, clearly not expecting company.

"Miss Stanton," he said with a puzzled expression. He glanced behind her, surely wondering what his friend's daughter was doing out alone at dusk. "Is something wrong?"

There wasn't time for formal pleasantries so she plunged in. "Oh, Mr. Davis, you have got to come quickly. The soldiers have arrested my father!"

His eyes widened in shock. "For goodness' sake! What for?"

"They didn't say. They just took him! They said they were taking him to Fort McHenry."

He pulled back the door. "Come in, my dear. Did you come here on foot?"

Julia nodded her head. "Yes. I ran the entire way. Lewis, our stable hand, is missing."

William Davis called for his wife. "Sarah? Will you come here, please?"

Sarah Davis emerged from the dining room. One look at Julia and the woman's face filled with concern. "My dear, what is wrong?"

"Will you please get Miss Stanton a glass of lemonade?" her husband asked.

"Certainly."

Emily was at the top of the staircase. Having heard the conversation between Julia and her father, she quickly raced down. "Oh, Julia, I am so sorry! This is simply unbelievable!"

Mr. Davis turned to Julia. "Give me just a few minutes to gather my things. I will drive you home. Then I will go to Fort McHenry."

Relief flooded her veins. "Oh, thank you, sir. Thank you."

Lewis brought the mare to an abrupt halt at the fort's outer gate. A sentry stepped out of his post.

"State the purpose of your visit," he said matter-of-factly.

Sam leaned forward so the guard could see him better. Lewis held the mare's reins. "I am here on behalf of a prisoner. A man arrested just this evening."

"No visitors," the guard said.

Sam pressed on. "I have evidence to prove this man's innocence. Please, if I may just speak with your commanding officer."

The guard studied him for a few seconds. "One moment," he said and he stepped back into his enclosure.

Lewis leaned in Sam's direction. "What evidence?" he whispered. "We don't even know what he has been charged with."

"You heard them say something about the bridges."

"Yes."

"That's all we have to go on at this point."

The guard stepped back out. Another came with him. He held a piece of paper and a pen.

"What is the prisoner's name?" the first guard asked.

Sam spoke clearly. "Dr. Thomas Stanton."

"Residence?"

"Mount Vernon."

The guard's comrade scribbled then he walked through the gate, presumably headed for the main section of the fort.

"Wait here," the remaining guard told them.

Sam nodded his thanks. Lewis continued to hold the mare. The guard stood in place, his eyes on them.

No one said a word.

Mr. Davis took Julia home then left immediately for the fort. After he had gone, Julia asked her mother if Lewis had returned.

"No," Esther said. "While you were gone I thought that perhaps he went to find Samuel."

"Oh, Mother," Julia cried. "That is all we need. If he is involved, they will end up arresting each of us."

"Hush, girl." Esther then sighed. "I imagine, though, if Lewis told him then he would have come here first. I suppose the boy just got scared and ran off."

"I suppose," Julia said. *Unless he did find Samuel and they went to the fort.*

The spark of hope the thought generated was quickly doused with the cold water of reality. *But there is nothing he can do. His presence will only make things worse! The Federal Army has taken my father prisoner for assisting runaway slaves!* She fought back tears. *Lord help us, please.*

The guard told Lewis to wait at the front gate. Another escorted Sam to the main fort. Uneasiness settled over him as he followed the man in blue. Darkness now shrouded the garrison. Lamplights flickered about windows. A campfire blazed in the center grounds. Around it, a few soldiers had clustered.

High above flew the American flag. Noticing it, he couldn't help but think of Francis Scott Key's words, the joy he felt to see the Star Spangled Banner still waving over Fort McHenry. Sam had to admit that tonight, for him, the flag invoked more apprehension than joy. The stars and stripes were symbols of power. Whether benevolent or despotic, he wasn't yet sure.

The guard led him to an area on the ground floor of the garrison. A long table furnished one end of the dimly lit room. At it, several Federal officers were seated. Dr. Stanton was standing before them.

He and the men turned in Sam's direction the moment he entered. Dr. Stanton looked glad to see him.

"Sam! What are you doing here?"

A man at the center of the table, a lieutenant colonel, beat a gavel. "The prisoner will direct all utterances to this board of inquiry."

Dr. Stanton turned back toward the men. Their eyes were now focused on Sam. Their faces were shrewd and cold. He stepped even with Julia's father. The guard that had escorted him into the room took up post at the door.

Sam noticed another was standing on the wall opposite Dr. Stanton.

For a night in June, the atmosphere was chilly. The musty smell of history past lingered in the air.

The lieutenant colonel spoke to Sam. "You are the person claiming evidence on this man's behalf?"

"Yes, sir. My name is Samuel Ward. I am a friend of Dr. Stanton."

The man nodded. "Lieutenant Colonel William Morris." The man looked to be about sixty or so, stern faced.

Sam nodded respectfully in return. "Thank you, Lieutenant Colonel Morris for the opportunity to speak with you."

"Quite to the surprise of some, we are not without due process here."

"Yes, sir."

He glanced at Dr. Stanton. The look on his face warned him to proceed with caution. Sam whispered a quick prayer. *Lord, give me wisdom.* Then he turned back to the lieutenant colonel.

"It is my understanding, sir, that Dr. Stanton has been apprehended in connection with the bridge burnings on the evening of April nineteenth."

"That is our concern," Morris conceded.

Sam noted he used the word concern, not charge. Before he could ask what the formal charges were, the lieutenant colonel continued.

"I am certain you are aware, young man, that this city has fallen on perilous times. Certain individuals wish to disrupt law and order. Some actively seek disunion."

"I am aware of such, sir."

"And you wish to offer evidence that the man beside you is not a person of such malevolent convictions?"

Sam chose his words carefully. "He had nothing to do with the bridge burnings, sir."

Morris looked doubtful. So did the others. He lifted up a sheet of paper for him to see, then he read its contents. "Dr. Thomas J. Stanton. Residence, Mount Vernon District. Treated wounded citizens following the Pratt Street riot. Son, Edward R. Stanton is a Maryland Guard member, enlisted with the Confederate Army."

Morris stared at Samuel, waiting for a reply.

He had hoped they would not know of Edward's enlistment. He looked at Dr. Stanton.

"That is all true, sir," Julia's father told the men. "I treated anyone in need on the day of the riot. I would have given aid to the soldiers, as well, had I come across any."

"And how did you know that the riot had taken place? How did you know where to go?"

Sam realized what Morris was getting at. Was the Pratt Street riot planned? Did Dr. Stanton have anything to do with it?

"My son and my daughter were at the train station that morning," Dr. Stanton said. "Mr. Ward was arriving from Philadelphia. They were caught up in the riot."

The lieutenant colonel looked at Sam. "Is that so?"

"Yes, sir."

"What business had you in Philadelphia?"

"I was attending a teacher's college. My graduation exercises were over and I was returning home." Sam answered the questions openly. He had nothing to hide, at least as far as the riot or bridge burnings were concerned.

The lieutenant colonel scribbled a few notes on his sheet. "And what did you do when the rioting began?"

"My foremost concern was for the safety of Dr. Stanton's daughter. We—"

"We?"

Sam clarified. "Her brother Edward and I, sir."

Morris waved his hand. "Continue."

"As I was saying, we struggled our way through the crowd until we reached safety."

"Did you alert anyone to the disorder?"

"We passed a squad of police officers. It was obvious that they were headed for the riot so we did not detain them or explain what had happened."

Morris turned his questioning back to Dr. Stanton. "And where do you come into this?"

"My children told me what happened. I retrieved my medical bag and went to help the wounded."

"And then you returned home?"

"Yes, sir."

The man looked at Sam. "And you were with him?"

"Yes, sir. I had dinner that night with his family."

"And you remained at the Stanton home for the rest of the evening?"

"Not the entire evening, sir."

Morris crossed his arms over his chest. "Then how can you be certain that Dr. Stanton did not leave his home that evening? What is to say that he did not meet at the Carroll Hall Armory and then participate in the bridge burnings?"

"Because, sir, he stayed home."

"Am I to take your word? You may be a gentleman, sir, but many a gentleman in this city would make war on the Federal Army. We already know his son is guilty of sedition. How do we know Dr. Stanton is not, as well?"

Sam swallowed hard. He knew this question would

come. He also knew what it might cost him to answer it truthfully. "Dr. Stanton was not at the armory, sir."

"Really?"

"I know this because I was at the armory."

Eyes widened. The officers all leaned forward.

Dr. Stanton tried to shush him. "Don't, son. Don't."

"You were at the armory?" Morris asked, looking quite intrigued.

Again Thomas Stanton motioned for him to keep quiet. Sam looked back at the lieutenant colonel. He would clear Julia's father's name even if it meant sullying his own.

"Yes, sir," Sam said boldly. "The city was near panic that night and when word reached me that more troops were en route, I went to the armory as a volunteer. At that moment, burning the bridges seemed the prudent thing to do to avoid further bloodshed."

"And so you participated."

"No, sir. I did not."

"No?"

Sam explained. "During the discussion, as plans were laid out, I thought better of the idea. It occurred to me that the act of protecting the city could be seen from the Federal Government's perspective as an act of sedition."

"So what did you do then?"

"I tried to convince those in my company that they should not proceed. That they should let the soldiers pass through to Washington."

"Obviously they did not heed your instructions," Morris said. "What happened next?"

"I was thrown out of the building." The officers stared at him in silence. Sam continued. "When I returned to the Stanton home, Dr. Stanton was waiting. He, too, agreed that burning the bridges was a bad idea."

Morris then asked, "And what of his son's enlistment in the Confederate Army?"

The scene of Julia standing in the foyer holding out her engagement ring flashed through his mind. He forced it aside. "Dr. Stanton tried to convince Edward not to go."

The table broke into whispers as the Fort's commander conferred with his men.

Sam and Dr. Stanton stood silently before them, waiting. They looked at one another, uncertainty on both of their faces.

The discussion quieted. Finally, Morris turned. "Dr. Thomas Stanton, step forward."

Julia's father did as he was told.

"You will hereby be set free provided that you agree to swear an oath of allegiance to the United States Government. Will you so swear?"

Relief must have flooded Dr. Stanton's veins for Sam certainly felt it.

"I will, sir," said Dr. Stanton.

Morris seemed satisfied. "Very well. Raise your right hand."

"I, Thomas Stanton, do solemnly swear that I will bear true allegiance to the United States and support and sustain the constitution..."

Listening, Sam breathed a sigh of relief and thanked God for such an outcome. Thomas would walk out a free man. He knew Julia was home praying. He imagined the look of joy on her face when her father returned.

"...So help me God."

The lieutenant colonel had Julia's father sign a written copy of the oath. "You are free to go," Morris said. He motioned to one of the guards. "Escort Dr. Stanton to the main gate."

The guard snapped to a salute then turned on his heel. Dr. Stanton did the same. He was smiling in gratitude as he stepped toward Sam.

"I can't thank you enough, son. You took an awful risk but I am grateful."

"You would have done the same for me." Sam turned to match the doctor's stride.

"Mr. Ward!" Morris called. "You are not dismissed!"

Color drained from their faces. Both men turned back to the table. Morris motioned to the guard at the back of the room. He stepped forward.

A sickening feeling swept over Sam. All of Julia's expressed fears about the Federal occupation ricocheted through his mind. He knew what was about to happen.

Dr. Stanton did, as well, and he did not hesitate to intervene. "No! You can't! He told you himself that he didn't have anything to do with the bridge burnings!"

The first guard took hold of his arm. Dr. Stanton resisted. The lieutenant colonel stood to his feet.

"May I remind you sir, that you swore an oath of allegiance. Go home. This matter does not concern you."

Dr. Stanton's eyes widened. He planted his feet. A flash of Edward and Julia's fire surfaced. "This does concern me!"

Now it was Sam who tried to shush his would-be father-in-law. "Don't do this," he said. "Just go. Things will work out."

He looked at Sam. "No. I won't leave—"

The guard tightened his grip on his arm. The second showed his musket.

"Sir, I advise you to leave peacefully," Morris said.

"Go," Sam urged once more. "Go home to Julia, to Esther."

The look on the doctor's face softened to one of pity.

Sam knew he had no choice but to obey the soldiers. The guard pulled Thomas Stanton to the exit. The other stood with his musket on Sam.

"I will get a lawyer," Dr. Stanton promised. "We will straighten this out!"

Sam nodded but legal proceedings were the farthest thing from his mind. "Tell Julia that I love her."

The wait was agonizing. Mr. Davis had left hours ago and still there was no sign of Lewis. Julia paced about the parlor. More than once she had wished for Edward and his army to sweep into the city. *They would put a stop to this! They would send those Yankees back where they belonged!*

In contrast, her mother had spent the time praying. When she had run out of her own words she began reading through the Psalms.

"The Lord is my shepherd... God is our refuge and strength... Hear my prayer, O Lord..."

Every carriage that rolled past their home, every horse that galloped by, brought Julia to the window. The carriage that now held her attention was no exception. To her disappointment, however, it was not her father. Shoulders slumping in defeat, she turned toward the chair opposite her mother. She picked up her own Bible, though she knew not where to turn.

Esther was now reading aloud the love chapter from First Corinthians. It was one of her favorite passages. The verses had been read at her wedding.

"Charity suffereth long, and is kind..."

Julia bristled at the words. In the work of Christ, she knew she was surely lacking in patience. She always had.

Her mother read on. "It seeketh not her own, is not easily provoked..."

Again, another area where I don't measure up. She sighed. *Now Samuel...not easily angered...that is his personality.*

"Beareth all things, believeth all things, hopeth all things, endureth all things..."

He trusts, Julia thought. *After all, the closing of his school did not alarm him in the least. He even called it a blessing. And as for perseverance...he continued to show kindness to Elijah and Elisha despite the soldier's warning.*

Her emotions swirled. Pain cut deep, bringing tears to her eyes. *But my father has been taken prisoner because of Samuel's choice of action.*

"And now abideth faith, hope, charity, these three; but the greatest of these is charity."

Julia went back to the window. The light from the streetlamp cast just enough glow. Her pulse quickened. She recognized the approaching mare.

"Lewis! Mother, it's Lewis!"

Esther joined her daughter at the window. Lewis stopped the mare in front of the house. Another carriage pulled in behind.

"That's William Davis," she said.

Their hearts leapt with hope but they dared not move until they were certain. They held their breath until the carriage door opened. Out stepped Dr. Stanton, unharmed. Both women let out a cry of relief.

"Glory be to God!" said Esther.

"Oh, thank You, Lord!" Julia cried.

The women raced from the parlor to meet him as he came through the front door. He was exhausted. His eyes were droopy but he met them both with a hug and a grateful smile.

"You are home!" Esther cried.

"Yes, my dear and glad for it."

William Davis stepped inside the house. He was carrying his big, black satchel. Julia looked at him. "Oh, sir, I cannot thank you enough!"

He took off his topper and held it to his chest. "It was not me. I am afraid I never made it past the front gate."

The women looked at him, then at Dr. Stanton.

"What happened?" Julia dared ask. "Did the soldiers just decide to release you?"

Her father shook his head. "Sam came."

Julia's heart fluttered. *Samuel was there?* "How? How did he know?"

"Lewis found him. They both came immediately to the fort. Sam convinced the lieutenant colonel that I was not involved with the riot or the bridge burnings."

"They thought you had been involved in the bridge burnings?" Julia asked.

"Yes."

Her spirit soared. *So they don't know about the runaway slave! And Samuel himself went to face the Federal Army! He defended my father!*

"Lord bless him," Esther said. "Where is he?"

"Yes," Julia now wanted to know, as well. "Is he with the carriage?"

She looked at him. Her father's expression stole the joy she felt.

"He is at Fort McHenry," he said.

"What do you mean?"

He turned to Mr. Davis.

"It seems the lieutenant colonel was willing to make a trade," Davis said. "The soldiers granted your father's freedom in exchange for Samuel's."

A tingling sensation began at the top of her head then spread all the way to her toes. One of the lamps in the foyer must have gone out, for the room was getting darker.

"I don't understand," she said, though her own voice sounded strange in her ears. "Wh-where is Samuel?"

"Child," her father said, slowly moving toward her. "Samuel took my place in prison."

Her knees buckled. The last thing she remembered was her father catching her in his arms.

Chapter Fourteen

After Dr. Stanton had been escorted from the fort, the guard marched Sam from the interrogation room back to the open air. He breathed it in deeply, fearing it may be his last fresh air for quite a while.

Lieutenant Colonel Morris had told him that he was being held on suspicion of disloyalty to the Union. It seemed Samuel Ward had been at the wrong place too many times and was acquainted with too many questionable sorts of people. He wondered what the Federal officers would say if they knew about Rose, the young runaway. He prayed that by now she had reached Pennsylvania.

Dr. Stanton had promised to send a lawyer. Sam asked Morris if he would be allowed to speak with such a man.

"Of course," the lieutenant colonel had said, "but in the morning."

So Sam would spend at least this night in confinement. Though, from the looks of things around here thus far, he expected the time would be longer.

Lord, I don't know why You have allowed this but I will submit to Your authority. I thank You that Julia's father was able to return home.

Much to his surprise and relief, the guard did not march him to the confinement cells within the Sally Port Prison. It was there Sam knew from his history readings, that the accommodations were less than hospitable. There were no windows and little means of ventilation. The cells were a constant source of mold and mildew, year-round.

Instead, he was taken to the old quarters within the star-shaped fort. A holding room on the second floor had been reserved for political prisoners. He climbed the staircase and walked toward a guard stationed at the far end of the portico. As he did so he looked to his right. Beyond the fort's walls lay the lights of Baltimore. For as much relief as he felt at not being taken to the confinement cells, Sam was still grieved. The city lay like a sparkling jewel, the signs of war unnoticeable except for the fort's guns pointed in her direction.

He wondered what Julia was doing at that moment. *Is she afraid? Does she know what has happened? Is she thinking of me?*

The guard at the end of the portico unlocked a door. "Inside," he ordered.

Sam stepped into the room where he was directed. A wall sconce offered a minimal amount of light but it was enough to get a feel for his surroundings. Eight bunks filled the room. Three of them were occupied by men of various ages. There was a chair in one corner, a wash stand and basin in the other.

"Pick a bed," the guard said. "First call is at sunrise."

The door shut and locked behind him. Sam chose an empty bunk, one closest to the window. He had been given a mattress and a wool blanket. There were no linens.

The man in the bunk next to him leaned up on his elbow. "Bridge burner?" he asked.

Sam took off his frock coat and unbuttoned his vest. "They say I am."

The man laughed. "I was following the orders of the police commissioners. Now, here I sit. I suspect the police commissioners will be joining us shortly." He stuck out his hand. "Name's John."

Sam gave it a shake. "Sam Ward."

"Good to know ya, Sam. Although I'd rather be making your acquaintance at the local tavern than here."

The guard rapped on the window. "Lights out," he said.

One of the men blew out the candle. Stillness settled over the room. Sam leaned back on his bunk, arms behind his head. Across the room, someone whistled the first line of the "Star Spangled Banner." John countered with a measure of "Dixie."

Sam lay in the darkness thinking only of Julia.

The soldiers took Samuel to the darkest, most inhumane cell in the fort. Mold covered one wall and the only comfort in the room was a dirty mattress on the floor. Samuel stood in a space barely big enough to turn around in.

"You will remain here until your scheduled execution," said the guard.

The iron bars clanged shut. The guard walked away. Samuel was left standing alone in the darkness.

"Samuel! Samuel!" she cried. "Oh, Lord, please! Samuel!"

"It's all right, dear."

Julia heard her mother's soft voice through the nightmare, felt a cool cloth on her forehead.

"Mother?"

"Yes, dear. It's all right. You are safe."

Julia's eyes swept the ceiling and then the room. She was in the shelter of her own home, the comfort of her own bed. The lace-trimmed pillows and brightly colored quilts were soft to the touch.

Her heart wrenched. *Samuel.* Where did he lay his head this night?

Esther sat on the edge of her daughter's bed. She removed the cloth and laid it in the washbasin on the table beside her.

"Are you feeling better?" She asked.

"Yes. I—I suppose so."

She may have recovered from her fainting spell but in truth Julia did not feel better. She thought the agony of fearing for Edward's safety on some unknown battlefield was the most terrible pain she had ever suffered, but knowing Samuel was deep in the confines of Fort McHenry was even worse.

She remembered Samuel saying he would die to protect her. Sally's words echoed through her mind. *If I were you, I would be happy he hasn't proven that yet.*

Guilt clawed at her heart. *He is there because of my family. He is there because of me, because I pressed him to show his loyalty.* Her stomach rolled. *I caused this.*

She looked at her mother. "Where is Father?" she asked.

"He is in the study. He and Mr. Davis are going through the law materials. They are going back to the fort in the morning."

Julia sat upright. Wrestling with her skirts, she swung her legs over the far side of the bed. "I want to go with them."

"Don't be ridiculous, dear. That fort is no place for you. Besides, you need to rest."

She stood. "I am fine, Mother. Really, I am. I want to go with Father. I have to."

Esther looked her squarely in the eye. "Assuming you could get in to see him, what would you say?"

The question cut her to the core. Julia bit her bottom lip. What would she say to Samuel if given the chance? She had no idea. It wasn't as though she had changed her mind about marriage. All she was certain of at this point was she did not want him to be held as a Federal prisoner. She could not bear the image of his solitary confinement.

He is loyal to the Union. Why can't the soldiers see that?

She realized her mother was still staring at her. "I don't know what I would say," she answered truthfully.

"Then wait for the words to come, dear. They will in time." Esther then said, "Your father is going to Samuel's house at first light to gather a few necessities. Why don't you go with him?"

Julia thought for a moment then took heed of her mother's advice. She didn't know what to say to Samuel but she could still do something.

"There is dough in the kitchen," she remembered. "I have time to make a loaf of bread. I could send it with Father, along with a jar of jam."

Her mother smiled. "I am sure he would appreciate that."

Julia went to the dressing table and peered into the looking glass. Her skin was pale, her hair a mess. She quickly brushed it out, parted it in the middle then crafted a bun. She hurried downstairs.

The lamps were glowing in her father's study. Dr.

Stanton and Mr. Davis were at the desk, poring over the law books. Julia's father looked up, his spectacles dangling from the end of his nose.

"Child," he said with surprise. "I am glad you are feeling better but why are you up at this hour? You should be sleeping."

She moved into the room. Mr. Davis did not even look up. He kept reading, stopping only every now and then to scribble on his pad of paper.

I hope he is preparing a good defense, she thought.

"I am fine," Julia said to her father. "Mother told me you are going to stop at Samuel's house before going back to the fort."

"Yes. He will need clean shirts and other items."

"I would like to help."

Dr. Stanton pulled off his spectacles. He fingered his mustache. Julia didn't realize that her mother was standing in the doorway behind her. She nodded approval to her husband.

"All right," he said. "We will be leaving about sunrise."

Mrs. Stanton quietly moved to the parlor before her daughter turned for the kitchen.

"Thank you, Father."

"You are welcome, child." And he went back to his books.

Julia took the lamp from the foyer and carried it to the kitchen. The dough she had been saving was warm and ready to be punched down.

She quickly set to work. With her hands covered in flour, she whispered a prayer. *Lord, please watch over Samuel. Please make the soldiers set him free.*

Sam did not sleep well in his new accommodations. One reason was because of the snoring coming from the bunks around him, the other was his restless mind. He had promised God that he would submit to His will but here in the darkness, surrounded by armed soldiers he found the promise more difficult to keep.

The Lord has allowed me to be here for some reason but at this moment I would much rather be home in my own bed. I would rather have plans to see Julia in the morning, her face happy and bright at my arrival.

He thought of how things used to be when he and Julia were engaged. She had been so eager to marry, so excited to begin their life together.

Then came war.

He thought of Edward. He wondered where his would-be brother-in-law was at that moment. *Has there been a battle? The newspapers aren't reporting any such events but what if the Federal Army is controlling what goes into print?*

He rolled over to his side. The mattress was lumpy. *I can't think like this. It will do no good to speculate. It will do no good to wish I were somewhere else. I am here, for as long as the Lord allows it. I might as well accept it, just like I have had to accept everything else that has happened.*

A guard passed by the window. Sam could hear the thump, thump, thump of his brogans on the portico. He rolled to his back, staring at the bunk above him. *Lord, help me to be patient. Help me to trust in You.*

As planned, Dr. Stanton and Mr. Davis finished their legal work by sunrise. Esther fixed them a quick breakfast of hardboiled eggs and cold ham. Julia sliced the fresh loaf of bread she had baked for Samuel. She wrapped it carefully in a linen cloth then went upstairs to change her dress before leaving with her father.

The streets were beginning to stir as they approached Samuel's house. Men were leaving for work. Women were opening windows, airing out rooms and beating rugs.

Mr. Davis waited in the carriage while Julia and her father went to the door. Samuel had given her father a key when he had left for his first semester of school just in case there would ever be a need. Julia knew Samuel had never imagined they would enter his home to gather items for his prison stay.

Her father popped open the front door. They stepped inside.

The Ward home had always been a quiet one but an unnatural stillness now permeated the place. The only sound was the creaking floorboards beneath her feet. Julia was unprepared for the emotions that met her. Memories stole her breath away. Every harsh word she had ever said to him came flooding back.

"I will gather the clothing," her father said. "Why don't you look about down here and see if there is anything he would like to have."

Julia could only nod in response.

He climbed the staircase. She stepped into the parlor. On the table beside the rocking chair were Samuel's watch and a stack of books. Julius Caesar lay at the top.

He must have been reading this when Lewis came, she thought. *I should send it with Father. Samuel will want to keep on with his lesson plans so he can be ready for school when he returns.* Doubt rose from deep within. *If he returns...*

She shook off the thought and reached for the Bible, which was next in the stack. Julia cradled the careworn leather respectfully as she sat down in the chair. She flipped through the delicate pages. A scrap of paper earmarked First Corinthians: 13.

Charity suffereth long and is kind, he had copied. *Lord, help me to live out such qualities. Help me to love as You love.*

Tears gathered in her eyes as Julia traced the words with her fingertips. Samuel had written them as a prayer. He was struggling to love, to remain full of faith. This war had taken more of a toll on his emotions than she had imagined.

She had been so concerned with her own losses; she had never once stopped to consider what he had lost. *Edward was his closest friend. They were like brothers.*

She shut the Bible then picked up the watch. Carefully she opened it. Her photograph was still inside. *Nothing about us has changed from his perspective. Nothing at all.*

A door shut. She closed the watch then carried it, the Bible and Julius Caesar to the foyer. Her father was coming down the stairs. His leg must have been bothering him again for his foot was heavy on the boards.

He had wrapped Samuel's shirts in brown paper.

"I have gathered up the clothing."

She held out what was in her hand. "He will want these."

Dr. Stanton took the Bible and the schoolbook. "Not the watch."

"It belonged to his father."

"That is why it should stay here. It's too valuable. Someone may steal it."

She clutched the golden bob in her hand. Memories of his smile, his laughter filled her mind. She tucked the watch into her own pocket.

"We should get going," her father said. "I will take you back to the house."

Julia hesitated. She couldn't explain why but she did not want to leave. "I would like to stay here for a while, if that is all right with you."

He studied her.

"The house could use a cleaning," she said.

Half a smile emerged beneath his mustache. "Lock the door behind me. I will come back to get you when we are finished at the fort."

"What about the seminary? Should we notify them? Samuel said they had hoped to relocate."

"I will speak with Dr. Carter at the first opportunity."

He tucked the parcel under his arm. She followed him to the door.

"Do you think the soldiers will let him come home today?"

"I don't know, child. We can only pray and then do our best."

"Mr. Davis is a good lawyer."

"Yes. God has gifted him with words." He reached for the doorknob. Before opening it, he turned back to look at her. "You know, last night as I was leaving, Sam asked me to give you a message."

"What did he say?"

"He said to tell you that he loved you."

Her eyes clouded. Her lip began to quiver and for the life of her, Julia could not formulate an appropriate reply.

"I will be back soon."

"Yes," was all she could manage.

He turned for the carriage. Julia bolted the door behind him.

* * *

Sam passed the first night, awaking to the sound of a bugle and the stirring of military men. His close-quarters comrades yawned and stretched as they, too, prepared to begin another day in captivity.

Having no clothes but the ones he had slept in, Sam did the best he could to tidy up. He tucked in his shirt. He put on his vest. It at least covered up some of the wrinkles.

After a breakfast of slightly undercooked beans, he was delighted to discover that prisoners of his kind were allowed some measure of freedom. They did not have to remain locked in their second-floor room. The window was opened and the door unlocked. Sam and his fellow prisoners were allowed out on the portico for sun and exercise.

His back was stiff and his muscles were sore from the mattress. He stretched his arms over his head and then walked to the railing. He gazed not over the fort but out beyond its walls, toward Baltimore. The air was humid. Gray clouds were forming to the west.

"Looks like rain," he said as John came to join him.

"That it does."

Sam turned to face him. "So what does the day hold for us?"

John huffed. "You have experienced everything there is to tell already, my friend. The real test of torture here is boredom." He leaned his back against the rail, rubbed his unshaven chin. "Get your family to send books, cards, anything to pass the time."

"How long have you been here?"

"Round about the time of the occupation. I'm a lieutenant with the Maryland Guard."

Sam's stomach dropped. He wondered if John had

been at the armory the night he was tossed out on his ear. He also wondered how well he knew Edward. He did not ask, though. There were Federal guards within earshot. The less they heard about his family, the better.

"You chose not to go south?" Sam asked.

"No. I'd planned to but I didn't leave when a good many of the others did. I foolishly waited. So here I am."

For the first time, Sam felt thankful for Edward's swift departure. *If he had stayed, he would be here, as well.*

John stretched, then rubbed out a knot in his own back. "The bunks here aren't much but I suppose they are better than the ones in the confinement cells."

Sam nodded.

"Reckon I'll get some exercise."

He watched as John walked the length of the portico then turned and retraced his route. Doing so, he had to step over two other men in their company—Richard, also a member of the Maryland Guard, and William. Sam did not yet know William's occupation. Both men were sharing sections of last week's copy of *The Sun*.

A guard climbed the stairs. His eyes quickly swept the other prisoners then stopped on Sam. "Samuel Ward?"

"Yes, sir."

"You have a visitor."

Julia, he thought for a hopeful split second, only to remember it was most likely her father's lawyer friend, William Davis. Grateful for any news, Samuel started in the guard's direction.

John called after him. "Hope they brought you somethin' good to eat."

The guard marched Sam to a room on the first floor.

To his surprise not only was William Davis waiting at the table but Dr. Stanton was, as well.

Sam smiled. "Sir, I did not expect to see you."

"I gave my oath to the Union," he said. "They aren't worried about me anymore."

Sam shook hands with both men then took a seat across from them. The guard took his place by the doorway.

"I thank you both for coming," he said.

Dr. Stanton chuckled. "You look a mess, son."

Sam smoothed back his hair and offered a sheepish grin. "Please pardon my appearance. This hotel does not provide shaving accessories and the tailor shop is closed."

They laughed.

"I see they haven't captured your sense of humor," Dr. Stanton said.

A brown paper parcel had been lying on the table. He pushed it forward.

"I gathered up a few necessities for you, along with your Bible and one of your history books."

"Oh, thank you. I appreciate that." He would find the comb and toothbrush as soon as he got back to the room. "I am not in a confinement cell," he told them. "They have us in a room on the second floor. There are bunks with mattresses and a window."

"That is a relief to know," Dr. Stanton said. "Still, if there is anything else you would like to have just let me know."

He was dying to ask him about Julia, but didn't. He looked to Mr. Davis instead. "Were you able to speak with the lieutenant colonel?"

"Yes. I demanded your release since no specific charges have been presented. He cited a great deal of military and political drivel but basically would not comply."

Sam's shoulders slumped. "How long will I be here?"

Davis shrugged. "It is hard to say. Evidently, in wartime the government has decided it can forgo legality. But I won't let you sit here. I will investigate other avenues. I will find a way."

Sam believed he would. "Thank you, sir. I appreciate all your efforts."

"And I will speak with Dr. Carter and the seminary," Dr. Stanton said. "I will let them know what has happened and ask them to hold your position until you return."

"Thank you. I appreciate that, as well. When I spoke last with Dr. Carter he said they were close to resuming studies."

The guard at the door pulled a watch from his pocket. "You have five minutes," he told them.

Davis glanced at Dr. Stanton. "I will wait outside for you." He rose from his seat then looked back at Sam. "I will leave no stone unturned," he promised.

Sam shook his hand. "I know you will."

"I'll return as soon as I have news," he said and then turned for the door.

"Four minutes," the guard called out.

Sam looked back at Dr. Stanton. Julia's father now had another package. It must have been sitting on his lap because Sam hadn't noticed it before. His spirit lifted immediately. Whatever it was, it was wrapped in a dishcloth, tied up with twine.

"Julia sent this."

The mere mention of her name brought a smile to his face. Sam quickly unwrapped the cloth. It was a loaf of bread and a jar of strawberry jam. He thought of what

John upstairs had just said about visitors bearing food. He laughed.

"She thought you might like it," her father said.

"I do."

It was a hopeful sign. At best she had forgiven him for implicating her family with abolitionists. Or at worst, she felt sorry for him. Whatever the motive behind the bread, at least she was thinking of him.

"How is she?" he asked.

"She is worried about you. She is at your house, cleaning."

"Cleaning?"

Dr. Stanton shrugged and smiled. "She said it needed doing."

Sam laughed. The thought of Julia in his home, in *their* home at this moment, then made his voice thick with emotion. "Tell her that I thank her."

"I will."

"Time is up," the guard announced.

Not wanting to leave the Federal Army's good graces, Dr. Stanton and Sam both immediately stood. They shook hands. Sam's throat was still tight.

"Thank you for coming," he managed.

"You are welcome, son. Don't worry. We will get you out of here soon. I promise."

Julia had scrubbed the kitchen and foyer floors and was working her way through the parlor when her arms and knees gave out. Sighing, she put aside her scrub brush and wiped her hands on her apron. Her eyes roamed the room. The curtains in the parlor entryway were now free of dust. The clock on the mantel held correct time. It ticked softly.

How often she had imagined housekeeping in this

home. How often she had thought of days filled with children and nights beside the one she had promised to love for all time.

But everything is different now. Everything has changed.

An empty ache filled her heart. The man she had promised to marry was now a prisoner at Fort McHenry, a captive of the Federal Army.

Sitting there in the empty house, all Julia could do was cry.

Sam carried his packages back to his room. His new friends were all waiting.

"What did they bring you?" Richard asked.

Sam grinned and laid the clothing on his bunk. He held out Julia's bread and jam.

John practically licked his lips. "From the lady of the house?"

"Yes." He offered him a slice.

John did not have to be asked twice. Neither did the others. Smacking lips and nods of approval soon filled the room.

"Good bread," John said. "What's her name?"

Sam felt pride and thankfulness both at the same time. "Her name is Julia."

John dipped his last bite in the jam. "I hope she sends more."

"So do I," Sam said.

The food was gone within a matter of minutes but the men had enjoyed every bite. Belly full and heart lightened for the first time in days, Sam spent the rest of the morning on the portico. Legs outstretched, he read the Scriptures. What a blessing it was to have his Bible with him.

The sound of the soldiers' cadence and the flapping flag faded from his ears. Rain was now drizzling but he did not mind.

Thank You, Lord, for what You are doing, he prayed. *Thank You that she has not forgotten me.*

Julia had returned to her housecleaning with a determined strength, as though she was personally at war with the dirt and dust that had dared invade Samuel's floors. By the time her father came back she had cleaned the staircases and all three floors.

"Did you see Sam?" she asked immediately.

"Yes. For a few minutes. He said to thank you for the bread and jam."

She felt a tear trickle down her cheek. She turned and quickly wiped it away so her father would not see. She moved toward the kitchen. He followed her.

"I am grateful his conditions are not as bad as I expected," he said. "He isn't in a cell. He is in a room with bunks and other political prisoners."

"It is still jail," she said. She took off the apron she was wearing, one she had found in a drawer belonging to Samuel's mother. She hung it on a peg behind the kitchen door. "When will they release him?"

"I don't know but William says he will keep at it."

"Do they know about the runaway slave?"

"No."

She sighed heavily. "Then there is no reason to hold him."

"The army will realize that in time."

But with how much time? She thought. *What if in the meantime they find out about his abolitionist activities? What if they keep him months or even years?*

The thought of Samuel being held at the fort for an

extended amount of time caused her hands to shake. Tears multiplied in her eyes. Soon she could no longer hide them.

"There now, child," her father said as he wrapped his arms around her. "Don't lose faith. God watches over him. The Almighty won't allow anything in our lives that isn't part of His ultimate plan."

"Even Federal soldiers?"

"Yes. Even Federal soldiers."

They stood there for several minutes. Julia clung to him like she had often done when she was small.

"It will be all right," he promised her.

Oh, Lord, she prayed. *Please, let it be so. Please let Samuel come home.*

"You have had a long day," her father said, finally. "We should go home."

Chapter Fifteen

❧

When Julia arrived home, her mother encouraged her to go upstairs and rest.

"You were up all night," she said, "and you have worked hard all morning."

"But what about the prayer meeting and the things which need tending to here?"

"Leave that to me. Go on now. I won't take no for an answer."

With a smile, her mother pushed her from the kitchen. Julia climbed the staircase, feeling the ache of every tired muscle with each ascending step. She went to her room and shut the door behind her.

She didn't even bother changing her dress. She simply unhooked her collar, loosened her cuffs and sat down on the bed. From her pocket, she took out Samuel's gold watch. It had run down and needed winding. After doing so, Julia tucked up her knees and laid her head on her pillow. She clutched his watch close to her heart and closed her eyes. She waited for sleep to come.

It did not.

Her mind was filled with images of Fort McHenry, of marching men in blue and musty old buildings where plans for war were made. Her father had told her that Samuel wasn't in a cell. For that she was thankful. Still, she wondered just what the conditions were like. She could not imagine they were very comfortable.

What is he doing at this moment? Is he lonely? Is he thinking of me?

She rolled over onto her back and stared at the ceiling. She had baked his bread and had scrubbed his floors all because she knew she must do something. Her acts of service, though, weren't enough. They did not fill the emptiness in her heart nor wash away the guilt she felt.

He is there because he defended my family. He was defending me. He said he would do so and I didn't believe him.

She winced, remembering that day in the churchyard.

"I would give my life for you, for your family, if necessary."

Samuel's eyes had been fixed on hers. She'd seen the hurt in them when she told him he was all talk. Julia now felt sick to her stomach, sick of heart.

Oh, God, forgive me for how I have treated him. He has done everything he said he would and yet I have done nothing but insult him. Sally said she believed I was making a mistake, that Samuel truly loved me.

She thought about the first time he had declared his love for her. It was April, only one year ago. War between the states was unthinkable. Spring was in full bloom and Samuel had just returned home on a semester break.

They had enjoyed a quiet family supper. While Edward was still in the dining room, finishing his dessert, Julia and Samuel had moved to the garden.

The sinking sun cast a soft glow over the daffodils.

Cherry blossoms swayed in a subtle breeze. Julia had reached up to touch their silky, soft petals.

"Aren't they wonderful?" she'd said. "So pretty."

He had watched her sniff a branchful.

"Not as pretty as you," he'd said.

She'd frozen, her cheeks matching the color of the flowers. She never knew how to respond when Samuel said things like that but she liked to hear them.

"Tell me, what news is there of Philadelphia?" she'd asked. "Have you visited all the historical places?"

"I have. I have even visited Independence Hall."

"Oh, how wonderful! What else?"

He'd led her to the bench. Julia's heart pounded at being so near him.

Samuel told of the Delaware River and Valley Forge, of George Washington and his brave yet humble men.

"What was Valley Forge actually like?" she'd asked.

"Primitive. I can't imagine how harsh it was for our soldiers wintering there. They had so little. I think it was only by the grace of God that they survived to keep on fighting."

"Imagine what the world would have been like if they didn't."

She'd fostered polite, intelligent conversation but the sleeve of his coat had been touching her arm. Her skin tingled and her ears were thudding.

Samuel went on to tell more and Julia hung on every word. She loved to hear him talk of history. His voice practically danced with excitement over the smallest details.

"I would love to see the places you have visited," she'd said.

He had smiled. "Then we will do so, one day."

The invitation surprised her yet she did not have much

time to ponder it. Samuel had then said, "You know, by this time next April, I will have completed my studies. I will have found permanent work."

He'd searched her face. Julia felt butterflies fluttering in her stomach. Her heart had beaten even faster as his words raced though her mind.

Then we will do so one day? I will have completed my studies? Could this be leading to...?

She'd held her breath, waiting, hoping.

Samuel glanced in the direction of the house, presumably making certain Edward wasn't approaching.

Don't let him come, she'd prayed selfishly. *Oh, please Lord, don't let him come. Make him stay inside.*

Samuel reached for her hand, running his thumb gently across her skin. She'd dared to meet his gaze.

He'd looked as nervous as she felt. His words then tumbled out.

"Julia, I love you. I have loved you forever it seems. When my studies are finished, when I secure a teaching post, will you consider, well, will you marry me?"

He'd stared at her, eyes wide.

She had not moved. She did not breathe. She could scarcely believe what she had just heard.

"Did you just ask me to marry you?" she'd asked, her voice trembling with emotion.

"Yes. Well, I must ask your father and I must find work—"

There was no telling how much longer he would have rambled on had she not laid her free hand on top of his. He'd stopped midsentence.

"Yes," she'd said.

At that, he'd looked as though he scarcely believed her. "You will wait for me?"

A surety unlike anything she had ever known before

settled over her. She wanted to be with Samuel. It seemed God had planned so from the beginning.

"I will wait for you," she'd promised.

Robins had chirped their approval as a smile moved over his face. Julia felt the warmth of his gaze, seen the hunger in his eyes.

No man had ever kissed her before. She bit her lip then realized that was completely the wrong thing to do in this situation.

Samuel leaned closer. Fear and yet anticipation made her hands tremble. He must have felt it. He squeezed them gently just before his mouth found hers.

Julia had never forgotten the sweetness nor the excitement of that first kiss. When Samuel held her in his arms he had the power to make everything else around them disappear.

But reality soon returned, harder and uglier with each dose.

Lying in the stillness, the safety of her own room, she sighed. *Did I just not realize then what I was promising? I didn't know how complicated things would become. Neither of us imagined war, let alone our family divided over it.*

She rolled back to her side, her eyes falling upon the Frederick Douglass book lying on the nightstand. Her father had asked her to read the small volume; but as of yet she had not. Julia sucked in her breath. By Samuel's own admission it was this man's words that had shaped his convictions and fixed his position concerning this conflict.

What was it this man said that convinced him he could not support Edward's cause? And if it is so important to him then why didn't he simply ask me to read it in the first place?

Her curiosity sparked, she swapped his watch for the narrative.

Propping up on her pillows, she turned to the first page. She was about to find out more information than she had ever imagined.

She just didn't know it.

John had been right. The real test of political imprisonment here at the fort was boredom. Sam had often wondered what it would be like to have unlimited hours to read. He had found out it was not as glorious as he had once imagined. Eyes grew weak, necks stiff. Julius Caesar and his Roman legions were not nearly as intriguing as they had once been. He soon found himself longing for the most mundane of physical labor, chopping wood or pulling weeds from the garden.

John passed him the latest copy of *The Baltimore Sun*. Sam glanced at the headlines and sketches. Short, bald General Butler had been replaced by Major General George Cadwalader and three regiments from Philadelphia. Sam scanned the article, learning it was partially this man's role which had led to his arrest.

Cadwalader had received orders from President Lincoln "to arrest persons under certain circumstances and to hold them prisoner though they should be demanded by writs of habeas corpus."

Sam had read enough of the article. He passed the paper back to John.

"I'm telling you," John said, "it is only a matter of time before we see more good citizens of Baltimore here in our company."

By the way the article had read, Sam was inclined to agree with him. He prayed the soldiers would continue to honor Dr. Stanton's oath of loyalty and that Dr. Carter and his friends in Fell's Point would be careful concerning their activities.

One of William's relatives had sent a checkerboard. The men took turns passing the time with the game. John, who by now had abandoned the paper, asked questions about Julia and her baking. It seemed he had an appetite as large as the Federal Army itself.

"Will she send more soon?"

Sam had not told anyone of what had happened between him and Julia. He did not want anyone to think ill of her. "I am sure she will when she is able," he said.

"Does she make cornbread?"

"Yes."

"Blueberry muffins?"

Sam smiled. "When the berries are in season."

John nodded. "We're coming into blueberry season here soon," he said.

"I will mention that next time I speak with her."

Sam didn't know when that might be but he did not let on so. He had thought about writing her but there wasn't much news to tell. The only things he did want to say to her, he had promised he wouldn't.

I said I would respect her wishes. I must do so.

He picked up his Bible and walked out to the portico. A summer storm was pelting the fort. Sam sat down on the buckling porch floorboards and stretched out his legs. He wondered when Dr. Stanton would visit again. He wondered if Julia would ever come with him.

He sighed, knowing deep down inside that she wouldn't. *Even if it was her desire to set things right between us, she is too afraid of the soldiers. The best I can hope for at this point is more bread.*

He watched as below, a squad of men ran double-quick across the grassy interior. Their uniforms were soggy. The men were slowed by the heavy, wet wool. A fellow at the end of the line tripped in the mud. He scrambled to his feet, hurrying to catch up with the others before anyone noticed.

They were once just ordinary men with ordinary lives. Now they are here and our entire nation is divided.

He thought again of Julia. He had purposely spared her the details of slavery. Many were too gruesome, too appalling to discuss. But he wondered what she would say if she knew the whole truth. *Would it change her opinions, her focus in this conflict?*

He sighed once more. *Even if it did, Edward would still be part of the Confederate Army. The family would still be divided. And slavery would still be legal here in Maryland.*

Julia continued to read, though she had been ghastly underprepared for the story the book told. In the first chapter alone, Frederick Douglass told how he was separated from his mother as a baby, which was the common practice in Maryland. Mothers were sold off to other plantations and the children given to old women who were too feeble to work in the fields.

Did such a thing happen to Elijah and Elisha? she wondered. *Do they even know who their mother is?*

Douglass went on to tell how men and women were whipped repeatedly by cruel overseers. Much of the time, the whip masters were drunk and swearing profanely.

Two chapters of the man's life were all she could take. Julia was now in tears; her eyes opened to a new world, a cruel and despicable one.

No wonder Samuel cannot support States' Rights, not if slavery is a right insisted upon. No wonder he felt he must aid the young runaway. Oh, Lord, please forgive me. I had no idea. Edward has no idea. She wiped her eyes, shivering as she imagined the gruesome scenes she had read about.

How many slaves are suffering such a fate here in Maryland? How many right here in Baltimore? I thought Samuel had been a coward. I even told him so. Tears rolled down her cheeks. She began to sob. *Oh, Lord, forgive me. I had no idea.*

Sam felt it as certainly as though John or William had nudged him on the shoulder. He laid his Bible aside.

I need to pray for her.

Bowing his head while the business of war circled about him, Sam once more prayed for Julia. *Whatever is happening to her at this moment, Lord, be with her. Give her wisdom. Give her courage to follow the path You have chosen for her.*

She had told herself she would not read another word. It was too disturbing, too heartbreaking, but she felt compelled to continue. Julia cringed at stories of slaves who had been murdered by their masters. Neither the justice system nor society treated the acts as a crime.

And then those poor girls...

A knock sounded on the door. Julia jumped. Quickly laying the book aside, she scrambled to her feet. "Come in."

Sally peeked her head inside.

Julia wiped her eyes with her handkerchief. "Oh, Sally, thank goodness you are here!"

Sally shut the door behind her. "Your mother told me what happened. I am so sorry."

She gave Julia a hug and then they sat down on the bed.

Julia drew up her knees and smoothed out her wrinkled day dress. "Oh, Sally, it's just terrible."

"Were you able to sleep?"

"No."

"Emily came to the prayer meeting today. She said that her father spoke with Sam this morning."

"Yes, but the soldiers won't release him."

"Oh, my."

"I went with Father to the house this morning. He was bundling up shirts. We sent him his Bible and one of his schoolbooks. I baked him a loaf of bread."

Sally smiled comfortingly. "I am certain he appreciated that."

"Oh, Sally, I have been so foolish! I should have listened to you when you said I was making a mistake. I should have gone back to Samuel right at that very moment and told him that I was sorry. Now I am afraid that it's too late."

Julia strangled the handkerchief in her hands. "I called him a coward. A *coward!*"

"Julia, if I know Sam, he has long since forgiven you."

"Do you think he could?"

"He loves you. You know he does."

Julia nodded her head yes. If there was one thing she was certain of now, it was that Samuel Ward loved her; though she could not for the life of herself understand why.

"It is worse than that," she said.

"What is?"

"I know why he has sided with the abolitionists."

"You do?"

"Yes." She drew in a quick breath. "I read that book."

Sally squinted. "What book?"

Julia pointed to the nondescript volume lying at the foot of her bed. "That one. It belongs to Samuel."

"Is it about slavery?"

"Yes."

Curiosity caused her to pick it up. Sally leafed through the pages though not really settling on any particular one. She then looked back at Julia. "Is this the man from up north? The one that set him thinking about abolition?"

"Yes. He was a slave on a plantation in Talbot County some years before."

"Truly?"

"Yes. Oh, Sally, he wrote all sorts of horrible things! I thought slavery was just about working in the fields, like farm hands but this man wrote of what life is really like for a slave. Things that I never imagined."

"Like what?"

"Like how they chain their hands, their feet, even their necks! How slaves are separated from their families and sold to different owners." She lowered her voice to a whisper. Her cheeks grew warm with embarrassment. "The women are bred like horses."

Sally blinked. "What do you mean?"

Julia found Frederick Douglass's own words and showed Sally the page.

Her jaw dropped and her face turned as red as Julia's. "The slave masters father the children and then they turn around and sell them? Do they do this everywhere?"

"I don't know," Julia said, "but it must be common enough if this man chose to write about it."

"That is absolutely disgraceful!"

Julia nodded. "Samuel kept saying that he could not support a Confederacy that allowed slavery. I am beginning to understand why."

"Then you should tell him that."

"Where would I even begin? It's so awful."

"Tell him what you have told me. Tell him that you read his book. You don't need to say anything more. He will understand."

Julia's shoulders rose and fell with a quick shallow breath. "Do you really think he will?"

"Of course."

Both of them grew quiet, contemplative. Sally picked up the book again and scanned its pages. Julia's breathing eventually settled to a more normal pace.

A half hour went by. Sally put down the book.

"I don't want to read anymore. I have read enough."

Their minds were full. Their hearts were heavy. With eyes opened to such evil, their consciences demanded a choice. They could not remain ambivalent as they had been and they both knew it.

"What do we do now?" Sally asked. "Where do we go from here?"

"I wish I knew. For the first time I understand the pressure, the confusion Samuel must be feeling. Slavery is wrong. I am convinced of that now but I don't like what the Federal Army is doing either."

Sally shook her head in disbelief. "I can't believe that they arrested your father. That they kept Sam."

Julia shuddered just thinking of it. "I don't know when or if they will let him come home."

"Just keep praying," Sally urged.

She tried to have faith. She tried to be brave but her thoughts immediately went to her brother. "What am I going to tell Edward?" Julia asked.

"What am I going to tell Stephen? I never knew slaves were treated like that."

They both wiped away tears. Sally then stretched out across the bottom of the bed and stared at the ceiling.

"There aren't any answers written up there," Julia said. "Believe me, I have looked."

Sally rolled onto her side. "Why did God allow it to get this far?" she asked. "Why did He let it come to war?"

"Perhaps He was speaking all along," Julia said. "Perhaps we just weren't listening."

The unspoken consequences of such actions blanketed the room in heavy silence.

"What will happen to our brothers?" Sally dared ask. "To our other friends? Not everyone in the Confederate Army agrees with slavery."

Julia thought of what Samuel had said about praying for Edward's safety. His words had angered her. Now she appreciated them more then she could ever have imagined.

"Like you said, we just have to keep praying."

"We should pray for them right now. We should pray for ourselves, as well."

Julia agreed. Sally pulled herself into a sitting position and they clasped hands. They pleaded for God's intervention in the lives of their brothers and for all of those they knew. They did not stop until His peace permeated the room.

Sally returned home just before supper. After the light meal, the doorbell rang. Dr. Stanton had gone upstairs, so Julia went to answer the door. She first checked the window for any sign of Federal soldiers.

On the porch stood Charles Moffit.

Oh, dear, she thought.

Taking a moment to gather her composure, she then opened the door.

"Miss Stanton," he said, quickly removing his topper and placing it over his heart. "I came as soon as I heard the news. The arrest of your father? Why, it is appalling! Those Yankees—"

"He is home now," Julia said, "and the matter has been concluded."

He breathed a sigh of relief. "I am pleased to hear that. I shall be returning to Annapolis today but if your family should have need of any assistance..."

Any assistance she may be in need of, Charles Moffit could not supply. She knew that now. "I thank you Mr. Moffit but that won't be necessary."

"I see."

Julia knew she had to speak plainly. "And as for our future correspondence, I am afraid I must decline."

His face fell. "I see," he said once again. "Does this have anything to do with your former fiancé?"

She was taken aback by his inquisitiveness. "It has to do with a great many things," Julia said. "Most of which would be improper to discuss."

"Of course," he said. "Forgive me. I understand." As credit to his social standing, he knew when it was time to leave. "I suppose then this is farewell."

"I am afraid so."

This time he did not kiss her hand. Julia smiled politely nonetheless.

"I do wish you happiness for your future," he said.

"Thank you, Mr. Moffit, and I you, as well. May God grant you safe passage home."

He turned for the front gate. She shut the door, thankful to have closed at least one chapter in her life.

"Was that who I think it was?"

She turned to find her father standing on the staircase. "Yes. I said that I did not wish to correspond with him."

"And why is that?" he asked, as he joined her.

Julia knew full well that her father wasn't asking because he thought she had made a mistake.

"I read that book…or at least, part of it."

His left eyebrow arched with intrigue. "Frederick Douglass?"

"Yes."

"I was hoping you would."

Images of women being whipped as young children were ripped from their arms made her shiver. She lowered her chin, feeling ashamed that for years she had thought nothing on the matter.

"I could not finish it," she confessed. "It was too disturbing."

"It is, indeed."

"I understand now why you helped that young woman."

"You do?"

"Yes."

His mustache rose with just the hint of a compassionate smile. He extended his arm. Together they walked to the study.

"Your mother and I came to the decision that slavery should be outlawed only a short time ago," he explained. "It was only as we became aware of how horrible the institution was that our opinions—or, rather, lack thereof—changed."

"How?" Julia asked.

"Partly because of Sam, the experiences he spoke of, the people he had met while he was away. We never had any real experiences with slavery. None of our close friends own slaves and the few that I have seen here in Baltimore appear to be well treated by their owners."

He continued. "But that perspective was limited. Sam knew people who had seen much more and the things that he told disturbed me greatly."

Julia mentioned only a little of what she had read in Samuel's book, the beatings, the separation of families. "Are those things common?"

"According to Sam they are and according to the various abolitionist literature that I have since read."

She sighed heavily. Her mind drifted back to that day in Fell's Point when she had stood arguing with Samuel and her father concerning their activities. How selfish and immature she had acted. She hoped the young woman upstairs had not heard.

"Father, what happened to Rose? Did she suffer such things?"

He nodded sadly. "She was a slave from a house on Hanover Street. Sam said that her mother lived on a plantation in Talbot County and her father had been sent to one on the Severn River."

Julia winced as though a bayonet had been run through her chest. She wondered if the plantation on the Severn could possibly be the Moffit's large acreage outside of Annapolis.

"I must admit, I was hesitant about helping," he said. "I was concerned about the potential consequences of doing so."

"What changed your mind?"

"The look in her eyes the moment I saw her. There was no way I could deny her care. My conscience would not allow it. She had been beaten more times than a man could count."

Julia shuddered and once more thought of Frederick

Douglass's description of masters and their methods for increasing the slave population. She was compelled to ask, "The baby she is carrying...the child doesn't belong to her husband, does it?"

"She doesn't have a husband."

Julia's heart broke for Rose and all the other young women like her. *And what of Elisha and Elijah? Who is their father? Could it be the dry goods merchant himself or someone even more cruel?* Tears filled her eyes.

Dear Lord, how could I have been so foolish? How could I be so focused on my own pleasures that I failed to notice what was happening all around me?

She looked at her father. "I understand now why Samuel felt that he could not support Edward."

"I see," he said slowly, "and where does that leave you?"

"I am not certain."

He smiled. "Well, I am confident that the Lord will show you and that in turn you will do what is right."

I hope so, she thought.

She loved Samuel Ward but did she have the courage to walk beside him? Could she travel his path without worrying about the opinions of her brother, her fellow citizens and the consequences of state and federal law?

Chapter Sixteen

The following morning dawned clear and bright. As the sunlight from the small window streamed into the room, the political prisoners yawned and stretched before beginning a new day. Sam put his feet on the floor. He had passed another restless night. This time it wasn't so much the mattress that kept him tossing and turning. It was dreaming about things he could not control.

He saw Edward on the battlefield, his tailored Maryland Guard uniform now tattered and covered in mud. He and his men were taking on fire. Trees were splintering. Julia's brother fell in a pool of blood.

The nightmare then shifted to her. She stood vigil over Edward's casket. She was dressed in black with a veil covering her face. Sam could barely see her through the heavy draping.

"I am so sorry," he'd said.

She turned her back to him. "Go away," she'd whispered, so as not to make a scene in front of the other mourners. "You are not welcome here."

He'd touched her on the sleeve. "Julia, don't do this."

Bitterness laced her words. "This is all your fault, Samuel. I wish that I had never met you."

Trying to shake off the haunting images, Sam dressed and combed his hair, mentally preparing for another day of confinement.

I don't understand why all of this has happened, Lord. But I choose to believe it is part of Your plan. I choose to believe this is for our ultimate good...Julia's and mine.

Julia finished her morning chores then traded her cotton work dress and corded petticoat for her hoop and silk. As she made herself ready for the noon prayer meeting her thoughts were churning.

She still feared the soldiers. She still hated the Federal occupation of her city. But she loved Samuel. She wanted to support him and his work. How exactly, she was not sure. Her legs were shaky, her steps uncertain, yet she knew she was finally on solid ground.

I will continue with what we have begun at the prayer meeting. God will give me further instructions when I need them.

She brushed out her hair then twisted it up into place, leaving just a few curls about her ears. Samuel had often told her that he liked her hair that way. She then opened the top drawer of her dressing table. She took out her engagement ring. She slid it on her finger, the action solidifying her resolve.

Whatever happens will be in God's hands.

She rode to church in the back of her father's carriage. Julia stared at the houses as they passed by. Not a symbol of seccession remained in Baltimore. The flags and bunting which had covered the streets of Mount Vernon before the occupation had all been taken down for fear of Federal imprisonment.

An ache moved through her heart. She wondered where Samuel was at that exact moment. Had the soldiers given him any sort of breakfast? Had they moved him to a confinement cell?

She had it in her mind that she was going to write him a long letter as soon as she got home from church, that she would tell him about reading his book and how she had come to see life from a different perspective. She wanted to tell him that she was sorry for the things she had said and that she now believed his decision not to join the Confederate Army was the right one.

But her fears nagged her.

What if the soldiers censor the mail? What if they confiscate it altogether?

There wasn't anything illegal about expressing anti-slavery sentiments but there also wasn't anything illegal about treating wounded citizens on Pratt Street.

And yet the soldiers came for my father.

Uneasiness made her squirm in her seat and her chin began to quiver.

What if I do or say something that will get Samuel into further trouble?

Clutching her Bible tightly in her lap, she bowed her head and prayed silently for him once more.

Lord, I don't know what to do or what to say. All I know is that I must do something. I can't let him think that I don't love him.

The carriage rocked side to side. She opened her eyes just as her father turned onto Charles Street. The church building came into view. Its large, white steeple punctured the hazy, late-morning sky. Dr. Stanton rolled to a stop and the three of them climbed out.

Sally's father had served as chaperone in Samuel's absence. He and his daughter were already at the table.

"Shall I stay with you?" Julia's mother asked, knowing she was anxious about resuming her duties.

"Thank you, but I will be all right." Julia said the words with more courage than she actually felt. She hoped there would be no blue uniforms in the vicinity today.

Esther squeezed her hand. "I will say a prayer for you."

"Thank you."

Her parents entered the church building and Julia joined Sally.

"I am so pleased to see you," Sally said, hugging her. "Your presence was greatly missed."

Julia smiled. Sally always knew how to make a person feel welcome.

"I missed you, as well, but I am certain that you managed just fine without me."

"Several people have asked about you," Sally said. "They all hoped you would return."

"Truly?"

"Yes."

Tears filled Julia's eyes but she blinked them back. Could it be she'd had the slightest impact for good, despite all of her mistakes?

Oh, Lord, You are so merciful, she thought. *So merciful.*

The noon bells chimed the hour and the congregants began arriving. Among them was a new face, Rebekah Van der Geld. She approached the table. The drab black bonnet still crowned her head yet Rebekah's face was far from judgmental. Kindness and compassion shone in her eyes.

"I wanted to tell you that I heard about Samuel," she said. "I am so sorry."

Julia touched the ring on her finger, thinking of that day at the sewing circle when she had been ashamed to tell her friends what Samuel's wartime position was. How foolish she had been.

"Thank you," Julia said. "That is very kind of you."

"I will pray that they release him soon."

"Thank you. I appreciate that." Julia moved to give her a hug, grateful for Rebekah's compassionate words. Perhaps the two of them could once again find common ground.

When Rebekah left the table to join her family in the church, Sally said,

"The spirit of God is moving."

"Indeed," Julia said.

Prayers were being answered. Hearts were softening. People were coming to Christ.

If only Samuel could see this. If only I could tell him about it face-to-face.

She and Sally handed out milk rolls and lemon tea cakes while Mr. Hastings served water to those on the street. The hour passed for Julia with a mixture of fear and joy. She kept a watchful eye, praying Elijah and Elisha would come.

At ten till one, she saw them, torn trousers and a sack of grain. Julia drew in a deep breath. Despite being warned otherwise, she started across the street.

Elijah and Elisha set down the sack. They grinned and tipped their caps.

"Miss Julia! We'z glad to see you!"

With tears brimming in her eyes, she immediately hugged them both. They smelled like stale hay. She could feel their ribs through their coarse, rag shirts.

"It is I who am pleased to see both of you," she said. "Tell me, are you well?"

"Yes'um," Elijah said. "We'z right as rain. We'z seen God!"

Julia blinked. "I beg your pardon?"

"We'z seen God! He came to our lean-to early one mornin' 'fore sunrise."

The boys were adamant. Julia had no idea what they were talking about but whatever they had experienced left them happy and excited.

Perhaps Samuel's conversations about Jesus have caused them to dream about Him. She then realized the problem with that explanation. *But both of them having the same dream?*

She looked at Elisha. He nodded seriously, eyes wide as his brother continued. "He answered our prayer."

"He did?" Julia asked. "How did you see the Lord, exactly?"

"Master Wallace said we weren't gonna git no bread that day but we'z hungry, so we prayed for somethin' to eat. And God brought us milk rolls for breakfast! He slipped it in our lean-to and then quick as a wink, He was gone!"

Julia glanced again at Elisha. He was still nodding.

"And that's not the best part," Elijah said. "He gave us stockins, too! Brand new! They fit just right!"

They pulled up their trousers for proof. Julia hadn't even noticed until now the burlap tied around their feet which served as makeshift shoes. On their ankles were gray knitted stockings, the ones she had given Samuel.

Tears filled her eyes and her heart swelled with love and admiration. *He found a way! Lord, bless Samuel for his kindness, his perseverance.* "What did your visitor look like?" She asked.

"He have white hair and a beard and a big fancy stovepipe hat."

She realized the man they were describing was Dr. Carter. Samuel must have passed the items on to him before his arrest. "That wasn't the Lord," she corrected gently, "but it was surely one of his servants, one of Mr. Sam's friends."

"Oh…," Elijah said slowly, not the least bit disappointed. "Miss Julia?"

"Yes?"

"Where is Mr. Sam?"

She did not want them to worry so she chose her words carefully.

"He had to go away for a while," she said.

"Is he a comin' back?"

Her body trembled at the thought of anything otherwise but Julia stood firm on faith. If God could change her heart, could he not also change those men at Fort McHenry?

"Oh, yes," she said. "He will return. Will you promise me something, though?"

They lifted their chins. "Yes'um."

"Will you pray for him until he does?"

They nodded, taking the request as a solemn honor. "Yes'um. We be happy to."

"Thank you, gentlemen." She handed them each a tea cake and a roll of candy. Her heart ached at what the rest of their day may hold. Though she wished to, she knew she could not keep them any longer.

Lord, thank You for answering their prayer. Thank You for answering mine. Please continue to watch over them.

"You had better go now," she said. "I don't want you to be late. Will I see you tomorrow?"

They flashed their milk-white smiles. "Oh, yes'um."

She helped them hoist the grain sack onto their shoulders then watched as they headed up the street. Not a soldier or a passerby had harmed them and the joy she felt at serving far outweighed her fears.

It gave her courage.

I must go to him, she thought. *I must go to Fort McHenry and tell Samuel that I love him.*

A peace washed over her that was beyond comprehension. She knew what she was about to do was right. She waited until the service had ended and their carriage was well on its way before she spoke of Fort McHenry. She knew her parents would not be comfortable with the idea of her visiting the fort but she prayed they would at least consider her request.

The summer sun gleamed bright and heat rose in rippled waves from the street. Julia opened her fan. Her heart was pounding.

"Father?" she asked.

"Yes, child?"

"Will you take me to Fort McHenry so that I may see Samuel?"

He kept his eyes on the road in front of him. A wagon loaded with lumber was crossing the street. He slowed to let it pass.

She wondered if he had heard her request. "Father?"

"I am not certain that is a wise idea," he said finally without taking his eyes from the road.

Julia bit back her disappointment, knowing beforehand this would probably be the response. Still, she pressed her position respectfully.

"Please? It is very important that I speak with him. I was going to write him but I was afraid that the soldiers would—"

"I noticed the ring," he said. "Does this mean you have changed your mind?"

She shuddered to think of all the hurtful things she

had said and done to him. "I was a fool to ever think otherwise," she said.

Her mother looked back at her and smiled. The feathers on her new bonnet swayed slightly. "We are all fools at some point, dear. The important thing is having the courage to change."

She appreciated her mother's encouragement. She leaned forward in her seat. She could tell by her father's wrinkled brow that he was at least considering the idea.

Oh, Lord, please...please let me set things right.

Her father drove the final blocks to home without saying a word. Julia sat on the edge of her seat the entire time, breathless. When they pulled in front of the house Dr. Stanton set the brake but did not climb from the carriage.

Holding on to that measure of hope, Julia did not move. Her mother sat still, as well.

"Thomas," she said slowly.

Dr. Stanton looked at his wife and then at Julia. He sighed. "I want you to wear your most understated dress and bonnet. Nothing too fancy. I don't want you to speak a word to anyone until you see Sam. Is that understood?"

Joy welled up inside her. She threw her arms around his neck. "Oh, thank you! Thank you!"

His face softened to a laugh. "If it were any man other than Samuel Ward I wouldn't even think of letting you do this." He patted her arm. "Go on now. Go inside before I change my mind."

It was by far the most humid day that Sam had experienced during his stay at the fort. Summertime in Baltimore could be sweltering and by afternoon the second story room of confinement felt like a furnace. He and his companions sought the shade and slightly cooler temperatures of the portico.

The men were far from talkative except for the occasional wish for a glass of water or lemonade. John and William tried to pass the time by playing checkers. Richard was pitching cards at an empty water bucket. Sam watched Fort McHenry's daily life unfold with its usual routine.

The soldiers on the parade grounds seemed to be moving in slow motion. As Sam followed their laborious movements he couldn't help but feel sorry for them. He and his imprisoned comrades were in shirtsleeves. The soldiers were in full uniform.

I imagine they wish they were anywhere else but here, as well.

He looked out over the hazy, bluish-gray horizon. Baltimore lay in the distance, her slate roofs soaking up the summer sun. It wasn't long before his mind settled on Julia. By now she would have returned from the prayer meeting.

He imagined her in the kitchen preparing dinner. The windows would be open. The house would be warm.

Afterward, she will more than likely go to the garden, sit on the bench beneath the cherry tree and finish a little sewing. He smiled to himself. *She will probably take off her shoes and stockings if she thinks no one is looking. She loves to sink her toes in the cool, green grass.*

"Look yonder," Richard said, interrupting his reverie.

Sam turned. The man had abandoned his cards and was now standing at the railing.

Sam got to his feet and looked in the direction of the inner gate. Five well-dressed men were crossing the yard under Federal guard.

"Who is that?" he asked.

"Not sure," Richard said, "but I don't think they are here for just a visit."

More political prisoners, Sam thought.

William must have thought the same. "Where are we going to put them? Our room is crowded enough already."

John abandoned the checkerboard and came over for a look.

"Do you know them?" Sam asked.

He squinted then nodded. The look on his face was grave. "That there is Marshal Kane and all four of his police commissioners."

Sam remembered John's prediction that the city leadership who had advocated burning the railroad bridges on the night of the Pratt Street riot would soon find themselves under arrest, as well.

John grunted. "This ain't a good sign."

Sam had to agree. *If Marshal Kane has been arrested then the Federal Army will be taking over the police department. How many more citizens will be arrested?*

His muscles tensed and his heart pounded as once more he thought of Julia. *Watch over her, Lord. And please don't let anything that I have done bring trouble on her or her family.*

Julia had done as her father asked and chosen the most nondescript dress in her wardrobe. She held it to her chin as she stood in front of the looking glass. The garment had wide pagoda sleeves but the fabric was plain and unadorned. The color was her least favorite.

I suppose this is an appropriate color for visiting a Federal Garrison, she thought. *Union blue.*

If she had her way she would choose the sea green

dress she had worn the day Samuel had walked her home. It was light and breezy, perfect for a summer's day.

I always thought you looked beautiful in that color, he had said.

He had made her blush with that compliment. Her heart had fluttered.

It was fluttering now, at the thought of seeing him again.

If only I didn't have to meet him while wearing such shabby clothing. Sighing, she slipped the dress on then fastened the hooks and eyes of the bodice. She adjusted her collar. She then tied her black bonnet on her head and hurried downstairs.

Her mother and father were waiting in the foyer.

"Are you ready?" he asked.

"How do I look?"

"Plain," he said. "And very supportive of the Federal Army."

It wasn't exactly what she wanted to hear. She glanced at her mother.

"Sam won't even notice what you are wearing," she promised. "He will just be happy to see you."

"I hope so."

"Don't worry, dear."

Julia's thoughts jumped from fabric to food. "Bread!" she said. "I must fetch some!"

She flew to the kitchen. She had baked a pan of cornbread the night before so she cut several slices. Wrapping them carefully she placed them in a basket alongside a jar of apple butter. Assuming Samuel's meal rations were poor, she gathered a bunch of fresh lettuce, a nearly ripe tomato and a tin of sardines.

There is no telling when the last time was that he had fish and vegetables.

Lastly, she filled a canning jar with lemonade.

When everything was packed just so, she returned to the foyer. Her father chuckled when he saw the overflowing basket.

"Well, he won't be hungry. That's for certain."

Smiling, Julia followed him to the sidewalk. Lewis had already brought the carriage around front. A shiver of nervousness, more than just the uncertainty of seeing Samuel moved through her. As she climbed into the front seat she could not help but think,

I am going to Fort McHenry.

She set the basket at her feet then shielded it from the hot sun by tucking her hoop and skirts over it.

"Ready?" her father asked.

"I believe so."

When all was secure, he gave the reins a click. Julia tried to think about what she would say when she met Samuel, but thoughts of soldiers in their brass buckles and blue wool kept invading her mind. The closer the carriage came to the gates of Fort McHenry, the more anxious Julia became.

How did I ever think I could do this? I can't even walk comfortably at the market where there are only a few soldiers at a time.

She folded her hands in her lap only to keep them from trembling. Her thoughts were churning and her fears were growing. *What if the soldiers question me before they let me see Samuel? They probably already know that my brother is serving in the Confederate Army. What if they ask about Edward's correspondence? What if they find out about Mr. Hastings and the mail?*

The carriage bumped over the cobblestones. The air

was so humid that she was beginning to feel sick to her stomach. She pulled a handkerchief from her reticule and dabbed at her face.

"Sam will be so pleased to see you," her father said.

"Yes." Julia tugged at her collar.

"Don't worry. It isn't much farther. We will be there directly."

She swallowed back the lump in her throat and tried to breathe normally. They turned on the road to the fort. Tents of occupying soldiers stretched in both directions, as far as her eyes could see. Her stomach rolled.

"Did you know they were here?" she quickly asked her father.

"Yes. They are the regiments from Pennsylvania."

Her hands were trembling so that she could barely keep them together. The sight of that many blue uniforms made her lightheaded.

Courage, she commanded. *I must show courage! I must do this!*

The fort's outer gate came into view. Guards were posted. Panic seized her.

What if they ask me about that place in Fell's Point? Father didn't think they knew about Rose but what if they have since learned about her?

She swallowed hard. Her mind was racing. *Even if they do not know of Rose, if Samuel continues to assist slaves then the likelihood of him being rearrested is almost certain. What will happen when we have children? I can't raise a family alone!*

Her father glanced at her, recognizing what was happening. He slowed the mare to a standstill on the side of the road.

"Do you want to go back?" he asked.

Julia stared at the soldiers guarding the gate. They

had muskets on their shoulders. She wondered how many more armed men were inside.

"Child?"

She stole a quick glance at the canvas tents along the roadside. A group of men was playing cards at a make-shift table. Two of them were staring at the carriage. A third man stood to his feet.

She shut her eyes, willing them to disappear. *We are surrounded by soldiers! Lord help us! They will arrest us all!*

Her chest was heaving. Her lungs begged for air. The next thing she knew the carriage was wobbling and changing directions. When Julia dared open her eyes, the soldiers were behind her. Her father had turned for home.

"I will take you home and then I will return to visit Sam," he said. "I'll give him the food and tell him what happened. I am certain he will understand."

Chapter Seventeen

From somewhere deep inside a determination rose, one that far outweighed her fear of the soldiers. Julia vividly remembered the promise she had made just that morning.

Whatever happens will be in God's hands.

"No," she said to her father. "Stop."

"Stop?"

She loved Samuel. She would stand beside him come what may. "Please, Father. I have to see him."

He pulled back on the mare. He stared at her. "Are you certain?"

"Samuel once promised me that he would give his life for me if necessary." She looked at him, her voice growing stronger. "He took your place in prison."

"Yes. He did."

"Then the least I can do is face a garrison of soldiers to visit him."

He tugged at his mustache, his eyes blinking hesitantly.

"You once told me that you were confident that I would make the right decision."

"Yes. I did."

"Well, this is it. I won't abandon him."

Her earnestness won over his apprehension. With a sigh and then just the hint of a smile, he gave the reins a click. He turned the carriage around.

"Remember what I told you," he said. "Don't speak to anyone until we see Sam."

"I won't."

Julia braced herself as the main gate of Fort McHenry once again came into view. The cobblestones were rough and uneven the last stretch of the way and sickening waves rolled though her stomach. Determined this time to ignore her fears, she squared her shoulders and stared at the route ahead.

I have asked the Lord for wisdom and this is where the road has led. He will continue to guide me, to guide us.

They came to the entrance. A uniformed guard stepped up to meet them.

"State the purpose of your visit."

Julia kept her eyes focused on the gate in front of her while her father spoke with the guard.

"We are here to visit a prisoner. Samuel Ward."

There was a second guard. He checked a list that he was carrying in his hand then nodded to the first man.

"Leave your horse at the hitching post," the first guard said as he pointed to an area to the left of the gate. "Private Higgins will escort you to the waiting area."

Dr. Stanton thanked the man and then urged the horse to the place that the soldier had indicated. Julia whispered a quick prayer before climbing from the carriage. Her knees were weak. Her father helped her down.

"Take my arm," he whispered. "Stay right beside me."

Julia did as he said, hoping his close presence would be enough to quell her trembling hands. It wasn't. She hid one in the crook of his arm. She clutched her basket with the other.

The soldiers at the gate stared at her as she approached. Julia did not make eye contact with them. She only stole a quick glance at the man who was to be their escort.

Private Higgins was a stone-faced young man who didn't appear to be much older than she. She wondered if he had been one of the soldiers at the train station the day the rioting began. She wondered if he had used the musket he was now carrying to fire upon her fellow citizens of Baltimore. A shiver ran through her.

"Your basket please," he said to her.

Julia's mind and body momentarily froze. Her father quickly gave the man what he had asked for.

"It is just a few food items," he explained.

Private Higgins searched. Her father patted her arm. She prayed, begging God for the courage to continue.

Higgins thoroughly searched the basket then handed it back to her. Thankful that he did not confiscate it, Julia managed a polite nod.

"This way," he commanded.

He led them through the main gate and up the path to the old Star Fort. Julia tried to focus on the backs of his shoes and not on her surroundings as they walked. Blue uniforms were everywhere. The private led them past the parade grounds, the quartermaster's department and the stables. The afternoon sun was high in the sky and the temperature was oppressive. The meager breeze drifting in from the Patapsco River did little to ease the heat or quell the odor of sweat and manure coming from the stables.

When they reached the fort, Julia caught her first glimpse of the guns that were pointed in her city's direction. Private Higgins marched right past them, taking the visitors to a room on the lower level of one of the buildings.

It was there that another guard was waiting. He looked a little older but was just as grim faced. Julia lowered her eyes as she passed by him.

"Visitors to see political prisoner Ward," Higgins told the man.

Julia winced at his words. Of all the titles that could be attached to Samuel's name, political prisoner shouldn't be one of them. She and her father stepped into the waiting area. The room smelled of mold and peeling paint and was even hotter than it had been outside.

If it is this dreadful in here what is it like where Samuel is staying?

Private Higgins left them both in the watchful care of the other armed man. Then he disappeared. The second guard stood attentively at the entrance. He scrutinized their every move.

Julia turned her back to the man and moved to the far side of the room.

"Will he be here the entire time?" she whispered to her father.

"Most likely."

She hadn't counted on such. The man's presence made her even more uneasy than she already was.

"Do you want to sit?" Her father motioned to the table and four wooden chairs in the center of the room. They were the only furnishings.

"I would rather stand."

She took out her lace handkerchief and once more blotted her face. She wondered how long it would be before Samuel arrived. She tried to think about what she would say to him but because of the guard and the heat, her mind was drawing a blank.

Lord, give me the words to say to him. Give me the courage to say what needs to be said.

They continued to wait. A horse whinnied in the distance and outside was the raucous sound of men's laughter. Julia stole quick glances toward the door, longing for what she prayed would be Samuel's familiar and friendly face.

The guard never once shifted his feet. He stood straight as a marble statue at his post. Her father, however, had taken to pacing about the room.

He is as anxious as I am, she thought.

Once Marshal Kane and his police commissioners had disappeared into the processing room, the men returned to their places. Sam picked up his Bible. He tried to read, tried to pray but he just couldn't concentrate. He had taken to lying on his bunk when he heard footsteps clomping up the outside stairs. Private Higgins appeared in the doorway. He took off his kepi, shook out the dust then replaced it on his sweating head.

"You have a visitor," he told Sam.

Sam jumped to his feet and quickly rolled down his shirtsleeves, fastening the cuffs. He buttoned his wrinkled vest.

"Hope that lady friend of yours baked you some more bread," William said, flashing a gap-toothed grin.

"Or blueberry muffins," said John.

Sam smiled in return then followed Higgins down the staircase. He wondered if Mr. Davis was bringing news of his case or if Dr. Stanton, as the men also hoped, was bearing some delicious baked good.

Private Higgins marched him across the grounds and

to the front door of the waiting area. Julia's father was standing just inside the entrance. Dr. Stanton smiled then nodded to his right.

Sam's eyes followed. His heart nearly came out of his chest. There in the far corner of the room was Julia. She turned around just as he stepped inside.

The look on her face was enough to put all of his fears to rest. There was a longing in her eyes that he could read even from across the room.

Dr. Stanton put a hand on Sam's shoulder. "I will wait outside," he said.

For a moment, Sam had forgotten that he was even there. Gone were the guards and guns, as well. Fort McHenry no longer existed. All he could see was Julia.

He stepped toward her, taking her hands in his. She was trembling but she was wearing his ring.

"Are you all right?" he asked when he came to his senses.

"Yes."

Her voice was breathless, barely above a whisper. She stumbled through her words. "I w-wanted t-to tell you that I am so sorry. That I am s-sorry for everything hurtful I said and did. Please forgive me."

Her eyes were soft, blue oceans deep with emotion. Sam's heart swelled so that he thought it would burst. "You don't even need to ask," he said. "Of course I forgive you."

She closed her eyes, a smile of relief on her lips. He wished to take her completely in his arms.

"I have missed you," he said instead.

"I have missed you, as well," she said.

She searched his face. His chin was unshaven, his hair out of place and she could tell that already he had begun to lose weight because of his meager meal rations.

His smile, though, was still the same—full of life and laughter. She let the warmth of it wash over her.

"I have not been able to sleep since they arrested you," she said.

"It's not that bad here," he promised. "I get fresh air and decent meals."

Though the guard standing at the door was watching their every move, Julia no longer cared. She reached up to touch Samuel's face. "They aren't feeding you enough," she said. "I brought you a basket of food."

He glanced at the basket on the table. He grinned. "Thank you. Does it include bread and jam?"

"Yes."

He chuckled. "My bunkmates enjoyed the last loaf you sent. They were hoping you would send more."

Her hand found his again. She smiled. "I will send two loaves next time."

"They would appreciate that."

There was a pause in the conversation and once more Julia could hear the sound of soldiers' voices coming from beyond the room. As happy as she was to be with Samuel she was reminded that they were in the middle of a war. The disturbing issues of such flooded her memory. She lowered her eyes. She wanted to tell him about everything that had happened but she did not want the guard to overhear.

Samuel lifted her chin so her eyes met his. "What's wrong?"

Julia remembered her father's warning. She pieced together her words, choosing them carefully. "I read your book," she said softly. "The one that you brought home from Philadelphia."

His eyebrows arched. She knew he knew exactly what

she was talking about. She could feel the fire building in her face.

"Father asked me to read it…to understand why you… well, I understand now."

"I am sorry that you had to learn about such things, Julia. I never—"

"Samuel it is I who am sorry. I had no idea what it was really like. If I did, I never would have asked you to go with…" She bit her lip, not wanting to say her brother's name in front of the guard. "I believe now that you made the right decision."

Sam's spirit soared. How he had longed to hear her say such words, to have her respect the choice he had made. He ran his fingers gently through her curls. At that moment all he wanted to do was kiss her.

"I want to support you," she said. "Honestly, I do. I just don't know how exactly. I am praying about such things and I am on the watch for God's answer."

"Oh, sweetheart."

"You have five minutes!" the guard behind him announced.

Sam glanced at him and then back at Julia.

"I cannot even begin to tell you how you have made me feel by what you have just said," he whispered.

Julia smiled brightly. "In the meantime I will continue with what we have started. Sally and I will bake bread for the church and her father and mine will assist us until you return."

Samuel did not take his eyes off her. He clasped her hands a little tighter. "I prayed that you would do so."

"I was there today. I saw Elijah and Elisha. They both were well and—" Tears danced in her blue eyes. "They were wearing stockings."

"Oh, they were?"

Her hands were trembling in his but this time he knew it was because of joy.

"Thank you, Samuel."

"Thank *you.*"

"It did my heart good to know that they were being looked after."

"It pleases me that you care for them so."

"I want to do more," she said.

He ran his thumbs gently across her hands. "So do I."

"Three minutes!"

Her jaw twitched and his heart was racing. Time was slipping away much too quickly. There was so much he wanted to tell her yet there was so little time. He had thought the sight of her would be enough to sustain him through his confinement, however long it was. Now he realized that the separation would only bring more agony.

"I love you," he said.

"I love you. I wish we had married when we had the opportunity. I am so sorry for the time I have wasted."

"Hush now," he said. "None of the time has been wasted. We have both grown in our faith, in our convictions." He smiled. "God has a way of taking our fears and mistakes and turning them into something beautiful."

"You have always thought the best of me...of us." She squeezed his hand. "When will they release you?"

"I don't know, but don't worry. They won't keep me here forever."

"One minute!"

She glanced at the guard and then looked back at Samuel. The pending separation was going to be difficult.

"Is there nothing we can do?" she asked, the emotions

in her voice growing. "You didn't have anything to do with the bridge burnings. You tried to stop them! Why don't they believe that?"

Tears silvered her lashes. They spilled down her cheeks. Samuel pulled her close, laying her head to his chest. His heart was pounding.

"Don't cry. The army will sort this out soon enough. In the meantime, just keep praying."

Julia buried her head in his wrinkled white shirt, wishing that they were anywhere but where they actually were at that moment. "I promise I will, unceasingly."

When the guard announced that their time together had come to an end, she wanted to scream. Samuel reluctantly pulled away from her. She could feel her heart ripping in two.

"I love you," she promised.

"I love you."

The guard stepped toward Samuel to escort him out. Julia watched in powerless silence as he was led to the door. Just before crossing the threshold, he looked back.

"I will be home soon," he promised. "Don't worry."

With tears streaming down her cheeks Julia stood in the center of the room until he disappeared from view. A moment later, her father and Private Higgins returned.

"Are you all right?" her father asked.

She wiped her eyes and tried to muster a respectable measure of composure. He took her arm.

"I know it wasn't easy but you did a good thing by coming here today," he said. "Did you see the look on his face when he first saw you?"

She summoned a small smile. The look on his face could only have mirrored what she felt by seeing him. "Thank you for bringing me here."

He smiled. "You are welcome, child."

"Follow me, please," Private Higgins requested.

The sunlight stung her eyes as Julia stepped from the building. Once more the sounds of marching men filled her ears. Just before passing through the inner gate, she glanced back.

On the second floor portico of one of the buildings, Samuel was standing.

He was waving goodbye.

John came up to the railing. "Is that her?" he asked as the woman in the blue dress disappeared beyond the gate.

"Yes," Sam said. "That's Julia."

"You married? You never did say. In fact, you haven't said much about her at all except that she bakes muffins."

Sam smiled as he turned from the future that awaited him to face the grim confines of today. "No. We're not married yet. We are engaged."

John nodded. "So when's the wedding?"

"As soon as I get out of here."

Julia replayed the moments with Samuel over and over in her mind as her father's carriage wobbled toward home. Her heart was overflowing with praise.

Oh, Lord, thank You! Thank You for giving me the opportunity to see him, for allowing me to set things right.

She was also relieved to find that the soldiers at the fort were not nearly as horrible as she had imagined. The ones she had encountered today were not Northern monsters. They appeared to be just ordinary men.

Private Higgins, for instance, had addressed her

father informally as he escorted them back to the main gate. Julia had listened in on every word.

"Pretty city you folks have," the young man had commented. "The Patapsco River reminds me of a place back home."

"Oh, really," her father said. "Where is that?"

"Maine."

"Is that so? Do you do much fishing up there?"

"Yes, indeed, my brother and I. And I can't wait to get back to it."

She had never once considered that the soldiers occupying her city were just as miserable as she. They, too, wanted this war to end so they could be reunited with their own families.

Although Julia could not commit herself to supplying the Federal Army with socks, she would now pray for them.

Sally was waiting for her when she arrived home.

"Your mother told me where you were," she said, practically beaming. "Was Sam pleased to see you?"

Julia grinned, giddy with excitement.

"I take it that is a yes," Sally said. "I suppose then you will have need of this." From behind her back she drew a skein of lace. "I measured. It is enough to complete your gown."

Julia's eyes widened. A delightful gasp escaped her throat. "How did you—?"

"The girls and I kept working on it. That is why none of us have been able to match your pace of knitting."

Her heart swelled. She was so touched by Sally's faith. "You kept working even when I had broken the engagement?"

"Of course. You know me. I don't give up easily."

Sally grinned and Julia hugged her. "I am so glad for that."

"I have something else for you." She pulled a letter from her pocket. "It is from Edward."

The letter was already opened. Julia let out a laugh and raised her eyebrows when Sally handed it to her.

"I am sorry," she said sheepishly, "but when you weren't here, well, I could not wait. I wanted to be certain he was safe."

"Is he?"

Sally grinned once more. "He is well."

Julia was practically dancing with excitement. *First Samuel, now Edward... Could this day get any better?* "What else did he have to say?"

"I don't know. I only read the first two paragraphs. The rest concerns you and Sam. I stopped reading when I realized it was so personal."

A tint of uneasiness clouded her bright outlook. Julia unfolded the paper for herself. She hoped Edward's words toward Samuel would be charitable. Yet, even if they were not, it would not change her feelings, her commitment to him. She slowly began to read.

I received a letter from Sam just today. He wanted to apologize for our confrontation the night I left Baltimore. He said that while he could not join this fight, he would continue to pray for me.

Julia breathed and continued.

It is I who should apologize, Julia. I never should have told you to reconsider marrying him. I was angry. I was disappointed but the truth is, now I am glad he stayed behind. Sam is a good man. It is a comfort to know that he is there to protect you.

Although our political views may differ, I wish you nothing but happiness for the years ahead.

Julia wiped tears of thankfulness from her eyes before passing the letter to Sally. Miles, war and prison may physically separate them but in her heart, her family had been reunited.

The Marshal and police commissioners joined Sam and the others late that evening. The bunks were now full with one man left standing. Sam voluntarily gave up his bed for the floor. Little could physically disturb him now that Julia had come. His only source of contention was not knowing how much longer they would be separated.

Sunrise dawned hot and hazy. The men had just finished Sam's greens and sardines when Private Higgins climbed the staircase. Eyeing Sam, he said matter-of-factly, "You are ordered to gather your personal items and follow me immediately."

The men on the porch stared at Higgins. They then glanced at Sam. He swallowed hard and stood to his feet. Anxiety washed over him in a cold sweat.

"I will do so," Sam said and he went to gather his books and clothing.

John followed him inside.

"What do you make of this?" Sam whispered as he rolled up his extra shirts and wrapped them in the brown paper that Dr. Stanton had sent.

John scratched his head. "They are either sending you home or you are being moved to a confinement cell."

His pulse raced. *Did the Lord allow me to see Julia because things are about to get worse? Do they now know of the role I played in assisting Rose?*

The thought of the damp concrete and cold iron bars in the Sally Port prison did not appeal to him but Sam tried to think positively. *Whatever the Lord allows will be for the ultimate good, for me...for Julia...for all of us.*

Drawing on his faith, he turned to face John. He stuck out his hand. "It has been a pleasure knowing you."

"And you, Sam. I think they are sending you home. Good luck with that young lady."

"Thank you and I hope that you are released soon."

John waved him off with a cavalier smile. "This war can't last forever, you know."

Sam scooped up his belongings and headed back outside. He bid the others God's blessings then he followed Private Higgins down the stairs.

"Where are we going?" he dared to ask.

Higgins wiped his forehead with the back of his hand. He adjusted the musket on his shoulder. "The lieutenant colonel wants to see you."

Sam's mind raced. *Perhaps John is right. Perhaps they are sending me home. If that is the case then Julia and I—*

He tried not to think that far ahead. He followed Higgins to the processing room where Lieutenant Colonel Morris and his fellow officers were once again seated at the long table. The men were in full uniform. Their brass buckles and boots shined.

Sam felt severely underdressed appearing in his wrinkled trousers and shirtsleeves, not to mention his growing beard and unkempt hair. He tucked his brown paper package in the crook of his arm.

"You wanted to see me, sir?"

Morris shuffled the stack of paperwork before him. "Samuel Ward, your whereabouts and activities on the night of April nineteenth of this year have been confirmed. As you previously stated, you had no involvement in the railroad bridge burnings of that evening."

He continued to read from the sheet in front of him. The man's tone was all business, the trademark of a career military man. "It has also been confirmed that you were not involved in any seditious activity at the Carroll Hall Armory and that you did in fact try to discourage your fellow citizens from participating in the destruction of railroad property."

Sam wondered how the man had confirmed such information. More than likely one of the police commissioners had testified on his behalf. He held his breath, waiting, praying that Morris's next words would set him free.

The lieutenant colonel stared at him. His face showed no emotion whatsoever. "Therefore it is the decision of this board of inquiry that you be released, pending you agree to swear an oath of allegiance to the United States government."

Sam breathed a grateful sigh. Relief flooded his veins.

"Will you so swear?" Morris asked.

"I will."

"Then raise your right hand and repeat after me..."

Sam did so but had little idea what he was actually repeating. His body was in the processing room at Fort McHenry but his heart and his mind were already in Mount Vernon.

When the procedure was completed Private Higgins escorted Sam to the main gate. To his surprise William Davis was waiting for him.

"I didn't know that you were here, sir."

"I had arrived to discuss your case," Mr. Davis said, "but the lieutenant colonel told me of your impending release and he said I could wait for you here." The man grinned. "I don't suppose you need a ride to Mount Vernon, do you?"

Sam returned the smile. "Would you mind taking me to my house first?"

"In need of a shave?" Davis said with a chuckle.

Sam itched his scraggily chin. "You could say so."

The lace was absolutely beautiful. Julia stopped every few stitches or so to run her fingers over the delicate edges. She had already finished adding it to the sleeves and neckline. The only thing left was the waist.

She smiled to herself. White wedding dresses had only recently come into fashion. She could not wait for Samuel to see her in the gown. She could not wait to be his wife.

She sighed contentedly as she then glanced about the garden. He would come. She knew not when but she was certain he would come. The army would release him and then their life together would begin.

Why he felt nervous he couldn't imagine. Perhaps it was because reality had yet to sink in. This morning he was a political prisoner. This afternoon he was a free man. Sam clasped his hands behind his back only to keep them still. He felt like he did that evening in the Stanton's garden, the moment he had kissed Julia for the first time.

He rang the bell. Dr. Stanton opened the door.

"Praise be to God!" he shouted as he swallowed Sam up in a fatherly embrace. "I can't believe it! Is it really you?"

Sam laughed. "It is, sir."

"What happened?"

"I am not exactly certain. All I know is that I was called to see the lieutenant colonel and the next thing I knew, I was free."

"Praise be to God!" he said once more.

Mrs. Stanton heard the commotion and came running. "Thank the Lord!" She gave Sam a hug, as well, then stepped back to give him the once-over. "My boy, the soldiers have not been feeding you."

Sam chuckled when Esther then added, "You look terrible."

"He looks a mite better than he did the last time I saw him," Dr. Stanton said with a grin.

Sam ran his hand over his smooth chin. "A bath and a shave do wonders."

They all laughed.

"Well," Esther then said, "I will fetch you something to eat."

"I don't think he came here for food," Dr. Stanton said. He then looked at Sam. "She is in the garden."

Sam did not waste any time. He quickly hurried through the foyer to the back door. He peered through the glass panels.

Julia was sitting on the bench beneath the cherry tree, sewing. The afternoon sunlight painted her in a warm tone. Her dark brown curls swayed slightly in the breeze.

For a moment Sam simply stared. She was the most beautiful woman in the world. *And she has promised herself to me.*

He opened the door very slowly and moved down the steps. He quietly snapped a red rose from one of the bushes then stole in behind the bench. Julia's head nodded slightly as she moved her needle through what appeared to be the lace-trimmed bodice of a white wedding gown. Knowing Julia, she would want to wear the latest fashion.

He moved in closer and slipped the rose over her shoulder.

She gasped and quickly turned. Tossing the gown aside, she bolted from the bench and ran for his arms.

"Oh, Samuel! I can't believe this! Is it really you?"

He covered her face in kisses, only stopping to tuck the fresh blossom behind her ear.

"I am home," he said. Taking her hands he then stepped back. He looked down at her bare feet and grinned.

She immediately turned three shades of crimson. "Don't look," she said and then she remembered the gown that she had left on the bench. "And don't look at that, either."

He laughed. "Then will you please tell me what I am permitted to look at?"

She smiled bashfully and he led her to her previous seat. Julia's stockings were tucked inside her shoes. She pushed them beneath the bench. She then tried to hide them and her pink toes with her skirts. Sam laughed even harder.

"When we read in the newspaper that Marshal Kane had been arrested we did not know what to think."

"Yes, I know. I felt the same. I was worried that the army would step up their fortifications, that there would be further trouble."

"I have been praying and praying." She sighed happily, eyes filled with contentment. "And now the soldiers have let you come home."

"I think one of the police commissioners put in a good word for me," he said.

"Thank the Lord."

"Yes, indeed. He is the one who is ultimately in control."

She squeezed his hand. "I have heard from Edward."

"You have? Is he well?"

"Yes. He received your letter and he greatly appreciated it. Would you like to see what he wrote?"

"I would."

She pulled the letter from her pocket and handed it to him. As Sam read, his forehead furrowed. Julia watched him, happily.

Oh, how I have missed that.

When he had finished reading, a peaceful expression filled his face. He placed the letter in the envelope and handed it back to her. "I am glad we have his blessing."

"I would have married you without it."

He smiled. The look in his eyes made her heart flutter.

"I have something that belongs to you," she said. She then pulled out his watch, which she had been carrying with her all this time.

He chuckled. "I was looking for that. I wondered where it had gotten off to."

"I kept it with me after they arrested you. It made me feel close to you." She placed the watch in his open palm then closed his fingers around it. "I am so glad you are home."

"You don't know how much it meant to me that you came to see me. I can't even begin to express what I felt," he said.

"You don't know how much it meant to me to be forgiven. You are a selfless and honorable man, Samuel Ward."

He brushed a soft curl from her face. "Do you know what I have always loved about you?"

"That I am foolish and impulsive?"

He smiled, then his expression warmed into something deeper. "That you determine what is right and then you stand on your convictions. You are a brave person, Julia."

"You would not have thought so if you had seen me at the front gate of Fort McHenry. When I saw the soldiers, Father had to turn the carriage around."

"But you came back."

"I had to. My future depended on it."

She laced her fingers through his. So much had taken place since they had last sat together in this garden. War still raged and uncertainty lay before them both but they were united in purpose, in faith and in love.

"We have the rest of our lives together," Sam said.

"I want that life to start right now."

"So do I."

He was ready to kiss her once more but he held off. "Dr. Carter visited me after you left the fort. The school has found another location, the old Catholic convent in Mount Washington."

"Oh, that is wonderful! When will your classes resume?"

"In two weeks."

She smiled slowly. "Then that gives us just enough time."

He moved in closer, sliding his arms around her. "Yes. Provided that your wedding gown is ready."

Her blue eyes twinkled. "I will sew all night if necessary."

Two days later the church bells chimed as Julia and Samuel descended the front steps for the first time as husband and wife. Their hearts were light and joyful. Sam shook hands with his guests. Julia hugged her parents goodbye before riding off in her husband's carriage.

Her father smiled at her but his eyes were misty with

emotion. "I knew this day was going to come," he said. "I suppose, though, a father is never quite ready for it."

Julia's chin quivered ever so slightly. As Samuel approached, Dr. Stanton gave him his daughter's hand.

"Take good care of her," he said.

"I will, sir. You have my word."

She tossed her bouquet of blossoms high into the air. It landed squarely in the grasp of Sally Hastings. Those in attendance cheered. Sally immediately blushed.

Sam leaned close and whispered in his bride's ear, "Is that a sign of what is to come?"

Julia grinned, her joy uncontainable. "I hope so."

He helped her into his carriage and, with a final wave goodbye, they drove away. The well wishes of their friends and family followed after them. Samuel traveled up Charles Street. Men on the sidewalk stopped to lift their hats and women waved their handkerchiefs as the young couple rode by.

Julia glowed with happiness as she snuggled close to his arm. The carriage rocked gently from side to side. She couldn't help but giggle.

"What is so amusing?" he asked.

"I was just thinking. Do you remember our first carriage ride together?"

"The one that Edward took us on?"

"Yes."

He leaned his head back and laughed. Julia could hear the love in his voice. "I will never forget the look on your face when I told you I wanted to make certain that you didn't fall out of the carriage."

She grinned. "The two of you had that planned. I am certain of it."

"No, actually, we didn't but it worked out in my favor."

"Did you know then that this is how it would all turn out?" she asked.

"I hoped it would," he said.

Samuel rolled the carriage to a stop in front of their home. Julia took a deep yet peaceful breath, knowing the rest of her life was about to begin.

"God has a plan for us, Samuel. I know He does."

He smiled at her. "That He does and I look forward to discovering it with you."

"As do I."

He jumped from the carriage and came around to her side. Before Julia could step to the cobblestone, Samuel scooped her up into his arms.

Her heart skipped a beat. Faith had sustained her. Love had led her home.

* * * * *

Dear Reader,

Thank you for choosing *Her Rebel Heart*. Ever since I can remember I have been fascinated by the American Civil War. Although one of the darkest times in our nation's history, it was also a time filled with spiritual awakening, great courage and sacrifice. At the beginning of this story Sam and Julia are at odds, yet they eventually find common ground for the sake of the citizens of Baltimore. With prayer and cooperation, lives are changed for the better.

In the twenty-first century, our nation faces its own set of problems and uncertainties. May we always remember that our strength ultimately does not come from military might or political power. It comes by way of God's Amazing Grace. It is my prayer that we may set aside our differences, be they church traditions or political ideology, for the sake of our country and future generations. How can we begin to do so? Seek God's guidance. Be kind to others in word and deed, then watch as miracles unfold.

Blessings,
Shannon Farrington

Questions for Discussion

1. Sam dislikes the Federal Army's tactics, yet he cannot fully support the States' Rights position of the Confederacy. Have you ever been caught between two opposing views? How did you decide which path to ultimately take?

2. In what ways did you sympathize with Julia's decision to break the engagement?

3. Julia is fiercely loyal to her brother Edward. How is family loyalty a good thing? In what ways can it be bad?

4. Sam is a sincere Christian yet he ends up breaking the law. Is there ever a time when it is acceptable for a Christian to do so? Are there any examples in Scripture to support your position?

5. Why doesn't Sam simply tell Julia the reasons why he is so opposed to slavery? Should he have done so?

6. How does the Pratt Street Riot and the continued presence of Federal soldiers in Baltimore affect Julia physically? Emotionally?

7. Why do you think Julia is attracted to Charles Moffit? In what ways does he differ from Sam?

8. Have political differences ever put you at odds with someone you love? How did you reconcile those differences?

9. Why didn't Sam allow Julia to speak up on behalf of Elisha? Why didn't he defend the child in front of the slave owner?

10. Why does Julia decide to visit Sam at Fort McHenry? How does she finally overcome her fear of the soldiers?

11. Which character changes the most in this story? In what ways do they mature in their faith?

12. Do you believe prayer can bring about reconciliation? Does God have a plan for each of our lives? For our nation?

INSPIRATIONAL

Wholesome romances that touch the heart and soul.

COMING NEXT MONTH
AVAILABLE JANUARY 10, 2012

THE COWBOY TUTOR
Three Brides for Three Cowboys
Linda Ford

AN INCONVENIENT MATCH
Janet Dean

ALL ROADS LEAD HOME
Christine Johnson

THE UNLIKELY WIFE
Debra Ullrick

REQUEST YOUR FREE BOOKS!

2 FREE INSPIRATIONAL NOVELS
PLUS 2
FREE
MYSTERY GIFTS

Love Inspired

HISTORICAL
INSPIRATIONAL HISTORICAL ROMANCE

YES! Please send me 2 FREE Love Inspired® Historical novels and my 2 FREE mystery gifts (gifts are worth about \$10). After receiving them, if I don't wish to receive any more books, I can return the shipping statement marked "cancel". If I don't cancel, I will receive 4 brand-new novels every month and be billed just \$4.49 per book in the U.S. or \$4.99 per book in Canada. That's a saving of at least 22% off the cover price. It's quite a bargain! Shipping and handling is just 50¢ per book in the U.S. and 75¢ per book in Canada.* I understand that accepting the 2 free books and gifts places me under no obligation to buy anything. I can always return a shipment and cancel at any time. Even if I never buy another book, the two free books and gifts are mine to keep forever.

102/302 IDN FEHF

Name	(PLEASE PRINT)	

Address		Apt. #

City	State/Prov.	Zip/Postal Code

Signature (if under 18, a parent or guardian must sign)

Mail to the **Reader Service**:
IN U.S.A.: P.O. Box 1867, Buffalo, NY 14240-1867
IN CANADA: P.O. Box 609, Fort Erie, Ontario L2A 5X3

Not valid for current subscribers to Love Inspired Historical books.

Want to try two free books from another series?
Call 1-800-873-8635 or visit www.ReaderService.com.

* Terms and prices subject to change without notice. Prices do not include applicable taxes. Sales tax applicable in N.Y. Canadian residents will be charged applicable taxes. Offer not valid in Quebec. This offer is limited to one order per household. All orders subject to credit approval. Credit or debit balances in a customer's account(s) may be offset by any other outstanding balance owed by or to the customer. Please allow 4 to 6 weeks for delivery. Offer available while quantities last.

Your Privacy—The Reader Service is committed to protecting your privacy. Our Privacy Policy is available online at www.ReaderService.com or upon request from the Reader Service.

We make a portion of our mailing list available to reputable third parties that offer products we believe may interest you. If you prefer that we not exchange your name with third parties, or if you wish to clarify or modify your communication preferences, please visit us at www.ReaderService.com/consumerschoice or write to us at Reader Service Preference Service, P.O. Box 9062, Buffalo, NY 14269. Include your complete name and address.

LIHI1B

SEE IT

and SAY IT

in SPANISH

Is one of the books in Signet's new language series—books that have been especially designed to meet the needs of the beginner.

Also available in Signet editions: SEE IT AND SAY IT IN ITALIAN, SEE IT AND SAY IT IN FRENCH and SEE IT AND SAY IT IN GERMAN.

A WORD ABOUT THE AUTHOR

MARGARITA MADRIGAL is one of America's leading language teachers. Author of the outstanding bestsellers **Magic Key to Spanish** and **Open Door to Spanish**, she is in constant demand as a lecturer in Europe and Latin America, as well as in the United States. Although she lives and teaches Spanish in New York City, she is equally at home in Rome, London, Mexico City, and Athens. An accomplished guitarist, she considers her guitar her "passport to the world."